AF374262

The Pairing of Beasts

C. Hebert

The Pairing Series - book one

TRIGGER WARNING

The Pairing of Beasts contains explicit language, violence, mention of blood, mental and physical abuse, sexual assault, trauma, and death.

This book also contains extremely explicit and detailed sexual scenes.

The Pairing Series is a 6 book fantasy series consisting of both prequels and sequels, beginning with The Pairing of Beasts.

Each book follows an ever growing story with multiple characters and stories intertwined in a fantasy world filled with magic, love, conflict, and, of course, beasts.

As you read the stories of these beloved characters, you'll experience every emotion and be left begging for more.

CONTENTS

To my fellow readers,
Try not to fall in love with all the characters.

C. Hebert

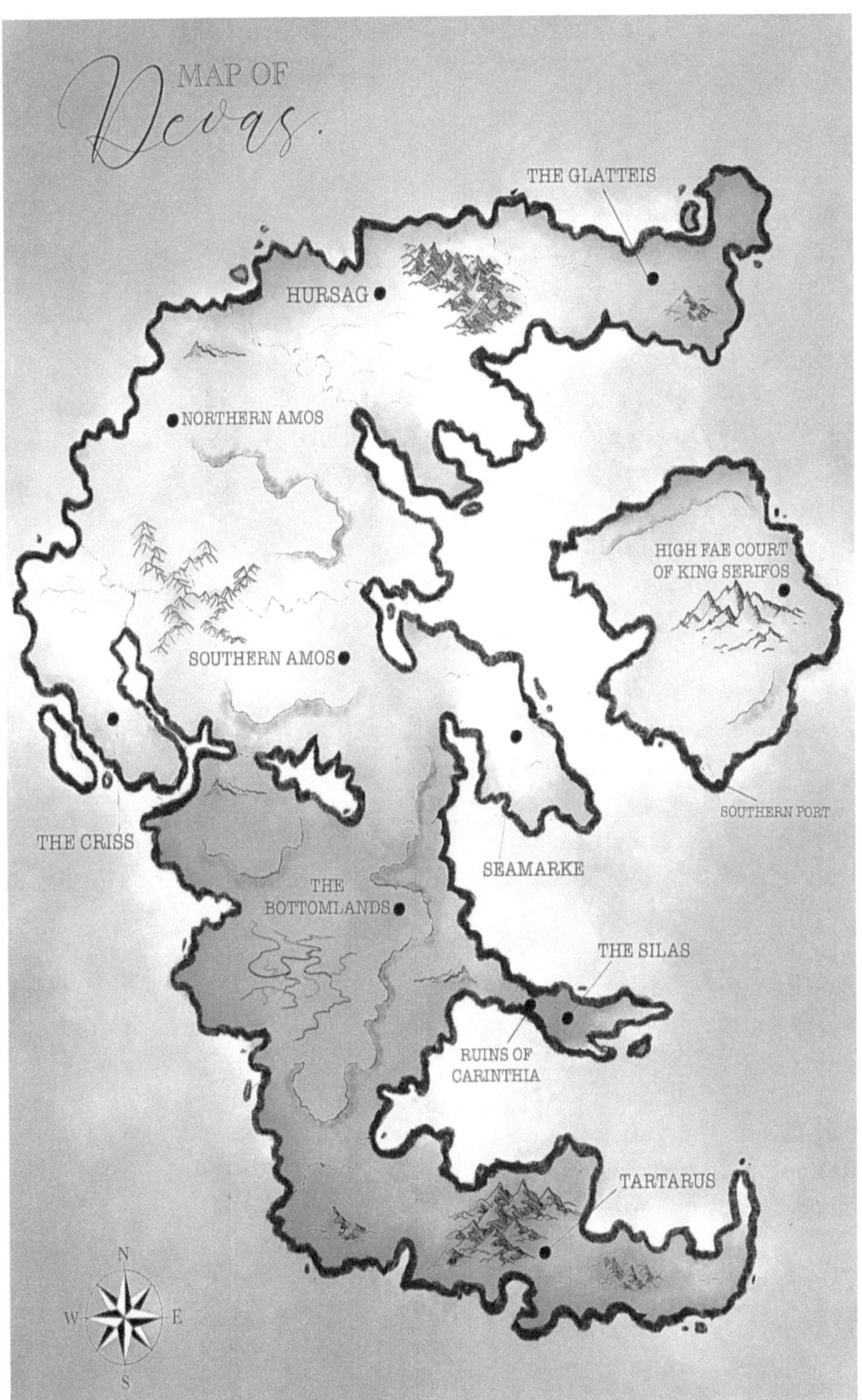

MAP OF
Devas
THE GLATTEIS
HURSAG
NORTHERN AMOS
HIGH FAE COURT
OF KING SERIFOS
SOUTHERN AMOS
SOUTHERN PORT
THE CRISS
SEAMARKE
THE
BOTTOMLANDS
THE SILAS
RUINS OF
CARINTHIA
TARTARUS
N
W
E
S

The Pairing of Beasts Characters
(In order of appearance)

Princess Cyrene (ky-reen)
Princess of Devas, youngest daughter of Queen Kea of the High Fae Court of Devas.

Princess Cecelia (su-seal-ee-ah)
Princess of Devas and Lady of The Glatteis, eldest daughter of King Serifos and Queen Kea of the High Fae Court, twin to Prince Keres.

Prince Keres (ka-ress)
Prince of Devas, Lord of Hursag, and commander of Devas. Only son of King Serifos and Queen Kea of the High Fae Court, heir to the kingdom of Devas and twin to Princess Cecelia.

King Serifos (sair-if-os)
Ruler of Devas and the High Fae Court. Married to Queen Kea and survived by his children, twins Keres and Cecelia.

Lord Emilios (e-mill-ee-os)
Ruling Lord of Northern Amos of Devas, distant relative to Lord Leander of the old Baldassare House.

Aodhan (a-o-dun)
Spirit animal in the form of a red tailed hawk, connected to the old Tartarian House of Lord Baldyr.

Captain Ivar (eye-var)
Rogue captain of Devas. Parentage is unknown to any, however he has deep connections to Seamarke.

The Sephtis
Mythical beast said to haunt the southern seas of Devas.

Fenix (*Jarloth*) (fin-ick)
Enemy to King Serifos and elder cousin to Lady Tove of The Bottomlands.

Lady Tove (toevah)
Ruling Lady of The Bottomlands of Devas, younger cousin to Fenix, and leader of an uprising against King Serifos.

Lord Leander (lee-anne-dur)
Ruling Lord of Southern Amos of Devas, ally to the uprising against King Serifos, and childhood friend to Lady Tove and Fenix. Distant relative of Lord Emilios of the old Baldassarre House.

Cormac
General and leader of Lady Tove and Fenix's armies in The Bottomlands.

Nox (knocks)
Spirit animal in the form of an inky raven, connected to Lady Tove of The Bottomlands.

Ydalia (eye-doll-ee-ah)
Druidess and leader of a rogue Vaud pack.

Farouk (fair-uck)
General and Tartarian warrior, younger brother to Lord Baldyr.

Lord Baldyr (ball-dare)
Ruling Lord of Tartarus of Devas and older brother to Farouk.

"You should be kissed, and often, by someone who knows how."

Gone With the Wind

Prologue

"I love the way you moan," he whispered, piercing my ear softly with his canines. I could feel his heart beating fiercely against my back as he sucked on my pointed ear. His lips slowly and effortlessly moved down my neck, releasing shivers across my skin.

"Don't stop," my sharp breaths begged. His rough, warm hands traveled delicately under my silk nightdress, casting shivers up my spine. He grabbed my hips roughly, pulling me closer to him, causing me to gasp. I could feel him pushed against me—hard, growing—as he traced my curves with those rough hands. Gods, my body wanted him.

For months I had experienced these forbidden, salacious fantasies in my dreams. Bodily bliss exchanged between my mysterious lover and me. I didn't know who he was, but my body *hungered* for him. The details of his sweaty, muscular body had always appeared so hazy. His blurry face was framed in wild, deep onyx waves just out of focus. My eyes never fully saw his face, but I *sensed* he was beautiful.

My lover caressed and traced my body, taking his time to worship every individual detail. His hands glided across my stomach, slowly traveling further down. Soft moans escaped my lungs, as I reacted to his touch. He yanked my thighs open, spreading them further apart, releasing a low, heavy grunt. The strength of his grasp and his desire to feel me made my center wet. A fire rolled through my core. My head rose as I gasped for air, wrapping an arm back around his neck. The other braced my body against him, my free hand firmly against his hip. He ran his hand under my night dress, across my breasts and caressed my nipple, feeling every detail. His other hand carefully traced up my inner thigh. I craved him. I *needed* more.

His fingertip circled along to the edge of my body, making its way to my center. I could feel his lips forming a sensual smile as he felt my wetness. A low, hungry snarl escaped from deep within his throat. My hands moved to firmly grip his waist, grinding my body against his. He squeezed my breast, growling into my ear as his fingers ventured lightly inside me, teasing. I bit my lip, digging my nails into his skin. *More.* He could sense my excitement as he gripped my neck, pulling me closer to him as he quickened. He thrust his warm fingers further inside me passionately with each new motion. His tight hold around my neck only aroused me more. Warmth swept through my body. My back arched and my nipples hardened in response to him. *Yes. Don't stop.*

"Harder," my voice rasped. He obeyed my plea. My moans couldn't be contained as he continued to enter me, adding another finger. He was taking his time, enjoying my pleasure. He knew my body.

My breathing quickened. I could feel my body burning, growing to a peak. *Oh Gods.* He pushed harder, faster. Cries of euphoria filled my lungs.

He leaned his face against my bare neck, biting me softly as he growed, "That's right, come for me, Princess."

His command only added to my overwhelming elation. My heart began to explode with ecstasy. *No. Fuck!* My throat burned from my screams as I struggled to catch my breath. I could feel him smiling, pleased with my reaction.

"Good girl."

He remained inside me for a moment, thrusting his fingers further with one final jolt. My body quivered. I couldn't breathe. He slowly pulled his drenched fingers from inside of me and examined them. "Look how wet I make you," he purred, lifting his fingers to his mouth and licking my wetness from his fingertip. I didn't want this moment to end.

My lover softly turned my shaking body to face him. He wrapped his large, muscular arms around my waist. His broad, tan chest was blurry but bare. My eyes were level to his chest, and I admired his physique. He was beautiful. My hand rose, tenderly tracing the sharpness of his chin, making my way down his neck. My fingers felt something hidden amongst his foggy frame. *What is that?* I struggled to make out the details, running my fingertips across his skin. It appeared to be a large scar. The scar stretched from the edge of his neck across his collarbone. My fingers followed the ridges. It felt old and deep. He softly raised my chin as if to look into my eyes. I peered at his filmy face, struggling, unable to make out his features.

Why can't I see you?

I laid my head across his warm, bare chest, inhaling his scent. Cedar wood with touches of cardamom and ginger. His smell was so comforting. He tightened his hold, pulling me closer. I didn't want to wake up. I wanted to stay with him in this heavenly slumber forever.

"Who are you?" I asked fainty.

"*Cymar,*" he whispered.

Cymar?

I woke soaked in hot, sticky sweat as my silk nightdress clung to my body. I groaned, my eyes struggling to open as my body rolled around in the bed. *Gods, I don't want to be awake.* A soft whimper left my mouth as my arms rose, rubbing the sleep from my eyes. My gaze drew across the bed chamber, my weary eyes struggling to remain open. Warm golden sunlight poured through giant glass windows on either side of the room, soaking the room in a glistening glow. A small fire crackled in the ivory fireplace. *What time was it?* My gaze lifted, admiring the pale powdery blue velvet curtains hanging from the canopy that draped over my spacious bed. Beams of warm sunlight flowed in the air above me. I reached my hands into the golden beams, inviting the sun to dance around my fingertips. My ivory skin glowed in the gilded light. I didn't want to be awake. I wished to fall back to sleep and rejoin my lover.

My eyes shut slowly, remembering how it felt when he touched me. I lightly ran my fingers up my arm to my neck, retracing each spot his lips kissed me, continuing down to my inner thigh, imagining how he felt against me, inside me. I gasped softly, daydreaming of him. His gentle rough hands traveling across my skin. His steady, hot breath against my neck. My breathing began to intensify. I yearned for him. My body began to peak when a hard knock against the doors of my room interrupted my fantasy.

"Princess Cyrene?" My hand retreated quickly, fumbling to adjust my nightdress.

"C-come in," I stuttered, trying to compose myself. A pack of my ladies staggered into the room, one after another, carrying a ridiculous amount of gowns and dresses.

"Cyrene, honestly, do you realize what time it is?"

Flowing gracefully behind my ladies was my older sister, Princess Cecelia. She was tall and slender, her pale skin resembling porcelain. Her long, straight snow-white hair fell delicately below her waist. She looked painfully regal. She bore an elegant crown composed of pure silver, forged into roses and thorns that twisted to a point atop her head. Each metal rose was adorned with pale moonstones mimicking water droplets on the forged silver petals. She was dressed in a long, deep blue formal gown, native to our winter region, embroidered with an intricate pattern of silver roses and thorns. A dark gray sheepskin cloak with winter furs was fastened around her long neck, trailing faintly behind her. Her piercing, muted blue eyes were striking against the dull, faded color of her attire. Cecelia's boots tapped softly against the stone floor. She examined the various dresses presented by my ladies with no emotion.

Tonight was the Spring Equinox. High fae had traveled from all across Devas and had gathered here at my father's court to celebrate.

"What time is it?" I groaned, stretching as my body rose.

"Midday is upon us. Now, hurry. We must get you dressed properly for tonight's festivities, Cyrene."

Fuck, had I slept all morning again? These dreams always drained me.

Cecelia pondered, observing the options presented in front of her before making her decision. She lifted her choice, revealing a full, dusty blue gown made entirely of tulle.

"This will do." She snapped for me to get out of bed, ordering my ladies to dress me. I hopped from the bed and stood, arms out, rolling my eyes as I obeyed her demands. My ladies gathered to my side.

Cecelia gasped as one of my ladies lifted the thin, silk night dress above my head.

"What in the Gods is *that*?!" She pointed, glaring at a hideous bruise below my right breast. It was a menacing, deep purple bruise the size of my palm. *Fuck.* My eyes glanced from the bruise to Cecelia. Her expression was full of rage.

"It's nothing," I snapped quickly, motioning for my ladies to carry on. "It must've happened when I tripped while roaming the gardens yesterday."

My skin could feel Cecelia's eyes watching me as my ladies resumed dressing me.

Gods, I hated being a princess, and she knew it. My whole family despised my wild spirit. My true passion was roaming outside the palace grounds, riding, hunting, and studying the history and lore of Devas. Pretending to be completely free. Naturally, my father disapproved of my behavior. He was determined to keep me locked inside these horrible palace walls where I was to bow my head and do as I was told. I was expected to look, act, and think like an obedient high fae princess, to one day marry some high fae lord and be shipped off to his lands. Forgotten.

Over time, I had learned to behave well enough in the presence of my father, but my soul longed for the adrenaline of an adventure. I would take every opportunity to sneak out of the palace and venture to the lands outside these walls. My heart craved experiences. To help my mind escape the daily strain of my boring position, I would read. I read every book in my mother's library. The most intriguing books were filled with tales and myths of Devas. Recently, I had begun reading about the Sephtis. The Sephtis were said to be an ancient, deadly sable sea serpent that stalked the sea just south of our island. I'd read countless books mentioning the fabled beast. Legend had it that this terrifying sea creature attacked lone, stray vessels daring enough to cross the southern sea at night, leaving no survivors. According to the tales, few had been lucky enough to spot the serpent from the shores of our land.

Not far from my father's palace was a ridge made of obsidian rocks and sea glass that towered high over the water. It was one of my favorite places to sneak away to and hide from my duties. I would read and watch the waves below, searching for a possible glimpse of the elusive beast.

Last night, I had camped in my usual spot along the rocks to read, hoping to sight the Sephtis. I was unsuccessful. Annoyed with my fruitless endeavor, I returned to the palace wall, paying no attention as

I attempted to climb over. My hands fumbled, and I fell over the stone wall, slamming hard on a stone bench below. I winced now as my ladies wrapped a corset tightly around my torso. The bruise ached as they pulled the laces, pushing the hard bone of the corset deeper into the fresh bruise. *Fucking bench.* I tugged at the laces of the corset. *Two hours just to tighten and lace this damn contraption, ridiculous.*

"One of these days, Father will grow tired of your ludicrous behavior and lock you away. It's time you stop acting so absurd, Cyrene. You're a princess of Devas, not some *beast* from one of the southern regions."

My eyes rolled in response to her statement, and Cecelia glared at me as my ladies finished lacing the back of the dress. I didn't doubt her warning.

My father, King Serifos, was ruler of the High Fae Court and Devas. He openly disapproved of my feral spirit. Truthfully, he didn't appear to care for me in any form. At times, I wondered if he secretly blamed me for my mother's death. My mother, Queen Kea, died shortly after my birth. My father may not have voiced such feelings, but my older brother Keres did. He constantly blamed me, showing only hatred towards me. Cecelia, on the other hand, was indifferent towards me. Keres and Cecelia were both older than me, though Keres loved to point out that he was the oldest of us all. Like my father, Keres loved power and control. He enjoyed being feared, and pushed everyone around, particularly his twin Cecelia. Being the eldest, they had been given their own regions to rule in my father's kingdom.

Cecelia was the face of the northernmost region of Devas, the Glatteis. Though our father had appointed her the ruler of this region, it was well known that Keres ruled through her. Keres was the ruler of Hursag, the Glatteis' neighboring region. The two northern territories created the largest known armies in Devas, and it was led by Keres.

"Sit up straight, Cyrene," Cecelia snapped as she examined me after several more hours of primping my hair and face had passed. My ladies fluttered about, preparing me for tonight's festivities, taking an extended period of time. Such pointless, boring nonsense.

The enlarged tulle sleeves of my dress fluttered off my bare shoulders and hung above my elbows. My chest was cinched too tight.

My lungs struggled to breathe, my breasts bulging from the constrained, itchy material. The thickly layered tulle skirts flowed from my pulled waist, down onto the floor, and pooling around me. My head turned to examine myself in the large, golden mirror. My bright auburn hair had been styled in an elaborate braid adorned with small delicate hair pins that sparkled. My hair glowed like fire in the warm sunlight. A humble silver tiara of blooming flowers and leaves sat atop my head. Simple, yet beautiful. One of the ladies approached me with a long gray cloak with elaborate silver floral stitching and fastened it around my neck. Cecelia clapped her hands together, clearing her throat as she ordered the ladies away.

"Now, come along, we can't be late. I don't wish to agitate Father."

She adjusted her dress, perfecting her already straight posture, and drifted from the room. My eyes glanced back at my reflection for a moment before reluctantly accompanying Cecelia out into the hall.

I followed closely behind my sister, dreading tonight's festivities. We made our way to the grand stairs, a voice trailing up towards us.

"Too close, Cecelia." My sister stiffened at the drawled voice. Peaking around her, I glanced down the lengthy, elaborate ivory stairs to see our brother Keres.

He stood tall, like a statue, at the foot of the stairs. His arms were crossed, his bulky muscles constricted against the tight dark gray formal tunic trimmed in all black. He wore an onyx crown of sharp thorns that contrasted boldly against his blazing white hair, fashioned back as a few stray hairs lay next to his dead, blue eyes. He looked menacing.

"Typical Cyrene, fucking everything up for the rest of us," Keres uttered sharply. I sneered at his words.

Prick. With no expression, Cecelia took my arm and forcefully led me down to our brother. Keres picked a piece of lint off his shoulder as we approached the bottom of the grand stairs.

"Can we continue?" Keres looked only to Cecelia. She nodded silently, motioning towards the ballroom doors ahead of us. Keres rolled his eyes as we all proceeded forward. Faint music and muffled voices could be heard behind the towering, ancient wooden doors. Keres and Cecelia stood tall beside one another. Trailing behind, lost in their shadows, out of place between the two of them, I followed.

"Behave yourself, brat," Keres hissed back as he stared forward.

"I shouldn't even be here," I whispered to myself, rolling my eyes and crossing my arms. I dreaded attending these events.

"I couldn't agree more." Keres' words stung. He meant every word.

Chapter 2

The tall wooden doors slowly creaked open as music poured from the ballroom, flooding my ears. High fae from each region of Devas filled the alluring room. They all were dancing, drinking, and mingling in celebration of the Spring Equinox. The ballroom was breathtaking. Giant crystal chandeliers bloomed from the towering ivory and gold ceiling, engulfed with thousands of flowers in every shade of blue, hanging from the crystal accents. The flowers branched from the chandeliers across the high ceiling, reaching down the ivory walls. Dusk flowed through the colossal windows that stood in the back of the ballroom near the open garden doors. It was dreamy. My gaze drifted across the busy room, watching as the high fae enjoyed themselves. It was such a spectacle. My focus shifted as a high fae male approached—my father.

King Serifos wore a dark gray formal tunic and trousers hugging his tall muscular frame. His clothing was stamped with a regal black and silver damask pattern. A frightening crown of entangled silver roses and black thorns weighed against his long alabaster hair, which was tucked tightly behind his pointed ears. His eyes were the same as Keres and Cecelia's—an intense pale blue. He cast a powerful and heinous shadow as he marched towards us. His appearance was intimidating.

The room fell silent as King Serifos cleared his throat. Every fae in the ballroom drew their attention to my siblings and me.

"Members of my beloved High Fae court," my father addressed the room, "it is my honor to introduce to you my children." He extended his hand towards us as he spoke. "May I present Prince Keres of Devas, ruler of Hursag and general of the northern armies." Keres grinned, smug and full of himself. "Princess Cecelia of Devas, ruler of the Glatteis." Cecelia bowed her head gently in respect. My father paused, turning his brutal gaze upon me. "And Princess Cyrene of Devas." I gave him a small curtsy. He ignored my response, turning back to face the sea of fae. "Enjoy yourselves, and may the celebrations of the Spring Equinox endure the night!" He raised a glass of wine. The crowd cheered and the music resumed as every fae returned to their own devices.

Keres and Cecelia walked forward, dissolving into the crowd of fae. My father, sipping his wine, returned to his ethereal throne that was perched in front of a grand fireplace. He watched the room quietly. I clung to the gaudy walls as I made my way around the ballroom, trying to avoid the other fae. A wallflower, preferring anything else to these ridiculous gatherings.

I happened upon a lengthy table overflowing with an elaborate banquet of exotic treats. My fingers picked at the garish, colorful creations, tasting a few as I watched the ongoing performance of fae before me. Everyone looked pristine, dressed in rich attire and dazzling jewels. Pairs of fae twirled and circled the dance floor, while others huddled together gossiping, discussing politics and gods know what else. I licked the sweet pastel icing from my fingertip, wishing to be anywhere but here.

"Princess Cyrene."

My head whipped around to see a strange fae standing next to me. The male fae was tall. He bowed, grinning, as my head nodded in respect. The high fae was strikingly handsome, staring down at me with intense deep brown eyes. His long black hair was partially tucked behind his pointed ears. The mysterious man wore a crimson formal tunic embellished with elegant black embroidery that traced the low cut of his neckline, exposing his tanned chest. A strange invisible force tapped at my shoulder as my eyes studied the fae.

"My name is Emilios Baldassare, Lord of Northern Amos."

Northern Amos. Amos was the largest territory in my father's kingdom.

The land had been divided into two regions, consisting of Northern Amos and Southern Amos. Both halves of Amos were ruled by Lords of the old Baldassare house, descendants of the late King Marius, my father's older brother.

King Marius was once married to Queen Eydis. They had two daughters who married the human lords of Amos. Their younger daughter, Hesperia, married Lord Hemlock of Southern Amos. Rumor was the two shared a *pairing bond.* A mystical bond that connected mates. Little was known about the pairing bond, but it was a magical bond said to be one of the most rare and powerful connections between mates. Unlike Hesperia, Marius' older daughter, Jacynthe, endured a miserable fate. She was married off to Lord Vicente of Northern Amos to secure the power of Northern Amos. There was no love or kindness in their union. I'd read stories of how her life ended in tragedy.

Lord Emilios gave a sensual smile as he examined my body. The invisible weight on my shoulders grew. *What is that*?

"It's a pleasure to meet you, Princess," he purred, snatching a cup of wine from a waiter. He took a sip, his brunette eyes remaining locked on me. "You are quite a sight, Princess, though I must admit, I expected you to resemble your siblings." He raised an eyebrow, taking another sip.

He wasn't wrong. Unlike my father and siblings, my hair was a burning auburn red and my eyes a rich emerald green. My appearance didn't resemble the other members of my family, aside from my mother. Cecelia had told me that my mother and I both shared the same ivory skin tone. I'd always heard of our mother's beauty. She had long wild chestnut hair and rich hazel eyes. The complete opposite of my father.

A strange force formed behind my lips, pushing my thoughts as I blurted out, "You're not so bad yourself, Lord Emilios." *Why did I say that?* My hand snatched a glass of wine for myself, taking a gulp to conceal my embarrassment. My cheeks flushed. He seemed to devour my hasty response.

"Tell me about yourself, Princess. I'm curious to know more of you. Not much is known of Princess Cyrene outside these palace walls, even less on the mainland of Devas."

He took another sip, gazing back down my body with hungry eyes.

My body shivered. It felt as though something was pushing me down towards the marble floor. My head slowly began to throb. I took another sip of my wine. *What is wrong with me?*

"Forgive me, Lord Emilios, but I think it would be best if I stepped outside for a moment."

As I attempted to retreat to the garden, Emilios grabbed my wrist, stopping me. He had such warm hands. My skin bristled at his touch.

"Would you at least allow me the honor of a dance before you retire, Princess?" My body was frozen. Something was holding me in place. I felt strangely intoxicated by his presence. Before I could deny his request, Emilios placed the cup from my hand on the table next to his. "Just one dance, I promise," he whispered as he stepped behind me.

He brushed my hair aside gently as he removed the cloak from my neck, exposing my bare shoulders and bulging breasts. My body shivered as his hands grazed across my skin. "You look ravishing, Princess," he breathed gently across the back of my neck. My heart raced.

Emilios seized my hand and began to lead me through the overflowing mob of fae. We weaved through them, making our way toward the dance floor. My mind felt dizzy. The music had faded from the previous dance as we approached the clearing in the center of the room. He softly turned me towards him. Other couples of fae gathered around, readying themselves for the next dance. He halted in the center of the floor and positioned our bodies close together. *What am I doing?* My body felt...controlled.

"Just follow my lead," Emilios whispered, placing my hand on his broad shoulder. He wrapped his free hand around my cinched waist, sharply clenching me closer. A chill ran down my spine. I gasped, loud enough for him to hear. He grinned. My head struggled to steady itself as the music slowly began, fear rushing through me. I didn't know how to dance. Emilios read the emotions across my face.

"Don't fear, Princess, I will guide you." His voice was so deep and desirable. His words entranced me. The music grew as I desperately clung to him, blindly following his silent commands. The room spun as he led me along. The intensity of the music began to grow. I had no idea what I was doing, yet my body moved effortlessly with his.

I felt bewitched.

Emilios gracefully spun me out and back into him. His chest pressed against my bare back as his arm reached tightly across my breasts, gripping my hand tight. My eyes closed. He smiled as his face nestled lightly into my neck. We swayed for a moment, moving with the music. He twirled me out and back around to face him. My free hand landed on his chest. He looked down at me, catching my curiosity as I thumbed the low neckline of his tunic. His eyes burned into my skin. My heart raced as the music gradually intensified.

Together, Emilios and I mastered each movement with fluid intensity. A strange power coursing through my body, controlling me, guiding me through the sensual dance. Emilios pulled me close to him as he dipped me back. His warm body leaned forward with mine as I dropped my head. My eyes closed as my body surrendered to the music, letting it wash over me. His hair lightly traced my breasts as he devoured the display. He steadily raised me back toward him, taking his time, consuming the sight of me. I lost myself in the music as we continued moving as one.

The dance neared the end as Emilios twirled me once more, our eyes meeting. For a moment, we stared at one another lost in the trailing beat. My eyes studied his face, his hands and his body.

Could he be the man I saw in my dreams?

My thoughts were interrupted by the sound of the surrounding fae applauding. Startled, I pushed myself back, breaking from his grasp and clapped in unison with the others. My cheeks burned as they flushed bright red. Emilios smiled, slowly clapping his hands together. His gaze remained on me.

"I must admit, you move elegantly, Princess." My head was throbbing. A pressure thickened as he spoke.

"I feel quite faint," I proclaimed, "I think it would be best if I take a walk outside. Maybe get some fresh air." I reached for my aching head.

"Shall I escort you, Princess?" He reached his hand out for me to accept. The heavy weight on my shoulders increased, my body eagerly wanting to accept his offer. I had to resist the strange urge to place my hand in his.

I desperately scanned the room, hoping that some wandering fae would meet my gaze and read my silent plea. My wandering eyes abruptly met my father's. He was leaning over the armrest of his throne, watching me. His gaze was frightening. Fear bubbled inside my stomach. I turned back to Emilios.

"I think it best if I go alone. Thank you for the dance, Lord Emilios." I stumbled, grabbing a handful of my skirts. I began to retreat towards the gardens.

"Of course, Princess."

My eyes glanced over my shoulders as I shuffled away. Both Emilios and my father remained in view, both still watching me as I scurried through the busy room.

I shoved and pushed my way through the crowd of fae, making my way towards the open garden doors located towards the back of the ballroom. I needed fresh air.

I felt instant relief as I lunged through the open, towering garden doors. The invisible weight released its grasp on me as my foot stepped onto the cold stone path. *Thank the Gods.* I closed my eyes and took a deep breath, inhaling the crisp fresh air. Relief. My headache slowly began fading away as the foreign presence dissolved.

The palace gardens seemed to glow in the evening air. My arms wrapped across my bare shoulders, clinging for warmth as my feet carried me further into the magical gardens. A faint breeze blew past and my body lightly shivered. *Damn, I wish I had my cloak.* I strolled through the gardens, inhaling the aroma of the fresh spring flowers and running my fingertips along the dainty petals. It was so peaceful. I came to the massive granite fountain in the center of the mystical garden. The water softly trickled down the old stone; the sound of the soft streams was calming. I sat on the cold stones at the edge of the fountain, absorbing the gorgeous surroundings.

The sun had set causing deep colors to drench the world around me, slowly soaking it in the colors of the night. Being outside had helped. My head was no longer dizzy, and my mind felt clear again. Sitting on the edge of the fountain, my body slowly began to fade back to its normal self. Feeling returned as the bruise on my torso screamed in pain from dancing. My hands clutched my chest as I inhaled deep, sharp breaths. *Fucking corset.* Breathing in the cooling night air, my mind wandered, replaying the beguiling exchange between Lord Emilios and myself. Something about him reeled me in.

The old bell tower above the palace rang, startling me. My bruise throbbed with pain as my body jolted.

I had been lost in thought for quite some time. *Fuck.* It had grown late and cold. My body screamed for me to remove the constraint around my chest. I grabbed a handful of the tulle skirts, lifting them over my knees as my feet hurried through the garden back towards the palace. My feet scurried carefully past the open doors, hoping to move past unnoticed as the festivities continued inside.

Past the garden doors, amongst the overgrown ivy along the palace wall was an old hidden, secret passage. I snuck through the aged rotting wooden door and stumbled into the tunnel. As a child, I hid from my siblings and played in the tunnels of the palace, memorizing every inch of the hidden pathways. This particular passage was my favorite. It led from the garden, past the ballroom, snaking through the palace and up to the hall outside my chambers on the second floor. The dark tunnel smelled of wet, moldy earth—a welcoming, familiar aroma. Creeping along the cold stone path, my skirts trailed behind, staining the hem with remnants from the dirty, dank floor. My instincts led me through the unused tunnel. Even in the darkness, my memory could navigate my way through the labyrinth. Faint music and muffled voices of fae from the ballroom could be heard through the thick tunnel walls. I was relieved to escape the ridiculous event. As I came to the bottom of the steel spiral stairs, a familiar voice stopped me in my tracks. The voice drifted from the other side of the stone wall beside me. My body inched closer, running my fingers along the cold wall searching for a small peephole. There were hundreds of them carved throughout the palace in the secret tunnels.

There you are.

My head leaned down to peer into the tiny spy hole. Faint light bled through from my mother's library. The room was massive. It reflected the aesthetic of the rest of the palace. Its towering walls were bursting with books and scrolls from all over Devas. In the center of the room was an old fire pit—fully ablaze—encircled with chairs. The familiar voice spoke again.

"I don't understand why we're still discussing this. There's no *real* threat." Keres walked into view and up to the firepit holding a glass of wine. The flames cast dark shadows onto his visibly annoyed face. "And even if there was, I told you what should be done."

My eyes surveyed the room, spying my father sitting in a chair facing away from the fire pit. He seemed deep in thought, legs crossed, as he sipped his cup of wine. Lord Emilios stood directly next to my father, hovering like a shadow.

"Still, my prince," he drawled, moving his attention from my father to Keres, "consider the benefits of such a contract."

"I think your proposal is ridiculous," Keres sneered, throwing his cup into the fire pit. The loud clunk of the impact made me jump.

"Enough," my father rose as he spoke firmly, "I'll consider your terms, Emilios. You'll have my answer within the hour. Now leave, *both* of you." He motioned the two fae toward the library doors, signaling them to exit. Emilios smiled as he bowed and left the library. Keres huffed as he bolted from the room. My eyes lingered, watching as my father approached the fire. He stared into the blazing flames, sipping his wine as the fire crackled in front of him.

Curious.

I withdrew my gaze from the peep hole. My breathing was strained against my cinched waist. My hands shifted the corset before continuing up the spiral stairs. At the top of the stairs was a small door hidden by a large tapestry that led to the halls outside my room. I carefully shoved the door open and pushed the thick, heavy fabric aside, peering into the hall before creeping to my chambers.

I need to get out of this damn dress.

My feet kicked the dirty, dusty blue tulle skirts aside, searching for my boots. My corset was thrown across the room. I had changed into my common green tunic and worn brown trousers that were kept hidden under my mattress. My hair remained braided, but all the tiny, glittering pins had been removed along with my tiara that sat on my vanity. Dragging my boots out from under my bed, old mud and dirt chipped from the soles as my feet shoved inside and I laced them. I snatched my small dagger and an old satchel from the vanity, sheathing the dagger as I hurled the satchel over my shoulder. Inside the bag was a small spyglass, an apple, and an old book from the library, *The Mythical Monsters of Devas*. I loved to sit and read atop the obsidian cliffs as waves crashed below. I was currently reading more tales of the elusive Sephtis.

My hands brushed old dirt from the chest of my shabby tunic, accidentally hitting my bruise. *Fuck.* I pulled a dark, tattered hooded cloak from under the mattress and clasped it around my neck before quietly easing open the door to my chamber. My head peeked around the door into the hall checking to see if anyone was near. Faded music and voices from the Spring Equinox festivities could be heard as they continued below. *Clear.* My feet tiptoed, dancing along the hall to the door beneath the tapestry, shoving the heavy fabric aside. As my body quietly slipped through the hidden door, the sounds from the festival faded as I ventured further into the tunnel. I carefully raced down the old spiral stairs and through the dark musty hallway, following the same path I had taken before, retracing my steps. The door to the gardens creaked as my hand pushed it open so I could peer past the thick ivy into the garden. The ballroom doors that led to the gardens were now closed and foggy. The air had become cold enough that I could see my breath floating in the night.

My back hunched down as I cautiously made my way to the far end of the garden. A large stone wall stood at the back of the palace grounds, overshadowed by an old oak tree. The tree grew from outside the palace wall and stretched over into the garden. My fingers felt along the wall, searching for little projections on which I could position my body. My feet stepped along the protuberances, and I braced myself as I climbed to the top, pulling myself onto the ledge of the stone wall. I crouched, hurling myself onto an outstretched branch of the tree. My weight shifted as I fumbled from one branch to another, awkwardly descending down the limbs of the tree. Lunging from one of the lower branches onto the ground below, my knees burned as my feet landed, hitting the earth below.

Made it. I wiped the dirt from my hands and pulled the hood of my cloak further down my face. The large obsidian cliff stood just east of the palace. The mountainous formation towered high above the water, overlooking the dark sea below. If I hurried, I should reach the rocks within the hour.

The waves crashed viciously in the distance, casting a strong breeze and filling the air with sea salt. The monstrous coal-colored cliffs reflected the moonlight. I carefully crawled the wet rocks, struggling to find my way to the top. I stumbled against the slippery smooth stone, eventually reaching the cold, flat top of the cliffs. My lungs inhaled the thick sea air, and I stepped further along the cliff, perching myself near the edge, my legs dangling freely in the cold windy night air. A cold mist enveloped my feet as waves roared below. I removed my satchel and dumped the contents onto the damp stone. My hands flipped through the pages of my book, searching for my place as I took a bite out of the crisp apple. My eyes glanced along the dark, vicious sea with my spyglass.

"Where are you?" I mumbled under my breath, hoping to spy the legendary sea serpent off in the distance.

The night grew late as the hours passed by. I had finished my book, slamming it with slight frustration. Once again, there was no luck spotting the Sephtis. My arm tossed the core of my apple into the ocean below with anger as I gathered my things, drew the cloak over my head, and stood in defeat. The night was bitter cold as a thick fog began to materialize across the base of the rocks. It was late. I needed to return to the palace before my father realized I was gone.

I began to descend the slippery obsidian cliff cautiously, trying to not fall. I leapt from the lower rocks onto the fog soaked ground, the smokey cloud dancing as my feet landed. My body shifted toward the palace when a familiar invisible weight stopped me in my tracks. A chill crept up my spine. I wasn't alone.

Retrieving my dagger from its sheath, my body crouched in a defensive position and peered through the dark fog. I held my breath listening for movement in the darkness. I could sense *something* was watching me. The invisible force pushed harder against my shoulders.

"Who's there?!" my voice shouted into the foggy night air. Hard foot steps crunched against the earth, growing louder from behind the rocks. I whipped around in the direction of the sounds, fully alert. A tall, dark shadow stalked in my direction through the smoky fog, stopping a few feet away from me. The figure slowly sharpened into view. Lord Emilios.

"Hello, Princess," he purred, inching closer. He was now wearing a thick black cloak atop his formal tunic. "I thought you had retired for the evening when you left the ballroom?" He tilted his head as his eyes shifted down, taking note of my changed attire. "What *are* you doing out here, *alone*, at this hour...dressed in such a way?" He seemed genuinely curious.

My body straightened, relaxing my posture. "Lord Emilios," I attempted to compose myself. "Forgive me, but I must be going. It's late, and I would prefer it if my father *didn't* know I was out here. Please, will you tell no one you found me here?" He didn't answer, only stared.

I hesitated, turning back towards the direction of the palace, when something grabbed my arm, forcefully holding me back. My eyes shot back to see Emilios' hand gripping my arm. He was so close, towering above me. He glided his fingers along the skin of my face, lightly tucking a stray hair behind my ears. "Allow me to escort you back, Princess." His hand drifted, firmly cupping my chin, raising my face to his. My brows furrowed as my heart raced. My body leaned into him, disobeying the voice in my head saying, *Run.* My instincts screamed, warning me to pull away, but I couldn't. My body was under a strange influence. His black hair fell across his face as he leaned in, closing the distance between us. Faint fear washed over my body.

"Please, let me go," I quietly demanded. He grinned devilishly.

"Is that *really* what you want, Princess?"

My heart beat echoed in my ears. The voice in my head yelled for me to run, but something about him kept my feet firmly unmoving. His grip on my chin tightened, frightening me.

"Release me." He ignored my command. My hand pulled the dagger to his throat sharply. His hold tightened around my other arm. "I said, *release me.*" My words resembled a growl. My hand pushed the dagger against his skin. His dark eyes sparkled with hunger as he glared down at me. His hand fell, releasing my chin as he reached for my dagger hand, gripping my wrist. He used his strength to overpower me, lowering my hand and dagger from his throat. I winced in pain as he turned my wrist, forcing the dagger to my own neck. A ghostly weight pushed harder against my shoulders preventing me from fighting. My hand struggled to resist. I tried to scream, but my voice wouldn't obey. That invisible force had taken over my body.

He leaned in close to my face as the dagger slowly pierced my neck. Warm blood leaked from beneath the blade.

"Stop resisting, Cyrene. You're only making this harder on yourself." Panic set in as my hand ached, straining to push back. Tears formed in my eyes as he watched me bleed. "*Stop fighting,*" he growled.

Never.

I spat in Emilios face, causing him to flinch and loosen his grip on me. Snatching my hands from his, I yanked the dagger away from my neck and directed it towards him, clutching my fresh wound. Warm blood slowly oozed under my hand, running down my neck. My feet stumbled as I steadied myself, feeling off balance. He wiped his face and smirked.

"I look forward to breaking your spirit."

I aimed the dagger higher in his direction.

"Back-the fuck-off, *Emilios.*" Rage burned as the warning escaped my throat. Emilios grinned with excitement as he abruptly lunged at me. *Fuck!*

I tried to run, but it was too late. Emilios yanked my cloak, choking me as my body fell back. He stepped around me and leaned down to grab my hand as my foot kicked him hard in the face. Emilios fell back. I scuttled from the ground, fumbling as I ran, sprinting toward the palace against the thick fog.

"You cannot escape me, Princess!"

As he yelled from behind me, my body seized. I had lost all control, becoming paralyzed. Horror filled my veins. Emilios' laughter echoed in the night as he walked behind me. He forcefully removed the dagger from my hand and tossed it onto the hard ground. My body struggled, trying to escape, but it was pointless. I had no control.

A wave of that invisible power washed over me, drowning me. I gasped, struggling to breathe under the intense pressure. Emilios stalked close. He snatched a handful of my hair back, forcing my head up as he whispered into my ear. "You will learn to bend to my will, Princess." I tried to scream. "You still don't understand, do you, Cyrene?"

Emilios released his grip and began to circle me like I was his prey. My body buckled as that powerful force slammed harder into me.

"I will *make* you surrender to me." He continued to pace around my frozen body. "Dear Cyrene, you lost the second I set my eyes on you. Now, I will admit you did surprise me, Princess. Your will power is *much* stronger than I had anticipated," Emilios stopped directly in front of me, "a mistake I won't make again." Of course. It all made sense.

Emilios was a *Pathos*.

Pathos were fae who had the terrible ability to enter the minds of others. They could manipulate emotions and take complete control of someone. All high fae and their descendants had extended life spans, but very few were blessed with such abilities. Even fewer, still, were gifted with multiple. These select few were known as *Seelies*.

Seelies were the most powerful high fae. The last known Seelie was the late King Marius, who had the abilities of a *Pathos* and a second unknown ability. Tales of his powers were great. My father and Keres had *Lout* abilities. They were strong, powerful, and skillful fae warriors. Brutes. My mother, Queen Kea, was a *Duende*. She dazzled all who set eyes on her, enchanting them. It was rumored that men and fae from all over Devas would fall madly in love with her, simply after catching a glimpse of her beauty. Cecelia was what was known as an *Unseelie*. Unseelies were high fae with no abilities. Ungifted. I myself had yet to discover my abilities...if I even had any. I didn't mind either way, though at this moment I wished to be a Lout.

Lord Emilios was a Pathos. The heavy weight I felt, the force that controlled me, the light headedness, the headaches. It had all been *him*.

"You see, Princess, I *need* you." Emilios clutched my arms as my limp body remained powerless. He shadowed over me as he spoke. "With you by my side, I would be crowned a prince. I could then use that power to lay claim to both halves of Amos, ruling the largest region in all of Devas. My power would rival that of your siblings, even your father!" I cringed with disgust at his claims. "We could rule Devas *together*. Overthrow your father and take the kingdom for ourselves. We would be unstoppable." He sounded so optimistic.

"My father would *never* let that happen," I coughed the words against his force. Anger washed over Emilios face as he gripped my throat with his hand, his eyes burning as he proceeded to choke me.

"If you won't join me *willingly*, I'll just have to *force* you to obey me."

I gasped, clinging to the night air. He leaned in, inches from my face. "Besides, he's already agreed." My eyes bulged with fear and shock. My nails frantically clawed at his hand as he squeezed my neck.

"P-please...s-stop," I begged desperately. Breaking the sounds of my desperate sobs, a bird screeched. It dove high from the sky, directly to Emilios' face, clawing at his skin. He was forced to release his grip as he battled the bird. Emilios' invisible hold over me instantly vanished. I coughed and gasped for air. My body fell into the dirt, and I scrambled away as the bird—a hawk—tore at his face, drawing blood. My neck screamed in pain, burning from his grip and the kiss of my dagger. I dug my nails into the dirt, gagging on the thick fog and cold night air as the hawk flew from Emilios.

"Where are you?!"

My eyes spied the dagger laying in the dirt only a few feet from me. I glanced back toward Emilios' voice. His eyes met mine. He charged toward me, his face bloodied, full of anger. I had to escape. Shifting my focus and mauling the earth, I frantically dragged myself toward the dagger.

Emilios sprinted to me, kicking my side. I groaned in agony as his invisible force returned, pinning me down against the ground.

"You see, dear princess," he leaned closer, "this agreement will not only benefit me but your father as well—or so he believes." My hands continued to struggle, clawing for my dagger. "Recently, an imposter from the Bottomlands has declared himself the rightful king of Devas. Your father didn't concern himself with this ridiculous matter, thinking it only to be a rumor, until support of this 'king' began to grow. So, naturally, *I* offered the king a simple solution. With this contract between us, we would have enough power to snuff out this foolish *Jarloth,* as they call him, leaving your father in debt to me. Then I could use that leverage to gain support and overthrow your father and siblings. It's the perfect plan really. Imagine ridding myself of this imposter under the guise of helping your father, only then to steal the kingdom for myself. Years of waiting for the perfect opportunity and here it finally is." Emilios chuckled smugly at his plan.

"You should learn to shut your mouth and pay better attention to your surroundings, Emilios."

He snarled down at me. My hand snatched the dagger as I lunged with all my strength. He howled in agony as the blade landed deep in his thigh. I scampered to my feet and sprinted back toward the palace.

I didn't stop to look back at Emilios. His cries faded in the night as I charged back toward the old oak outside the palace wall. *Gods, please, don't let him follow me.* I frantically scaled the tree, tumbling down and over the side of the stone wall. My head slammed against the hard stone bench as my body fell. *Fuck, not again!* I screamed at myself to get up, groaning in agony, as I rose and limped my way through gardens to the hidden door. I shoved the ivy curtain aside and flung myself into the dark passage. Once inside, I paused to catch my breath. *Keep going, Cyrene.*

My body screamed as I forced my way through the tunnel and up the stairs. I came to the hall outside my chambers and inched open the hidden door. The hall was silent and dark. My head was in agonizing pain as I crept towards my room. *Almost there.* My hands pushed the large, heavy wooden doors open. Moonlight beamed through the windows, filling the room with a hazy blue. *Made it.* I pushed the door shut, locking it immediately. My head pulsated as my body sloped against the doors, struggling to catch my breath.

My head throbbed immensely as the room began to spin. My arms pushed against the door, struggling to hold my weight. My knees buckled and gave in, causing me to collapse. I fell, hitting the cold marble. My body laid partially sprawled on the floor, unable to move. My vision blurred with each pulse of pain in my head. I could feel my consciousness slowly fading away as the room began to spin. My eyes blinked as a faint figure of a man suddenly appeared, walking toward me.

Oh no.

It couldn't be Emilios, could it? Fear conquered me. My body laid helpless on the floor, an easy target. My body shook from pain, exhaustion and coldness. The tall blurry figure was so close.

"I'm here."

My ears recognized his voice instantly. My fear dissolved.

How could he be here? Had I hit my head that hard?

My dream lover lifted my dirty, limp body with his large, dark arms.

He held me close. I could smell him. *Cedar wood, ginger, and cardamom.* It felt so real. He cradled me as he carried me to my bed. My mind battled the darkness, trying to keep my eyes open as he placed me atop my soft ivory mattress. My mind began to fade further. My hand reached out, searching for him.

"Wait..." I whined. *Don't go.* His warm hand gently embraced mine, the other caressed my forehead with care and tenderness.

"*Rest.*" His voice was so deep. I was exhausted. There was no strength left for me to fight the darkness.

"*Rest.*"

So I did.

I awoke with a ringing headache. My weary body shrieked in agony as I slowly rose, wincing. My hand touched my neck. The wound was stinging, embedded with crusty, dried blood and dirt. Fuck, it hurt. My eyes scanned the room and noticed my dirtied boots and cloak tossed in a pile next to the bed. The room was dark except for a faint glow in the fireplace. How long had I been out?

A delicate knock on my door broke the silence. A faint voice seeped through the thick wooden door.

"Cyrene? Are you in there?"

My legs dropped over the side of the bed. "Unfortunately so," I groaned. Cecelia gracefully entered my room, holding a lit candle that flickered in the thick darkness.

"Cyrene, what in the Gods is the matter with you?!" Cecelia was dressed in a simple, pastel blue silk nightdress draped with a pale shawl. Her chalky hair was braided casually down her back. "After you wandered off, Father became enraged. He sent Keres and Lord Emilios to search for you." *Well that explains why Emilios was at the cliffs so late.* "When Lord Emilios returned early this morning, Father demanded to know why he was injured. Emilios told Father when he tried to bring you back to the palace, you attacked him?! Cyrene, you *stabbed* him with your dagger!"

Fucking Emilios.

My blood boiled with rage. I needed to warn Father of Emilios' real plan. Once he heard the truth, he would dissolve the damn contract between us. Cecelia inched the candle closer peering at my face through the darkness.

"Cyrene? What's happened to you?"

My body struggled to stand, wobbling as I grimaced in pain. Cecelia covered her mouth, gasping at the sight of me.

"What time is it? Where's Father?" My sister fell back, numb with shock. "Cecelia, *please*, it's imperative!"

"I-it's almost twilight..." *Twilight? I was out for an entire day?! Fuck.* "F-father is in the library. What's going on, Cyrene?"

There was no time to explain. I needed to see my father immediately. My body shoved past Cecelia, darting down the grand stairs, my bare feet hitting the cold floor as I marched past the ballroom in the direction of the library. I hoped I wasn't too late. As I neared my mother's library, the giant doors swung open and Keres rushed out, vexed.

The color drained from my face as my bare feet halted. Keres narrowed his blue eyes at me. He was still dressed in his gray formal tunic, his crown no longer sitting atop his head.

"Just the *bitch* I was looking for!" He stalked in my direction. I didn't have time for him to berate me.

"Please, Keres, I need to speak to Father. Whatever you've heard, I—" Keres cut my words short as he enclosed the distance between us.

"Oh, you've done enough." He towered over me, emitting such power. "Did you honestly think we wouldn't find out what you did to Lord Emilios?!"

My feet slowly stepped back as he shadowed my steps. "Keres, please—" my voice fell faint like a whisper.

"Silence!" his words boomed. I had never seen him so enraged. "You have embarrassed this family enough. I warned Emilios of your absurd behavior, but he was so persistent to possess you...though I feel Father was relieved at the idea of ridding himself of you."

Possess? Excuse me?! My brows narrowed. "I am not some object to be given," my voice growled back at him.

He scoffed at my words. "Yes, you are."

We sat in silence for a brief moment, glaring at one another.

"I must speak with Father at once. Move aside, Keres," I tried to stride past my brother.

"You will do no such thing." He grabbed my arm and shoved me back, causing me to stumble.

"Keres, *please,* you don't understand! Emilios is going to use this marriage to take control of Northern *and* Southern Amos. He plans to gain enough power to rival Father!"

Keres bellowed. "Do you *actually* think that *halfr*, human-fae bastard, could accomplish such a thing?!" He crossed his arms. "Father knows exactly what he's doing. Emilios is just a pawn in the long game. Same as you. Now, return to your chambers. You are to accompany Emilios back to Northern Amos in the morning."

Like hell I was. Keres could read the discontent across my face. "You don't have a choice, Cyrene. You should be on your knees thanking Father for allowing such an esteemed marriage. You see," he lowered his arms, slowly stepping around me, "I personally believe you should be shipped off to that *Jarloth* creature. Let him distract himself with you and have his way. I hear he's a real beast, slumming in those nauseating Bottomlands swamps. But, alas, Father agreed to Emilios' terms," he stopped in front of me, glaring down his nose, "though you don't deserve such pleasantries."

"I know you dislike me, Keres, but what have I done to merit such hatred?"

He shook his head. "Hate you? No, I *despise* the very thought of you." His words burned. "You're an abomination, Cyrene. It's time you learn the truth." *The truth?* "Sadly, our poor mother fell victim to her own ability," he pointed in my direction, "and *you* are the product of such a crime. As if existing wasn't disgusting enough, you drained her life as you drew breath. You should burn for the sins of *your* father!" Tears filled my eyes as my eyes stared at the face of my repulsed brother. *My father?* "Take your pathetic, wretched self back to your chambers and assemble your things. We will finally rid ourselves of you at first light."

I choked back a burning pain as tears clouded my eyes and scurried down the hall, back up the stairs, and into my dark room like a defeated animal.

The door slammed behind me as I retreated into my room, leaning against the wooden doors, replaying everything Keres said to me. My mind struggled to process his bitter words. *King Serifos wasn't my father...*

Tears rolled down my dirty cheeks. My existence was a walking reminder of the violation my mother endured. A monstrosity. My stomach grew sick.

You don't belong here, Cyrene.

Pushing myself from the doors, I rushed to grab my filthy boots, shoving my feet inside as I laced them quickly. I threw the tarnished green cloak over my body and carefully clasped it around my neck, avoiding my wound. I took no possessions with me as I quietly swung the doors of my room open and charged towards the tapestry masking the passageway door.

It was time for me to leave, to *escape*.

The palace and its occupants lay dormant in a deep slumber. The secret tunnel was dark, cold, and silent. I forced myself through the passageway, attempting to ignore the suffering pain from my body or Keres' words as my feet moved. *Focus, Cyrene.* I made my way to the door that led into the gardens, slowly creaking the door open when his voice stopped me.

"Don't fret your pretty little head, Lord. She will be within your grasp soon." I peeked past the vines and spied Keres. He was speaking to Lord Emilios. Emilios stood next to him, his face shredded and bruised, his leg wound was tightly bandaged. He held a lit torch, grimacing at my brother while Keres toyed with my dagger.

"I still can't believe the bitch attacked you," my brother sneered. Keres sheathed the dagger into his belt.

"Alas, Prince, every creature has a breaking point," Emilios snarled. "I will find hers soon enough."

"Excellent." Keres smacked Emilios shoulder, snickering as he trotted off back into the palace.

The small tunnel door slightly gave. The sudden creaking broke the silence, snapping Emilios' attention towards the thick ivory. *Oh fuck.* I held my breath and stiffened. He aimed the torch in my direction, illuminating the vines to peer through the shadows in the direction of the concealed door. I could hear his boots crunching against the stone path as he slowly limped in my direction. There was no way to escape him again, I was too weak. My heart accelerated as my mind scrambled, contemplating my next move.

"Lord Emilios." One of the king's servants scampered to Emilios, distracting him. "King Serifos wishes to speak with you."

His eyes glared at the servant, then shifted back in my direction. "Is there something back beyond the ivy?" He asked, pointing unknowingly to the passage door. The fae glanced towards me, unaware of the hidden door.

"No, my lord, it's just a wall of ivy." Emilios stared for a moment before trailing behind the fae as they returned inside the palace. My lungs exhaled heavily with relief. *Thank the Gods.* I waited a moment before bursting from the door and sprinting through the winding garden to the back palace wall.

Clambering up the rough stone wall, my hand reached for a branch of the old oak and missed, once again, falling from the tree. My body howled in agony as it slammed into the ground below. There was no time to stop and rest. I struggled to stand with a grunt, plucking twigs and leaves from my tangled hair. My mind raced with thoughts. I couldn't remain on the island... Everyone here knew my face; I would be recognized and returned to the palace just to have Keres ship me off to Amos. There had to be a way out. I needed a ship. My breath huffed as my eyes peered through the darkness scrambling to think of something.

Emilios and his court would be departing from the western port. It would be impossible to find a ship there without being spotted. It was too risky. I scoured my brain for a second option. The southern port. It was smaller and less traveled, but it would have to do.

My eyes looked up at the cloudy night sky. The southern sea port lay a few hours south. If I set a good pace, I should be able to reach the port before sun up. My lungs inhaled the misty night air before bracing myself, hastening toward the southern edge of the island.

Soon I would be free of this place. My prison.

An hour or two had passed as a soft drizzle began. I continued traveling south, toward the smaller seaport. My clothing had become completely drenched from the cold rain, my boots soaked in mud. I hugged my body tight, shivering. The port couldn't be much further.

The rain grew into a heavy downpour as thunder boomed in the distance. My body ducked under a lone tree, seeking shelter from the storm, stopping to rest a moment. The rain thickened, challenging my sense of direction. *Where is the fucking port?* Hugging the base of the tree, my eyes strained to see which direction I should continue. I needed to hurry.

Scanning the darkness ahead of me, my eyes searched for any trace of the seaport when a loud, piercing screech rose from up the tree. My body recoiled, glancing up to see a familiar red-tailed hawk perched on a branch. It was the same hawk that had attacked Emilios. *Strange.* The bird remained still, observing me with his black eyes. He had the most beautiful rich brown feathers and a cinnamon red tail. *Why was he here?* The hawk's sight remained fixated on me, as if waiting for a response to its screech.

"Don't suppose *you* know where the southern port is now do you?" I asked sarcastically. The hawk stared deep into my eyes and shrieked, as if responding to my question. The reply startled me. Did the bird understand me? I squinted, looking out into the darkness then back to the hawk and hesitated, "Can you guide me to the port?" The hawk squawked, flapping his broad brown wings and shooting into the sky. He was fast. I instinctively trailed behind, struggling to keep pace.

I followed the hawk's shrieks, shadowing him as he sliced through the thick downpour. We continued moving south, making our way closer to the sea. I could hear the waves roaring in the distance. The hawk screeched and landed on a large cluster of rocks. My body leaned against the wet formation and scanned the distance ahead. The outline of a vessel sharpened into view. *The seaport.*

"Thank you." My eyes met with the bird's as he observed me. "Do you wish to join me?" The hawk tilted his head. I cautiously reached my arm out, and the hawk instantly jumped, landing on my arm with such force causing me to jolt. He was large and solid. His feathers glowed in the darkness like a small, beautiful fire. "I shall call you Aodhan."

He shrieked in acceptance of his new name. With the company of my new friend, we made our way through the darkness, closing the distance between the port and ourselves. We needed to remain unseen if we were to sneak aboard the ship.

Sailors of all ages were bustling around the docked vessel, shouting as they rushed. The men were fighting the rain in their preparation to sail. Prancing down the dimly lit pier, my body weaved behind various cargo and barrels. A sailor rushed past me as I ducked quickly behind a large container, attempting to remain hidden. My heart rate increased. *Too close.* Peeking over the box, I could see the ramp leading onto the ship ahead. *Time to hurry, Cyrene.* Suddenly, Aodhan screamed and shot into the sky, out of sight.

"What do you think you're doing?!" My head turned to face a tall, slender man. He was glaring back at me with deep, soothing brown eyes that matched his dark chestnut skin and shaved black hair. He was dressed in a long dark tattered brown jacket over a beige tunic. "I *said*, what do you think you're doing?" He shook me as the rain drenched us both.

"Please, sir, I need to leave the island—"

"Ahh, no stowaways on my ship." He tossed me aside as he trudged towards the ship's ramp.

"Please," I followed after him, "I cannot stay here! I promise I won't cause any trouble, sir. Please, I beg you!"

He spun around swiftly. "What business have you aboard my ship? Do you even know where we're headed?" The man crossed his arms, waiting for my response. He was watchful of my answer.

"Your destination is unimportant to me...as long as I leave this island *tonight*." His gaze remained fixed upon me for a moment. Thunder boomed in the distance. "How do you expect me to let you aboard? Do you have any payment?" *Shit.* I hadn't thought about bringing money with me. The man read the concern across my face. "That's what I thought," he huffed and turned back to the ship. He respectfully barked at a few sailors as they ran by.

"May I at least know you are headed, sir?"

The man shouted over his shoulder, "Seamarke."

I didn't know the Lord of Seamarke well, but I knew there would be a way to arrange some form of payment from the Lord upon my arrival. "I can get you payment!" The man turned, raising an eyebrow as he glanced in my direction. "If you let me board your ship, I can get you whatever payment you require…once we arrive in Seamarke. You have my word."

The man studied me for a moment. "What makes you think I can trust your word?" I sighed, pulling back the hood of my cloak revealing my face, my hair, and my pointed ears. The man's eyes met mine, as a glint flashed across his dark irises. He instantly stiffened in recognition. "Princess? Forgive me, my lady," he bowed in respect. My hands pulled the hood of my cloak back over my face shielding before the sailors could spot me.

"Sir, please, can you help me reach Seamarke?"

He grunted in acknowledgment. "You may call me Ivar. Welcome aboard the Herskip, my lady." He motioned for me to board the ship as I nodded my thanks. "We leave in just a moment's time. Please, make yourself comfortable in my personal quarters." I ascended the ramp and boarded the Herskip.

The sailors stared as my boots cautiously stepped onto the boat, Ivar directly behind me. "Oy, listen up! This is an old friend of mine. Show her the same respect as you do me. Understand lads?"

"Aye, captain!" The men shouted in unison. As the sailors rushed to resume their tasks, Aodhan called. My eyes shot high as they spied him nestled in the rigging above. He soared down, landing roughly on my shoulder.

"Ah, how nice of you to rejoin me, little sir." He purred as my fingertip lightly stroked the tiny feathers atop his head. "Let's get warmed up and out of this damn rain." The crew prepared to launch from the pier as the captain showed me to his private quarters.

My body was exhausted. It was time for me to rest.

I found myself wandering the most beautiful woodland, surrounded by moss covered trees that branched high into the sky topped with thick canopies of leaves. Moonlight peaked through entangled branches, casting white beams across the forest floor as fireflies danced around like shooting stars in the dark woods. The scenery was so magical—yet so familiar. It felt as though I'd seen this place before.

My eyes closed, absorbing the beauty around me. A soft night breeze circled me, rustling the greenery. Inhaling the woodsy smells around me, I recognized his friendly aroma immediately. *Cymar.* His scent instantly ignited a flame burning deep inside me. I drank it in, thirsting for more. *Where are you?*

Tiptoeing across the forest floor, leaves and twigs snapped under my bare feet as I frantically searched for any sign of him. He had to be nearby. The burning grew as a strange gravitation pulled me, guiding my every step. My body obeyed that foreign sense, exhausting itself searching. I came to a large, old moss-covered stump, stopping a moment to catch my breath, gasping for air. My throat burned. I had forgotten about the wound on my neck. My finger lightly touched the laceration. I exhaled sharply as a hand delicately turned my head. My eyes stared up, recognizing his blurry face.

His long black hair lay loose around his face as my head rested in his warm hands. My eyes strained to make out the details of his. *Were they glowing?* His bare arms bulged as he held me. He gently examined my neck, eyeing the deep cut and dark, painful bruises from my scuffle with Emilios. I winced in pain as his thumb barely traced the dagger cut. A low, deep growl emerged from within him, *"Who did this to you?"*

"It's not that bad," the lie left my lips like a whisper. He knew I was lying. He grabbed my battered hands and examined my injured fingertips. My nails were torn and bloodied from my struggle back on the island. I tried to snatch my hands from his. "I said, *I'm fine.*" I was embarrassed and tired. My body just wanted a release.

My hands attempted to break free from his grasp, but he was too strong. He held onto me tightly, growling as I tried to tug free. "I'm not some helpless damsel in distress waiting for your ass to rescue me!" I felt frustrated and annoyed. Eventually, he released my palms, causing me to stumble back, huffing. I shot him a furrowed glare and turned away, stomping towards a cluster of thick old trees. *Screw this shit.*

I had only traveled a few feet away when he suddenly appeared in front of me. He whipped my body around, shoving me hard against the trunk of an old tree. The back of my head smacked the hard wood as he pinned my arms above my head with one hand against the bark. His other hand squeezed my waist, tugging me closer to him. He tightened his grip around my wrists, as if struggling to control himself. His face hung above mine, his hair falling onto my face. He slowly breathed down my ear as the tips of his lips traveled lightly down, across the side of my injured neck. He licked the wound, sending a wave of pain and pleasure through my nerves, causing me to shiver. His mouth ventured further south to pull the strings of my tunic with his teeth, exposing parts of my chest.

He kissed my injuries gently as he made his way down my body. He traced up my sternum with his tongue as he tightened his hold on my waist. He lifted my tunic, my bare breasts falling free. His tongue found its way to my hardened nipples and traced them, lightly biting the tips. A small moan escaped my throat. His mouth finally found its way to mine, inhaling me. My heart struggled to stay calm as he breathed me in.

"Is *this* what you want?" His warm voice whispered through our intense kisses. His touch fueled a fire deep inside me, causing it to burn with an unspeakable carnal desire. My body shuttered and ached for more.

"I *want* you to fuck me." His lips form a devilish smile, exposing his canines.

"*As you wish.*"

He scooped my body up, throwing my legs around his waist, gripping my ass tightly. My arms wrapped around his neck as he carried me back towards the old tree stump. He dropped me onto the stump, forcefully pushing me onto my back as his rough hands grappled with my thighs. He spread my legs wide apart, causing me to gasp in excitement. He smirked. My trousers didn't stand a chance as he ripped them effortlessly from my body.

"I'm going to devour every last drop of you, Princess," he whispered through heated kisses, making his way down my leg to my inner thigh. I gasped, fighting back moans of delight. He faintly bit the skin of my inner thigh. I winced, enjoying the feverish pain. He kissed his bite mark before steadily moving in between my legs, focusing his warm tongue on my center. My lungs inhaled sharp breaths as he snaked his way inside me. He took his time, tasting me, consuming my wetness as he quickened his tongue, then slowly he retreated from my soaked body and forcefully yanked my body close to his. He was pressed hard against my center, as his lips met mine with lust. I breathed him in as we continued to consume one another, desperately craving more. My nails dug deep into his lower back. My back arched as he grunted, pressing harder against me. I wanted him inside me. My hand slid from his back and gripped the top of his trousers. As my fingers attempted to untie his trousers, I faintly heard Aodhan. I paused, confused. He continued to kiss me as Aodhan screamed again.

"Cymar?" I glanced up at my lover as his voice fell silent. The dream quickly began to dissolve. *No.*

My eyes shot open. Aodhan was flapping his wings, shrieking, alerting me. My body groaned in frustration as someone knocked on the door to the captain's quarters. I rose from the humble bed and stumbled to the door, cracking it slightly. The light from outside seared my eyes. Standing on the other side was Captain Ivar.

Ivar was holding a pile of folded clothes. "Sorry if I woke you, my lady. I just wanted to bring you some fresh clothes. It's not much, but they're better than those tattered rags you've got on now. Plus, they'll keep you warm." He extended the pile out to me. I hesitated a moment before accepting the clothing. "When you're dressed, you should join me. It seems we finally outran that damn storm." I nodded, thanking him for the clothes. He retreated to his crew as the door shut.

Captain Ivar's room was small and plain. Dull sunlight peeked through the windows above the captain's bed. At the foot of the small bed was a simple wooden arm chair and desk covered in maps, papers, along with a few lit candles emitting a glow across the room. A small table stood on the other side of the chamber with a pitcher of water, a wash bowl, and a small hand mirror. The room may have been a bit common, but it was warm and cozy.

I placed the pile of folded clothes on the chair as Aodhan perched at the top. He watched me curiously, as I filled the wash bowl and splashed my face. The water turned a deep, nasty brown color. I hadn't realized how dirty I'd become. My neck stung as the water rinsed my wound. I slid my filthy clothes off and wiped down my entire body, flinching as my hands cleaned around the many bruises I'd collected. My hand grabbed the fresh clothes from the chair and quickly dressed.

The large, thick tunic was a faded maroon, the trousers a stiff boring brown. The warm clothes sagged, concealing my smaller frame. I ripped some of the fabric from the bottom of the tunic and bandaged my neck, hoping to keep the wound clean. I managed to find a small brush and detangle my wild hair, removing a few twigs and leaves gifted by that damn tree, and styled it into a simple braid draping down my back. My pointed ears remained concealed under my thick hair in the hopes of keeping my identity a secret. I made my way towards the door of the captain's quarters and took a breath as my foot stepped through the doorway and onto the deck. Instant brightness burned my eyes as the sunlight momentarily blinded me.

"Aye, you made it. I was a bit worried you may have fallen back asleep." Captain Ivar approached me. My eyes squinted against the bright light, slowly adjusting, revealing the Eastern Sea. It was magnificent. I was mesmerized by the sight before me. The water reached as far as I could see, and the sky was the brightest blue. Birds flew overhead as the sea roared on, salt filling the air burning my nostrils. I had never traveled so far before.

"First time at sea, is it?" My head shot in Ivar's direction, stunned. "I can always tell when it's someone's first time crossing the great sea. There's always this mix of fear and excitement in their face." He wasn't wrong. The sea seemed powerful yet frightening. It was truly breathtaking.

"Come." Ivar motioned for me to follow alongside. We casually strolled to the bow of the ship, gazing at the waves as they crashed against its hull.

"How far are we from Seamarke, Captain Ivar?" *We had to be close. The great sea filled my sight in every direction.* He peered up to the clear sky for a moment.

"I believe we're about halfway there, Princess. As long as the sea and Gods allow, we should arrive around this time tomorrow." *Almost free.* The captain looked around a moment and then leaned closer. "If you don't mind me asking... Why *are* you fleeing the island, Princess?" The color drained from my face and my smile disappeared. How *does one* even explain what happened? Could I even trust Ivar with the truth? Sensing my discomfort, he shook his head. "Forgive me, Princess. I meant no offense. It's none of my business."

"No, it's okay, I just... It's hard to put into words." I paused for a moment, replaying all that transpired before my escape.

"Are you in danger?" Ivar asked, seeming genuinely concerned.

"All will be right, once we reach Seamarke."

Ivar stared blankly ahead. "I'm not sure Seamarke is the safest place for you, Princess," he spoke cautiously.

"Why is that?"

Captain Ivar continued to stare ahead with an intense expression, eyeing the sea ahead. He didn't look at me as he spoke.

"Devas is unstable at the moment. The Lord of Southern Amos has pledged himself to the Jarloth from the Bottomlands...and I hear the Lord of Seamarke is considering shifting his loyalty from the crown." *What was it about this Jarloth?*

"Lord Agwe has always been faithful to the king, a true, steady ally. There's no possible reason for his fealty to change so easily. This Jarloth is a nobody. Why would such a powerful region consider following him, breaking their vows to follow their king?"

Captain Ivar glanced back at me. "Forgive me, Princess, but you have no idea what's really happening in Devas, do you?"

My eyes glared at the captain as I crossed my arms, "Explain it to me, Ivar. Why would any region give this *usurper* a second thought?" He chuckled lightly, raising his brows.

"This Jarloth isn't some random fae rebelling against King Serifos. No. See, he claims to be the son of the late King Marius. Which, as you know, would make him the rightful heir to the throne—*not* your father. The rumors say that not only is he seeking to dethrone the king, he's seeking revenge for the death of Marius. He claims King Serifos murdered Marius for the crown."

"What utter shit! How could anyone actually believe such blasphemy?! Marius was Serifos' older brother. He may be powerful, but he would *never* harm his own brother." Serifos may not be my father, but I knew the king well enough to know this was a lie. He would never hurt Marius. He idolized him.

"Regardless, Devas is unraveling, Princess. Rumors alone can destroy a country. A few of the southern regions have already pledged themselves to this Jarloth. Truth or not, the people welcome any excuse to turn on our king."

My head snapped in his direction, "What has he done to earn such *treason* from his people?" Father or not, the nasty rumors disgusted me.

Captain Ivar sighed, "Well, for starters, the king has always ruled Devas with fear. His anger knows no limits. Queen Kea shielded the people from him, but after her death, they were no longer protected from his wrath. Over time he lost interest in torturing his people, handing the continent of Devas off to Prince Keres and Princess Cecelia to rule in his stead. Unfortunately, Keres oversees the regions with hatred, while Cecelia does as she's told. Keres does whatever he pleases and doesn't care who he hurts." *Typical Keres.* "The king is a dark shadow perched atop his throne, keeping all of us in a dark suffering, while he enjoys his pleasantries on his island. Forgive me, Princess, but the people of Devas deserve better."

It was known the king rarely left his court, but I didn't realize how bad things really were.

"But, Ivar, the rumors of King Serifos *murdering* his brother Marius… those can't be true."

Ivar shrugged. "Who knows? But if this Jarloth is the late King Marius' son—"

"Then he would be the rightful heir to the throne…" My words trailed in the wind as I stared out into the sea ahead.

"I'll get you safely to Seamarke, Princess, but if you need anything from me, please, let me know. I vow to guarantee your safety." I nodded, thanking him for his service. He was too kind. Captain Ivar excused himself.

I sat atop a large wooden crate at the bow of the boat, listening to the waves crash as my mind wandered, replaying everything Ivar had said to me. *Could this Jarloth be telling the truth? Was he really Marius' son? Serifos couldn't have murdered his brother… Could he?* My mind looped through the information, pondering for hours.

The sky slowly darkened, fading into deep oranges and magentas, painting a peaceful sunset across the great sea. My chest filled with anxiety. I was nervous but excited to reach Seamarke and begin a new life.

My stomach broke my thoughts, aching and growling with an immense hunger. It had been a long while since I last ate. I hopped from the crate and made my way to the captain's quarters. As my hand reached for the door, it swung open. Captain Ivar was exiting the room.

"Oh, apologies, Princess. I just wanted to leave some food on the table for you." He pointed back into his quarters. "It's not much but I wanted to make sure you had something in your belly." Ivar turned back before he left. "By the way, Princess, your bird really is magnificent."

I smiled, "His name is Aodhan."

"*Little fire*, very fitting." He returned my smile, bowing lightly before he turned to leave.

"Ivar?" He stopped, turning back to face me. I hesitated, "Would you care to join me? Aodhan is great company, but it would be nice to hold a conversation with someone who can actually speak." Ivar released a faint laugh.

"It would be my honor, Princess." I pushed the door open, motioning for him to enter.

On the desk was the meal Ivar had left for me—a small bowl filled with a warm stew and a plate containing a simple biscuit and humble sliver of salted pork. Next to the food was a cup of rum. Aodhan shrieked with excitement as we both entered the candlelit room.

"Aodhan seems to have taken a liking to you, Captain Ivar." He flew over to the desk, prancing along the wood to Ivar as he cautiously stroked his head. "Seems you've made a new friend." Ivar continued petting the hawk, admiring his friendliness. I smiled, sitting down as I looked at the plain meal. It might not have been as glamorous as what we were accustomed to eating at court, but my stomach was grateful for it. I tried to offer some of the meal to Ivar, but he waved my gesture off. "I'd love to hear a tale of the infamous Captain Ivar," I teased lightly. Ivar laughed, smiling as he spoke of his adventures, how he became a captain, working his way up the ranks, eventually earning his boat, the Herskip, how he had traveled to every region in Devas and even ventured to the seas beyond. His life sounded exciting.

I listened as Ivar spoke of Seamarke being his home as I picked up the small, warm bowl and began slurping the watery stew. It felt marvelous running down my throat. I downed the flavorless liquid as it warmed my hands. I took a bite of the dry biscuit, breaking off a small crumb for Aodhan. He softly pecked my hand as he gobbled the morsels. Ivar and I exchanged stories of mythical beasts and monsters that were said to haunt the great seas of Devas. He was pleasantly surprised by my knowledge of such creatures.

"I'm thankful to have you both as my companions." Aodhan purred as my finger brushed his smooth feathers. Ivar leaned close, placing his hand on my shoulder.

"I'll get you safely to Seamarke, Princess, you have my word." I nodded, thanking him for his time. He excused himself, leaving Aodhan and me to our musings.

My hand picked up the strip of salted pork and I took a bite out of the chewy meat. Aodhan and I sat in silence as I continued consuming the simple meal while chugging the rum. My hunger was monstrous, devouring the entire meal within minutes.

My eyes peered across the room and out through the foggy windows above the captain's bed. The sky had fully darkened, bringing the night with it. *Time to rest.* I stood and walked to the bed, settling myself in for the night. Aodhan flew to the window above me as my body curled up.

"Goodnight, little sir. Tomorrow we will reach Seamarke and begin a new adventure." I pulled the thick blanket over my body and closed my eyes as a faint drizzle began, tapping at the glass of the window. Aodhan remained perched above me.

Those soft taps continued, slowly lulling me to sleep.

Thunder boomed, startling me from my sleep. My heart raced as I frantically shot up in the bed. The ship was moving furiously as loud voices could be heard from outside. *What was going on?* The floor of the quarters was drenched in a thin layer of water as the boat creaked and rocked. I could hear rain fiercely pounding against the window above me. Peering through the glass, I could see only darkness. I hadn't been asleep long. Lightning cracked, followed by more thunder. A sudden burst of light outlined the dark angry sea. The waves slammed into the ship launching me from the bed onto the cold, wet floor.

Aodhan shrieked loudly as crew members shouted, rushing past on the deck outside the door. I tried to steady myself on the wet floor, as I wobbled toward the door. Aodhan perched himself on my shoulder. My hand gripped the handle of the door, opening it just as an overshadowing wave smashed into my body. I struggled to keep my hold on the door. Aodhan flapped his wings, gripping his claws into my collarbone, faintly piercing my skin, as he tried to steady himself. The boat leaned the opposite direction swinging us back with the door as the ship shifted. My eyes struggled to see outside. Rain slapped my face as mighty wind and waves continued crashing into the boat. Lightning was the only light we had to navigate our way through the night. I threw my body from the door and lunged out into the darkness. Thankfully, my body fell, landing firmly against a coiled pile of ropes. Aodhan struggled to keep his hold on my shoulder as I tried to fight the waves and steady myself against the ropes.

The boat continued rocking back and forth with the angry sea. Lightning struck across the sky once more, illuminating monstrous waves as they rose high over the side of the boat and washed along the crew. The sailors yelled as they fought the water, desperately trying to stay on board. The sky turned dark in between lightning strikes as heavy thunder roared, echoing through the night air. I could hear Captain Ivar yelling from the quarterdeck above. He was shouting for his crew to tie themselves down as he strained with the wheel, attempting to steer the ship away from the storm.

Aodhan's claws gripped tighter into my shoulder, as my hands fumbled along the lines, trying to make my way to the captain. Another powerful wave crashed into us. I coughed and spat the sea water from my mouth. The salt stung my neck and eyes. I struggled to see through the rain and sea water. My hands desperately clung to the lines.

Aodhan screamed and shrieked, but I couldn't focus on him. We needed to reach Ivar. He aggressively flapped his wings and continued to squawk at me.

"What is it?!" My throat burned as I snapped at the bird, coughing the words from my mouth. Aodhan blasted into the night sky with a screech. My eyes strained trying to follow him as lightning struck. The flash revealed the cause behind Aodhan's screams. Terror overcame me as my eyes widened. I watched as it slowly rose from the dark sea. Thunder echoed as the sky fell black again.

"CAPTAIN! STARBOARD!" I frantically screamed up to Ivar through the storm, my eyes fixated on what was lurking in the darkness. Ivar struggled to see the cause for my fear, peering to the right of the boat. A low, deep terrifying rumble filled the night. My heartbeat echoed in my ears. I could hear it approaching the boat, swimming through the sea. Another lightning strike revealed the frightening beast. *Gods, it was real.* The ancient serpent towered high above the ship. Its pitch black scale-covered body bled into the dark night. Piercing white eyes narrowed down at us. The monster released a frightening low growl, revealing a mouthful of long sharp teeth. My books couldn't have begun to prepare me for what stood before us now.

"SEPHTIS!" Ivar yelled down, warning his crew as they stood frozen in terror, gawking at the great beast. Just as the sky went black the

Sephtis released the most blood-curdling, deep shriek. I covered my ears, wincing, as it continued to screech. Suddenly, the serpent became oddly silent. *Why did it get so quiet?*

The serpent released another low growl as lightning struck. My eyes stared up at the monster as it lunged directly at the boat, mouth wide open. Fear washed over me as my bones ached in absolute horror, unlike anything I'd ever experienced before. I tried to flee but my ankle was tangled in the rope. Screams of terror filled the night as the Sephtis' fangs burrowed deep into the middle of the ship, completely snapping the boat in half. My body slammed into the wooden floor of the ship, my foot still tangled, as the stern of the ship began to rise. Sailors desperately clung to various parts and pieces of the boat as the two halves separated and began to sink. The Sephtis slithered through the sea, sending waves across the broken pieces of the ship, knocking the sides. The impact flung men from the ship into the sea, allowing the serpent to easily devour them. It felt like a nightmare.

"PRINCESS! Hold on to something!!" Captain Ivar was hanging from the helm, yelling down at me. I tried to dig my nails into the wooden floor as the ship turned, but it was too slippery. The Sephtis slammed hard into the side of the ship, finally tipping the rear half of the broken ship onto its side. The monster coiled its body around the broken half of the ship, constricting what was left. My hands desperately clawed at the ship, trying but failing to find something to grab onto. *No, no, NO!*

The Sephtis crunched the ship completely apart, snapping the lines. The ropes flew from the rigging, twisting my ankle, causing me to yell in pain. My body fell with the ropes and slammed hard into the cold, dark water. I struggled to hold my breath, splashing and clawing against the sea. The lines finally released my injured ankle as another wave pushed me back under. I forcefully swam my way back above the water. As my head broke the surface of the sea, a wave rammed a broken piece of the ship into my face, knocking me back under for a moment. My head rang as immense pain pierced my skull. I paddled against the sea hoping to escape the Sephtis that was still destroying the remnants of the Herskip.

Blood poured from my wounds as my head throbbed. I spotted a chunk of driftwood nearby and swam to it. I attempted to hurl my body onto the wood, but it was too wet. I slipped, falling back into the water. My hands tried to grasp the driftwood again but failed. A scream emerged from my throat, as I used all my strength to pull myself onto the piece of wood. My body was ablaze with indescribable pain. My hands burned as claws began to tear from beneath my bleeding skin, digging into the wood. Every bone in my body felt as if they were snapping and breaking. I roared in agony against the rain and waves.

What the hell was happening to me?!

I stared at my hands in horror as hair began to sprout from my skin, when something caught my eye. My head shot up to see a chunk of the ship's mast headed straight for me. I clawed into the driftwood and tried to duck the soaring debris as it bludgeoned straight against my face.

Darkness.

My body jolted awake, as I shot from the bed panting and clutching my bare chest. My skin was drenched in sweat and my head throbbed from a sudden migraine. *Fuck.* I rubbed my temples, groaning and trying to ease my head pain as I steadied my breathing. The nightmare felt so real.

"Fenix?" A voice trailed through the room as my door swung open. Her hair glowed like fresh blood as she leaned against the open door frame.

"It's time to get up, Fenix." Despite being my younger cousin, Tove had always taken care of me. She was strong and ruthless, a warrior. Her father, Harold, raised us together here in the Bottomlands. Harold was the late lord of our region. After his passing, Tove inherited his position and gained the title Lady of the Bottomlands, though she despised being called a lady.

"Come on now, your council has gathered in the great hall." I leaned over the bed as she tossed my tunic straight at my face.

"You know, some privacy would be *greatly* appreciated."

She scoffed, rolling her eyes. "Unfortunately, it's nothing I haven't seen before." *Ass.* I chuckled to myself, pulling the black tunic over my head, rising from the bed. "Besides, someone has to keep an eye on you."

I tucked the faded tunic into my dark trousers. "I can take care of myself, Tove."

She scoffed. "Yeah, until you do something stupid. *Again.* You're not invincible, Fenix." I ignored her, dragging my worn boots across the floor.

Tove straightened and tilted her head, concern filled her voice. "Are you okay, Fenix?" My focus remained on the floor as I grabbed my coat from the end of the bed.

"Yeah, just dealing with a headache." Tove stepped towards me as our eyes met. Her golden irises glowed in the dimly lit room. Her face was overshadowed by a giant scar that reached from her temple, across her eye, nose and onto her cheek.

"Are you *sure*?"

"Just a bad dream, cousin, I'll be fine."

"Alright then, suck it up!" She whacked my arm. "You may be our fearless leader, but let's not keep your counsel waiting." She turned and left the room, her sheathed swords across her back clanking as she moved. I smirked, rubbing my arm and followed behind her.

Tove spoke over her shoulder as we wove our way through the stone palace. "Leander received word from his spies up north. He wants to speak with you after the meeting."

Greatness. "Have we heard back from the Criss?"

She shook her head. "Lady Delmare has yet to acknowledge any of our proposals." *Of course.*

"What of her uncle, Lord Agwe?"

She sighed, "Seamarke is taking its time. Last we heard, Lord Agwe was considering our terms, though I wouldn't expect any changes for sometime" She glanced back at me. "He's watching us, Fenix. "

"I know. He wants to ensure the best for his region. I respect him for it, but we're running out of time. My patience is growing thin, and we need to know who our allies are." We continued making our way to the large closed wooden doors in silence.

Tove shoved the old doors open as she made her way into the great hall. Opposite the doors stood a large stone fireplace fully ablaze. The castle walls were adorned with tapestries and weathered shields paying tribute to past warriors. Candlelit chandeliers stretched along the vaulted ceiling, casting a warm glow over the old room. A large wooden table stood in the middle of the great hall. A small group of men hovered over the long table, sifting through pages and maps as they mumbled to one another. I'd chosen the most loyal members of our region for my counsel.

The room grew silent as we made our entrance.

Tove strode to the table, picking up a full cup of ale. "Thought you didn't drink this early, Leander." She chugged the ale and chunked the empty wooden cup down the table. Leander appeared from the group of men, snatching the cup before it could fall from the table. *These two.*

Leander was the Lord of Southern Amos and my oldest friend—aside from Tove. The three of us had grown up together, traveling between our two regions. We always seemed to find ourselves in some form of mischief. Tove loved to give Leander a hard time, and I think he secretly enjoyed her attention. The two had an odd chemistry between them, but I didn't mind. They might have annoyed the shit out of me, but they were my family.

"Ignore your cousin's ridiculous accusation, Fenix," Leander huffed in Tove's direction, "I haven't had a single drop. You know I don't like to drink this early."

"*Especially* after last time," Tove chuckled under her breath as Leander shot her a glare. I threw my sword onto the table, plopping myself down in my chair. I lifted my legs and crossed them over the table, signaling the members of my counsel to take their seats.

"Relax, Leander, I'm here to talk strategy, not bust your balls. Besides, *you* of all people know how Tove can be." My focus shifted to Tove as she rolled her eyes and tossed her swords next to mine.

"Honestly, I wouldn't mind a drink right now myself." Leander instantly stood, retrieving the ale and began to pour me a mug. He always looked so out of place here. His clean, formal green tunic clashed against our region's dark, common attire. He handed me the full mug. I nodded, taking a generous gulp of the bitter drink. *Hopefully this helps my fucking headache.*

One of the older men in my counsel cleared his throat, "Lord Fenix, we really need to discuss our next move."

I continued to drink the ale, my headache slowly dissipating. "I already know our next move, Cormac." He huffed as the empty mug slammed against the table. "We *need* more power. Since Seamarke and the Criss have chosen to test my patience," my eyes scanned across the seated members, "it's time we negotiate with the Vaud packs from the Silas."

Cormac and the other men instantly began shouting, vocalizing their displeasure. The room filled with disagreeing voices fighting to be heard. Tove eyed Leander, then me. Her eyes were wide with anger. My heart ached at her pain as she spoke.

"You can't be serious, Fenix... Why the *hell* would we ever do such a thing?!"

"Silence!" My voice boomed as my hands slammed into the table so hard they pulsated, showing a small glimpse of my power. The men silenced in fear. My head angled towards my cousin. "You may be the leader of this region, Tove, but know your place." My words thundered as her golden eyes burned with rage. She didn't speak, only nodded in submission. I turned my focus back to my counsel.

"The Vaud are powerful. They have control of an entire region in Devas. If we can convince even *one* of the roaming packs to join our cause, we would stand a far greater chance of defeating Serifos."

"And how, *dear cousin*, do you suggest we convince members of an unruled region, infested with those rabid wolves, to care enough about our cause and join us?" Tove spat her disdain filled words at me.

"We agree to give them the Silas, free from my rule. We would allow their kind to maintain their freedom within the borders of the region."

Tove scoffed with disapproval.

Leander leaned forward, "How would we avoid conflict upon approach to even speak with them? The packs are filled with uncivilized, shape-shifting humans who prefer their beast form to humanity and recognize no authority outside their own."

The man next to Cormac spoke, "Perhaps we could send a subset of warriors? Ones who have experience dealing with these packs."

The counsel took turns speaking. "Experience or not, the Silas is nothing like the Vaud strays we encounter here in our lands. Even our strongest warriors aren't strong enough."

"The Vaud are scavengers, searching for their next kill. We don't stand a chance." Leander looked back at me, "Fenix, you're our leader and this is your plan. What do *you* suggest?"

I exhaled a deep breath, "I will go myself."

The entire room protested my words. Leander studied me in silence, trying to decipher my blank expression as Tove erupted from her chair, standing tall.

"I will join you."

The side of my lips curled into a grin as I crossed my arms. "I figured you'd say that."

Tove leaned across the table and pointed her finger at Leander, "Your ass is coming too."

"Whatever you say, Lady Tove." Leander smiled as he leaned back in his chair. Tove snarled at him.

The men shifted in their seats as Cormac spoke, "Forgive me, Jarloth, but even with your cousin and Lord Leander joining you, would you stand a chance—"

"Are you questioning my judgment or insulting my power, Cormac," I growled, "or *both*?" He quivered in fear.

"Neither, Jarloth! I simply meant—"

"What Cormac *meant* to say," the older man seated next to Cormac started, "is that it *is* concerning, sir. We'd be sending our Jarloth, our lady, *and* the lord of a neighboring region into a risky situation. It's a costly gamble that would leave us and Southern Amos unprotected against Serifos and his allies."

"The tribe can protect our region while we're gone. Lord Leander has forces in place back in Southern Amos for situations like this. And your *lady* expects complete obedience from you. You will do as your Jarloth commands." Tove's words were firm. The men of the counsel nodded in submission.

"It's settled. Leander, Tove, we leave at first light. Cormac," he rose as I spoke, "I'm leaving you in charge during my absence. Continue things as I would, and by the Gods, don't make me regret this." Cormac bowed. "Now, if there's nothing else to discuss..." I rose from the table, "leave us." The remaining counsel members stood, bowing as they shuffled to exit the great hall.

My palms rested against the wooden table, my head bowed as my dark hair fell in front of my face. "Forgive my outburst, Tove, but you cannot question me like that again, especially in front of my counsel."

"I would never question your lead, Fenix," she walked to my side, placing a hand on my shoulder, "but I do not trust the Vaud wolves... not after everything that happened..." her voice trailed. My eyes studied the pain across her face.

"I know, you should've said something before announcing it in front of the whole counsel." My eyes scanned the deep scar across her face, our gazes meeting briefly before she sharply turned away from my sight.

Leander cleared his throat, "There's something more we need to discuss, Fenix." I sighed, rolling my eyes. *Of course.* "I've received word that Emilios has visited Serifos at the high fae court."

Fucking Emilios. "Yes, Leander, I'm aware of Emilios' plan. He left Devas to meet with Serifos, wishing to secure a marriage with Princess Cyrene." My voice fell flat. Leander's weary eyes stared at Tove. "Unfortunately, Serifos has agreed." Tove's eyes widened as Leander stiffened his posture. My body stiffened, turning my back to the two of them.

Tove stepped towards Leander, "But if Emilios is allowed to marry the princess, he—"

"He would gain enough power and influence to overthrow my own, potentially gaining control over both halves of Amos," Leander choked on his words. "We wouldn't stand a chance against him. Serifos may have complete control over the northern regions of Devas, but Emilios would be able to rival him, potentially defeating the northern armies." His words stung.

The fire crackled as we stood in silence for a moment.

My eyes stared at the stone floor as I spoke to Tove, "Send Nox. We need to figure out what Emilios' next move is. Find out where he is and when he plans to marry the princess." She nodded, releasing a high pitch airy whistle. Not a minute later, a large inky black raven soared through the open doors and gracefully landed on Tove's shoulder.

"Ah, there you are. I've got a special assignment for you, Nox." The raven croaked in excitement. "I need you to spy on Lord Emilios. Find out as much as you can, then return to me." Nox shrilled, flapping her dark wings, shooting from the great hall.

My head turned, facing Leander, "Send your men to do the same. We need to find a way to stop this. Emilios *cannot* be allowed to marry the princess." He nodded and marched from the room.

Tove grabbed her swords, returning them to her back. "We need to be careful, Fenix. Serifos, the Vaud, Emilios… This fight was dangerous enough, but it's becoming something else."

I paced around the great hall, stopping in front of the fireplace. My eyes burned as they glared into the dancing flames.

"He cannot be allowed to marry her, Tove." The words stung as they escaped my throat.

"I know, Fenix."

"Gods, Fenix, what happened to you?" Tove tossed a pack over her saddle as I tightened the buckle on my own.

"Couldn't sleep."

"Figures. Probably just nervous for today's adventure, huh?" She bit her tongue, smiling as she hurled herself onto her painted horse.

"Not today, Tove. It's too damn early."

"Maybe for an old fae like you," she pulled out a waterskin and began chugging the contents, "but some of us are still enjoying yesterday's splendors."

"You've got to be one of the classiest ladies I've ever met, Tove," Leander cackled sarcastically, carrying a bundle of supplies over his shoulder. Like Tove and me, he was dressed in a casual tunic and trousers draped in thick traveling furs. It was odd seeing him so casual.

"We all know you haven't met other ladies, Leander. That would require you actually speaking to another female…and we both know you're too timid and up Fenix's ass to do that." She urged her horse forward.

I spoke over my shoulder as I mounted the onyx horse, "As entertaining as it is listening to the two of you, let's save that energy. It's going to be a long day." My calves gently squeezed the horse's ribcage as I trotted after Tove, Leander following closely behind.

Stars slowly dissolved as the world around us woke from its slumber. We traveled east across the Bottomlands and toward the Silas. Once we crossed the border, we would set up camp at the Carinthia ruins for the night. The ruins were ancient and the only remnants of Lady Carinthia's rule over the Silas.

Lady Carinthia was the last established ruler of the region. Unfortunately, like the rest of the territory's inhabitants, she had become a victim of the infestation of the Vaud. No one, fae or human, was able to escape the horrific slaughter. The fucking dispersers murdered *everyone*. After the massacre, they burned the bodies, setting fire to the whole region. It reeked of death for months. My face grimaced at the memory. After the inexcusable slaughter, Serifos declared the Silas uninhabitable and forbade anyone from ruling or living in the region. Now, over a hundred years later, mangy Vaud packs, lone wolves, and stragglers were the only living beings left in the eerie land. The ruins were the last remaining skeletons of Carinthia's palace, resting a few miles inside the region's borders. Vaud wolves were rumored to avoid the ruins believing the destroyed palace to be haunted by the spirit of Lady Carinthia herself. Superstitious humans.

If we kept our pace and didn't kill each other in the process, we would arrive at the ruins by nightfall. We would camp for the night and seek out a rogue pack in the morning. Truthfully, finding a rogue pack willing enough to hear us out would be the real challenge.

"I'll gather some wood and get a fire started." Tove stated as she hopped from her horse pulling an ax from her storage bag. "Don't want you ladies freezing now do we?" She grinned as she sprinted toward the nearby woods.

"Fucking hell, Fenix, did she have to join us?" Leander complained as he and I dismounted our horses.

"I would have *loved* to see you try to stop her from joining us," I smirked at Leander, "but I'd put my money on her." He huffed, setting his gear down with his pack.

"She's mighty, I'll give her that, but showing respect isn't a weakness, Fenix, even if she tends to perceive it as so." His whole demeanor changed. "She may be one of my oldest friends, but despite our differences, I'll *never* lay a hand on her...you know that." He stared into my eyes, his dark eyes full of emotion.

"I know, Leander," I turned away, untying my bedroll, "why do you think my money's on her?" I flashed him a light smile that seemed to melt his broody mood. He nodded and continued unloading his horse.

The sky had grown dark as violet strokes painted the air. A cold wind crept through the Silas, bringing with it a dense layer of fog. The Carinthia ruins felt eerie. The crumbled structure barely provided enough protection from the frigid gusts. Leander and I continued setting up the camp, rushing to finish before the sun fully set. We worked in silence, constantly peering over our shoulders as paranoia seeped in. The Silas felt unearthly, a sinister presence lurking in the air. Distant howls sent chills up my spine as we remained alert.

What was taking Tove so long?

"Do you really think we'll be safe here for the night?"

I could sense a thin layer of fear behind his question. I didn't answer. Leander accepted my silence and straightened his bed roll across the cold dirt. A twig snapped just beyond the ruins. Leander instinctively crouched, grabbing his sword. I peered through the thick fog in the direction of the woods.

Where was Tove?

The sun had fully disappeared as night took over. Leander and I struggled to make sense of our surroundings in the darkness. We crept around the weathered stone pillars toward the woods as murky fog encircled us. We cautiously waded through the ruins. Leander stepped just outside the ruins, his sword in hand with his back to me. I slowly paced ahead toward the trees. My lungs inhaled multiple deep breaths, searching...but there was no trace of Tove's scent. I sniffed the air once more, catching a whiff of a musty, wet dog. The stench grew, quickly traveling east from the woods. *Fuck.*

"LEANDER!"

Instant snarls erupted from within the fog as a ragged wolf launched in Leander's direction. He whipped around as I slammed into the dog, sending it firmly into the ground. Howls broke in the distance as two more wolves crept out from the woods, circling us from either side.

"Fenix, I got this. You go find Tove." Leander held his position, angling his sword. The lighter wolf charged him, snarling. He swung, slicing the wolf down with mighty grace. "Go, Fenix!" The other wolf aimed at Leander.

As they fought, a larger wolf appeared. *Mine.*

I slowly stalked away from Leander as he and the other wolf continued fighting. The large wolf kept its eyes glued to me, as I shuffled cautiously toward the woods. I *needed* to find Tove. The larger wolf growled, suddenly lunging in my direction and slamming into my arms. Its mouth opened wide, baring long sharp teeth, clamping its jaw in hopes of biting my flesh. Its heavy body clawed at mine as I grappled its mouth with my bare hands. The creature struggled, biting, fighting to break my grasp. My hands clutched both parts of its jaw and forced its mouth completely open. A pain-filled shriek escaped its lungs as the bones snapped within my grip. I slammed the wolf's head hard against my knee as its skull crumbled beneath my force. The beast went limp. I kicked the carcass across the dirt and looked back at Leander. He ripped his blade from the dead wolf and marched to my side, panting.

Howls erupted from deep within the woods. "I guess we found our rogue pack." We stared at the dark woods ahead.

"Not a pack," I sniffed the air, "there's a hoard of Vaud wolves in those woods."

Leander glanced at me puzzled. "Vaud wolves don't have hoards... They can't function together in large groups like that. "

I spat at the dirt and shuffled towards the woods. Leander followed without hesitation.

"They do now."

Leander and I trekked deep into the dark woods. Moonlight barely reached through the thick leaves, leaving us vulnerable in the darkness. We cautiously inched further into the forest, wary of our surroundings. There was no sign of Tove.

Rage boiled under my skin as I fought to control my feelings. "She couldn't have wandered off this far," I whispered to Leander. He nodded, his eyes surveying the treeline. We stepped a few feet further when a rumble of low growls stopped us. Three wolves emerged from behind the trees ahead of us. Leander lifted his sword, slowly advancing forward.

"Wait." My arm swung back, stopping him from charging. He reluctantly obeyed, holding his position ready to strike. My focus turned back to the wolves ahead, ominously creeping closer. My voice deepened, "Where is she?" The wolves ignored my question, and continued to close the distance between us. "Tell me," I growled as my muscles bulged with power, "I'll gladly take my time killing each of you until someone tells me where she is." Power rippled through the veins of my body.

The wolves halted, sensing my ability. The middle wolf erupted with a tumultuous howl. "What are they doing? Why did they stop?" Before I could answer Leander's harsh whispers, a figure appeared from behind the trio of wolves like a shadow, slowly stepping into a beam of moonlight revealing herself. The tall ebony woman positioned herself between the three wolves.

"You're either very brave or very ignorant to wander this deep into our land," the woman tucked her long, bistre dreads behind her ears as she spoke. She stroked the middle wolf's head, studying Leander and me with subtle turquoise eyes. They glowed in the darkness similar to that of Vaud eyes. "It's not often we get many visitors," she stepped further ahead of the wolves, "and even more rare to stumble upon an *Alpha*." She stopped directly in front of me, glaring up into my eyes.

"Where. Is. She?" I clenched my fists to subdue the rage of my ability. The woman grinned, ignoring my harsh demand as she turned and strolled back to the wolves.

"A debt must be paid," she spoke over her shoulder.

"Oh fuck this." Leander swiftly charged from behind me.

"Leander, *wait!*" It was too late. She turned sharply, raising her arm. Her fingers flexed and curled, as the earth rumbled beneath Leander's feet. He struggled to stand as branches reached from the trees above, growing like vines, pinning him down against the dirt. He groaned as the branches tightened their grip around his limbs, constricting his ability to move. I marched towards the woman in retaliation. The wolves snarled as she lifted her other arm, her focus now on me. Numerous thick branches grew from the canopy above, snaking down towards me. I grabbed each extension, ripping them harshly from their trunks. She stepped back cautiously regaining her posture.

"You know better than anyone what must be done!" She raised both her arms, the earth quaking in response to her power. Immense cracks began to form in the dirt around us. I charged toward her as rage boiled inside. "A life for a life, Alpha!" She swung her hands, whipping thorn-covered vines in my direction. "You cannot stop this!" I tore through the weeds like they were air. My arm raised, power surging through my veins as I aimed in the woman's direction. She showed no emotion as she gripped her throat, gasping for air as she fell to the ground.

"She is not yours to claim," I growled, crushing her further into the earth as my power constricted her. The color began to drain from her face. Two of the wolves sprinted towards me. I smiled, moving like a shadow, and broke both the wolves necks. The woman looked up as I stood, towering over her, the third wolf dead in my firm grip. No fear lurked in her face as she glared back at me with her glowing eyes.

"You kill me and you'll never find her," she spat. My eyes seared into hers.

"She owes no debt. *I* murdered that bastard." I threw the dead wolf at her feet. "Now take me to her. You want a debt paid, I'll pay it," I leaned closer, "but she goes free." Her eyes remained on me as I released her from my power. "Now," my voice trailed as she coughed, the color returning to her face, "take me to her."

The woman digested my words a moment then slapped her hands together.

"FUCK!" Leander gasped as the branches and roots of the trees released him, shrinking and retreated back to where they came from. He stood, coughing and panting, attempting to steady himself.

"What in the fuck are you?!" he yelled, his arm shaking as he attempted to raise his sword.

"She's a Vaud druidess."

"My name is Ydalia, and I am *no fucking Vaud,*" she hissed. *Interesting.* Ydalia turned to the bodies of the dead wolves as Leander lowered his sword and approached me.

"If she's not part of the Vaud, what *is* she?" We watched as she closed each of the wolves eyes and kissed their heads.

"It seems that she's a Vargr." Leander jerked his head and gawked at me. I stepped over the dead wolves and kneeled next to Ydalia as she sat, stroking one of the deceased wolves' fur. "Take me to her."

She glanced at me from the corner of her eyes. "You know I cannot disobey you, *Alpha.*"

I sighed, "I am not an alpha."

Ydalia turned and studied me. "You may deny it, but it is what you are." She glanced back towards Leander. "Why do you travel with a *halfr*?"

"He is my oldest friend...next to the woman you stole."

"She is no woman, Alpha. You know this."

"Fenix. My name is Fenix. My friend there," I pointed behind me, "is Lord Leander." I stood, reaching my bloodied hand out to Ydalia. She hesitated a moment before taking my hand, rising.

"My people won't take too kindly to your presence, Fenix."

Leander spoke up from behind us. "Just take us to our companion."

Ydalia growled at him. "My tribe doesn't welcome outsiders." She glanced back at me, our eyes frozen on one another. "Fine, this way," Ydalia reluctantly turned, gliding further into the woods. "Stay close, you never know what's lurking in these woods." Leander and I trailed closely behind.

It wasn't long before the smell of smoke choked the night air. The scents of wolves and humans danced in the wind as we traveled towards a faint glow in the distance. Faint voices could be heard in the distance, growing louder as we neared a clearing. "Don't try anything stupid. You're outnumbered here, *Alpha*," Ydalia whispered back as we stepped to the edge of the woods opening to a large glade. Caravans and tents filled the open space. Campfires glowed as dozens of people moved and mingled. This wasn't a Vaud pack or hoard—it was a Vargr tribe.

One by one, the members of the tribe looked up to Ydalia, watching Leander and me with caution. Ydalia silently led us through the tense campsite. Low snarls and growls broke the silence as we walked past the growing crowd of onlookers. She took us further into the winding camp until we came to a large, wooden caged wagon. Inside sat Tove, chained. Our eyes met. She had blood across her face hiding a fresh bruise across her cheek. She looked worn and hurt. I pushed towards her with anger as Ydalia strained to stop me.

"NO!" She glanced around. "They are watching you," she whispered. I shoved her hand from my arm.

"Release her."

An older man with white hair and dark skin stepped forward from the gathering crowd of humans.

"You *all* must pay a debt!" He spat at our feet as others shouted in agreement.

Leander turned to face the older man, "Like hell we will." The tribe bellowed with anger.

"You murdered our kind before and now you return murdering more. You all must pay!" The old man shouted as the crowd cheered him on. Ydalia was shoved aside as a group of men pushed towards us.

"Don't fight them, Leander."

The men herded us toward the barred wagon. Our wrists were chained as they shoved us inside the wagon with Tove, locking the cage. The group left, praising one another as they rejoined the crowd. Music and chatter filled the night as everyone resumed their ongoings, celebrating our capture. Ydalia gripped the wooden bars.

"Don't even try to escape. The wagon and chains are enchanted. Only I can break them. You shouldn't have come here, Alpha."

Tove spit in her direction. Blood stained her lips. "We came here to give you a chance at freedom," she wiped her mouth smearing blood across her face, "but you fuckers are too foolish to see what's really going on. You and your stupid Vaud traditions—"

"We are not part of the Vaud!" Ydalia's bright turquoise eyes narrowed at Tove. "My tribe has been fighting the Vaud for years. We may have been born Vaud wolves in this wretched land, but we choose to live as Vargrs."

"Then why are you holding us captive, huh? Explain that." Tove leaned forward annoyed, her chains hitting the floor of the wagon as she moved.

Ydalia stared at Tove, glancing back at me, "You *know* why." Her eyes returned to Tove. The two women glared at one another for a minute.

Leander broke the silence, "It's not our fault your wolves attacked us at the ruins. We only traveled here to make peace. Both of our people face a larger enemy."

Ydalia broke her gaze. "What enemy?"

My posture straightened, my chains dragging against the floor of the wagon as I moved, "Serifos."

Ydalia ruptured in laughter. "Ah, the mighty King Serifos. Do you really think any of us here in the Silas fear that fae bastard? He dubbed these lands ours for the taking after the fall of Lady Carinthia." She put her hands on her hips and peered up at the stars, "No, Alpha, we do not fear him. But I do fear losing our only chance at rebuilding this region due to some high fae that decided they wanted to step over the border into *our* land, slaughtering *our* kind." She pointed in our direction through the bars, "You three die first thing in the morning." Ydalia grinned as she stepped away, her cyanic eyes glowing as she faded into the crowd beyond the caravans.

Leander shifted to Tove, his chains clanking as he raised his cuffed hands to her face. His fingers hovered over her bruised, bloodied cheek. "What did they do to you?"

She winced as he carefully wiped the blood from her swollen bruised face. "I deserved it." Her words stung.

"Don't *ever* say that," I growled, anger itching beneath my skin. "You did *nothing* wrong." Tears filled her eyes as she nodded.

My eyes lingered on the deep scar across Tove's face. The painful memory flashed across my mind's eye.

"I killed Lazar...and I'd do it a thousand times over for what he did to you."

I knew my actions would come back to haunt me one day.

Almost a century ago, when we were young and just coming into our abilities, Tove and I would gallivant all across the Bottomlands. We would take off for days, creating our own adventures and living life to the fullest. Leander would join us when he could but remained more reserved and tamed—typical son of a lord behavior.

It was the night of Tove's mother's death. She had sneaked into my room and sat at the foot of my bed. She was broken. Her eyes were red and swollen, tears rolling down her face. I could hear her whispered cries. I leaned across the bed, attempting to comfort her, but she acted like a ghost. She told me she wanted to run away just the two of us and leave everything behind. I tried to convince her to stay, to tell her she couldn't escape the terrible pain inside her heart, but she was too stubborn. She was filled with such intense raw emotion, no one could change her mind at that moment. My reasoning couldn't stop her; she was too determined to escape her pain. She left without me, cursing me for not supporting her rash decisions.

I knew I should've joined her.

The following morning, my senses woke me. The smell of blood filled the air. Tove was lying next to me, facing away with her knees curled into her chest, quietly sobbing into a pillow. I turned around and placed my hand gently on her shoulder, slowly turning her to face me. Her face was swollen and bruised, a deep, fresh gash across her face resembling a claw mark. She had cuts all across her skin and numerous dark bruises that covered her neck. She looked as though someone had strangled her. Her entire body was blanketed in deep bruises and cuts, her clothes dirty, shredded, and torn. She pulled away from my touch and hunched back into herself, crying. I begged her to tell me what happened, but she refused to speak, only continuing to cry to herself. Seeing her broken and defeated made my blood boil.

Over the next few days, I remained by her side, silently caring for her. She wouldn't allow anyone else near her, only me. I had carefully treated her wounds, remaining patient when she would retreat from my touch and burst into tears knowing I meant her no harm. I'd given her the space she needed without leaving her. Each night she'd toss and turn, screaming as she woke, reliving the nightmare she experienced. I'd tried to comfort her, to reassure her that she was safe, but she'd pull away from me, hesitant to allow me to be close to her. She resembled a beaten animal and it broke my heart.

As the days grew into weeks, she slowly began to bloom back to life, eventually allowing me to be close to her as her trust in me was reestablished. I could see the light in her soul reignite to its full glow. Finally, one day she sat me down and told me what happened. I struggled to control myself as she spoke about that night, recalling the horrors she endured. After storming from my room that fateful night, she had left the palace and initially made her way east. Along the way, she stumbled upon a small wandering pack of Vaud wolves that had trespassed into our lands, led by a man named Lazar. He appeared drunk as he teased Tove, making revolting remarks about her body and describing the heinous things he wanted to do to her.

She struggled to speak, choking back sobs as she recalled what he did to her, how she could see his face when she closed her eyes, and how he haunted her in her sleep. How she could feel his glowing, gray eyes burning into hers as he assaulted her. Tove hadn't stood a chance against Lazar and his mangy pack of dogs. She hesitated, fighting back tears as she whispered to me what happened. How his men laughed while holding Tove down as Lazar beat and raped her. How she fought as he mauled her face, while he fought against her resistance, determined to take what he wanted before leaving her for dead. My stomach grew sick, wrath and shame filled my body.

I kneeled before Tove, my head low and tears falling from my face, "I'm sorry, cousin. I should have joined you—protected you. I failed you."

She softly touched my chin, lifting my head. Her golden eyes stared into mine, the gash across her face slowly healing, "I survived." My heart ached at how strong she was.

Later that night, I summoned Leander to the Bottomlands. Tove was cautious of his presence but knew he wouldn't harm her. He sat across the room giving her space yet still watching over for her. I thanked him for coming, gripping my sword as I made my way to the door. Tove jumped from my bed and followed.

"Where are you going?" I couldn't face her. "Fenix?"

I could feel her wide eyes lingering on me, silently begging me to stay. Leander cautiously took her hand and led her from the door. My heart ached at the sound of her voice as she pleaded for me to stay.

"I'm going to kill them for what they did to you." Before she could stop me, I rushed from the room.

Seething anger fueled me as I hunted Lazar and his pack. I had scoured for days, refusing to rest until I located the fucking bastards. After almost a week of combing the Bottomlands, I found them. The men had taken over a small tavern near the southern border. They were inebriated, openly raving about how they stole the innocence of a young girl and how she had asked for it. I remained silent as I entered the tavern, drawing my sword. I flew into a rage, slaughtering every individual in the room. Innocent or not, every person and fae in that tavern paid for the sins of Lazar and his men. I saved Lazar for last. I wanted to make him suffer as he had made Tove suffer and then savor his death.

Lazar lay flat on his back, choking on the blood pooling in his mouth. He desperately tried to wriggle away, petrified of what I would do to him. He struggled to speak as I stood over him, glaring down at his bloodied body.

"Why are you doing this?" he coughed, gagging on his words. Without faltering, I swung my sword high, slowly digging the blade deep into his heart. He screamed in agony as I smiled, taking my time as I shoved my sword further with all my power until my blade pierced the floor beneath his body.

"You made the mistake of hurting someone I love," my sword remained buried in his bleeding chest as I lifted my leg, "and now I've come to return the favor."

"You kill me, you'll have a debt to pay," he spat, "they'll come for you."

My smile grew. "Let them." His eyes widening with fear as my foot slammed into his skull. His blood splattered as I continued stomping away all trace of his pathetic life.

Tove and Leander ran to me at the entrance to the palace when I returned home. "Thank the Gods, Fenix!" Tove hugged me, tears rolling down her face. She pulled back as she looked me up and down, her face horrified at the realization of what I had done. My body was soaked in blood. Leander carefully retrieved the bloodied sword from my grasp, setting it aside.

"Are you okay?" Tove asked softly. They both stared at me unsure of how to react. My eyes met Tove's as she understood my silent expression.

"I am now."

I would never forgive myself for what happened to Tove.

If these wolves required a debt to be paid for the murder of Lazar and his men, then I would pay it.

"We need to find a way out. Screw talking to these people, we need to get out of here." Leander shadowed Tove's every move with concern.

"I have to pay my debt," the words faded from my lips, "it was only a matter of time before this happened."

Tove sat next to me, her chains hitting the wooden floor. "We can't change Devas without you, Fenix. I understand you *feel* that you need to do this, but there is no debt to be paid. *He* took from me...but you evened the score. Leave it behind and let's focus on making this world safer for everyone."

"I'm not a hero, Tove. I'm not doing this to save the world. I'm righting a wrong. Serifos *murdered* my father for a fucking crown. He is no king," I rose as my chains clanked, "I'll get you two out of here, but you must leave without me. If I survive the trials, I'll return home. But Tove—," she looked up at me with sorrow, "you must continue this if I fail. Find the princess."

She sighed, "I'll do whatever you ask of me, Fenix."

Footsteps caught our attention as two men approached, dragging someone behind them to the wagon. Ydalia followed, her hands extended and fingers arched, ready to strike if anyone made a wrong move.

"No funny business, Alpha," she said as the men unlocked the cage, tossing the struggling man inside. "Busy morning tomorrow." Ydalia smirked as the men locked the door. Then the three of them left, returning to a camp fire off in the distance. Our focus shifted to the man at our feet, a halfr. His hands were bound with rope, tied in front of his waist. He groaned, struggling to sit up. His clothes reeked of sea salt intertwined with another faint aroma that immediately caught my attention.

"Who are you?" The question jumped from my mouth. Tove and Leander eyed me, surprised at the tone of my voice, looking back to the mysterious man. His dark face had a deep, fresh wound across his nose. His weary brown eyes met mine, glinting in the dark.

"My name's Ivar."

Ivar winced, adjusting himself against the bars of the wooden cell. He closed his eyes, steading his breathing, before looking at the three of us. He studied each of us carefully, his eyes meeting each of ours, before stopping his gaze on me.

"You're the Jarloth aren't you?"

"What business of that is yours?" Tove harshly addressed Ivar. He smirked, nodding his head at her quick response.

"That would make *you* Lady Tove of the Bottomlands." She huffed at her formal title. Ivar's eyes twinkled as he observed her. He shot his sights to Leander, "You must be Lord Baldassare...Southern Amos, if I'm correct?" The three of us remained silent. "Figured. I'd heard stories of each of you," he pointed first to me, "of your features, specifically. Glowing gold eyes, pitch black hair and a pure white streak. Hard to miss. And you," he pointed to Tove, "your scar brands you." Tove winced at the painful mention of the permanent reminder from Lazar. "Not to mention the protection you have for your Jarloth. But you," he aimed his finger at Leander, "you don't exactly resemble your relative Lord Emilios as I expected you too."

Leander released a disapproving gust of air, "We may share blood, but that is all. That fucker can burn for all I care."

"I'm curious, how did you end up here, Ivar?" He looked up at me at my words.

"A few nights back, my ship was attacked...by the Sephtis."

My eyes widened.

"My crew and I were sailing from the island of King Serifos' high fae court to Seamarke. The first night was a bit rough, trying to escape the threatening storm as we sailed. We were lucky enough to outrun it, unaware of the treacherous waters we were sailing into," his words faded. "It attacked out of nowhere... Had she not warned me—"

"She?"

He gazed at me with sad eyes. "Princess Cyrene. She spotted the beast first and tried to warn me...but it was pointless." His head fell. Leander's eyes observed me as Tove inched closer to Ivar.

"What was the princess doing on your ship? She's supposed to be sailing to Northern Amos with Emilios." My breathing intensified as they spoke.

"I caught her trying to stow away before we cast off. She was desperate, seeking refuge. Wouldn't tell me what happened, but someone had hurt her—badly. She wanted to escape. I didn't question her much, but I offered to see her to Seamarke."

"Where is she now, Ivar?" Leander and Tove both leaned in questioning the man.

He sighed, "She fell from the ship when the serpent attacked. I lost sight of her when she hit the water...not long after I too went under."

Tove groaned, punching the bars, "FUCK!"

"Hey, I tried to help her! When I woke up, I found myself washed ashore on this wretched land. I had wandered for a few hours when I caught sight of her—"

"You saw her? She's *here*?!" Leander stood, smacking his head against the roof of the caged wagon, "Ah fuck!"

"*Was.* I tried to run to her, but these large brutes came out of nowhere and took her—"

"Brutes? Not the people here?" Tove seemed confused.

"No, these men were bigger. Stronger. They had strange markings plastered all over their bodies and wore thick furs. They found her lying unconscious on some driftwood. One man examined her arm, motioning to the others. After studying her for a moment, they carried her off to their boat. I don't who they were—"

"Tartarians." Everyone looked at me as I spoke the word softly.

Tartarians were barbarian-like warriors. They feared little and were amongst the strongest, largest, and most skilled warriors to exist in Devas. If they took the princess, she would be in Tartarus by now.

"Please," Ivar begged, his bound arms stretching out towards me, "can you help me rescue her?"

"Why would I help you?"

He rubbed his hands across his partially shaved head, groaning. "I promised to help her...and I failed. She may be the princess, but she is also a good person. We need to protect her. Who knows what those men will do to her."

I felt sympathy for Ivar. Tove's chains clanked as she shifted to my side, placing her hand on my shoulder, the thick metal links hanging from her wrists brushed against my arm. I reached my hand to hers, our chains hitting one another.

"I know, Tove," I squeezed her hand. "One day I'll pay my debt, but not today." She smiled and nodded.

Leander, now seated, motioned us to lean in close as he whispered, "How do we escape? You heard Ydalia, the chains are enchanted, as is the wagon."

Tove motioned to me, "Fenix, can you break it?" My muscles and hands flexed as my power flowed through my veins as I tried to physically break the cuffs. It was no use. "Damn it, Fenix! I thought you were more powerful!"

"Not my fault, Tove. She *must* be a strong druidess if her enchantment is making *me* work for it." I tried again. "Just give me a moment," I groaned, grinding my teeth as I strained against the enchanted chains. My muscles bulged as power surged through my body.

Tove sniffed the air as I attempted again, "Fenix." The stench hit my nostrils, followed by screams. We peered through the wooden bars across the crowd to see what the source of the commotion was. Men and women ran past the wagon in a hurry as others shifted into wolves. Suddenly, a loud explosion erupted just ahead, rocking the wagon. Wolves sprinted toward the explosion as debris shot through the bars.

"What the fuck is happening?!" Ivar tried to shield his face with his bound hands.

Tove inhaled deeply, "Vaud—but they're not alone." I glanced at Tove, reading her expression as their scent filled the air.

"Okay, we need to leave *now*." I gathered my power and continued grappling with my strength, trying to break the enchantment. "Come on!" I strained as the spell continued fighting my force.

"Hurry up, Fenix!"

"I'm trying!!"

Leander slammed his chains against the bars, attempting to break them as Ivar tried to wriggle free of his bindings. Another explosion landed closer to the wagon, sending it onto its side. Our bodies fell hard against the enchanted wooden roof.

Vaud wolves tore through the remaining people and began attacking the Vargr wolves as arrows flew overhead. Tove grunted in pain as a stray arrow landed sharply in her shoulder.

"Just my fucking luck!" She ripped the arrow from her arm and examined it. "Leander," she handed the blooded arrow to him.

"Is it..."

"Emilios." His expression darkened with anger. He tossed the arrow aside, rushing to Tove and applying pressure to her wound. "Fenix, we need to leave *now*."

I closed my eyes and focused all my strength on the chains. The enchantment tried to stop me, but I had had enough. I forcefully pushed back with rage, groaning as I pulled my wrists against the cuffs. The chains shattered and fell from my wrists.

"About time."

I snarled at Tove, focusing on her wound.

"I'm okay, Fenix."

I nodded and crawled to the door of the wagon. Leander struggled to support Tove, his chains slamming into hers as they made their way to the back of the cage. My hands gripped the bars and began to pull against the enchantment when Ydalia appeared.

"NO!" she yelled, panting hard. Her face was covered in dirt and soot, and she spoke with a bloodied lip, "You brought them here!" She raised her arms in anger. Before I could respond, she blasted me with a wave of dirt and rocks. Tove screamed from behind me as I stumbled back.

"No, we didn't! These are the people we tried to warn you about!"

"You're all the same!"

Another blast. *Fuck.* Leander tried to shove me aside but I pushed him back, shielding him with my arm.

"The ones attacking you are your enemy, not us. *They* are the ones who need to pay! They are the ones who allowed the Vaud to overthrow the Silas." Ydalia listened to Tove, slowly lowering her arms. Another explosion boomed behind us as wolves continued fighting.

"Ydalia, listen, we want to help. Join us and you can have the Silas. You're not like the Vaud; you have a whole tribe of people who want to live a good life. Let us go, and we'll help protect your people. We can end this—"

"Fenix, get down!" Arrows whizzed past my face. I turned and watched as Ydalia fell to the ground, arrows embedded in her stomach.

My hands clutched the bars, my power pulsating through them as I roared. The cage door crumbled beneath my strength. We hopped from the wagon and ran to Ydalia. She was holding her stomach trying to apply pressure against her wounds, arrows sticking out from deep inside her flesh. Blood was pooling beneath her. I motioned for Tove and Leander. The both of them and Ivar ran to my side to help, still bound by their chains and rope. I examined the wounds as blood flowed from Ydalia's body.

"We need to remove the arrows."

"Do it," she sputtered. She raised her hand, shaking as she flicked her fingers. The chains on Tove and Leander's wrists fell and Ivar's hands became untied. Ivar and Leander gently held her arms down as Tove grabbed a stick and placed it in her mouth. She bit down hard, signaling for me to proceed. I gripped one of the arrows, taking a deep breath as I yanked the first arrow from her abdomen. She yelled in pain, baring her canines as she bit down on the branch in her mouth. I ripped another arrow from her abdomen.

"Almost done." I pulled the final arrow from her stomach.

She cried in pain as she lifted her hand to her wounds. A faint fiery glow emerged, flickering from her palm as she attempted to heal herself.

"Let me." I placed my hand over the gashes and focused. The small pool of blood around her slowly seeped back into her wounds. I tore her dress around her abdomen and examined her, "You're no longer bleeding, but you need a healer." Ydalia spat the stick from her mouth and tried to sit up, Leander and Ivar offered to help her.

"You didn't have to help me," she winced, slapping the men away, "but you did." She struggled to stand, refusing our help. Her eyes met mine, "Your debt is paid."

I slightly bowed my head in respect. "You need to rest, Ydalia." She shook her head in defiance.

"I *need* to protect my people. We can't fight with you if we don't survive the night."

"Spoken like a true Vargr." Tove and Ydalia exchanged a smile.

Ivar stepped forward, "I'm sorry, but what's the plan here?" Everyone turned, looking at me for an answer.

"First, we need to protect Ydalia's tribe. It appears the Vaud has decided to join Emilios in this fight. Leander, Ivar, find some weapons. The three of us need to clear Emilios' men and the Vaud wolves to allow Ydalia's people to escape. Tove, you and Ydalia get her people to safety." I turned to Ydalia, "Is there somewhere your people can go?"

"No, this was our home. Our horses are tied to a hitching post outside a small caravan of supplies just north of here, but that's it."

"We can take them back to the Bottomlands."

I shot a surprised look at my cousin. "Tove, that's a long journey. You're in no shape to travel—"

"I can do it, Leander!" She looked at me, "You can't stop them all. Hold them back long enough while we get everyone out of here. I'll lead them back to the Bottomlands, they'll be safe there. I can do this, Fenix." I nodded, believing in her strength.

A group of women ran past as Ydalia stopped them, directing them towards the horses and yelling at others nearby to do the same. Ivar and Leander searched for weapons to use. My eyes met Tove's as she grabbed my arm.

"Once it's clear, head to Tartarus."

"Tove, I can't leave you—"

"No, Fenix! Ivar needs you, the *princess* needs you. Promise me you'll go to her?" I didn't respond. "Fenix, PROMISE!" She aggressively shook my arm, pleading with me.

"I promise."

She released her hold and turned, watching Leander. "Keep him safe, Fenix. We both know he's not the same as us." She turned to me once more, "I'll send Nox to find you once we return." She began to sprint north towards Ydalia, speaking over her shoulder, "And next time feel free to heal me too, asshole." I smirked as she shouted for Ydalia's people to follow her.

Ivar and Leander returned to my side, their weapons in hand. Leander tried to hand me a sword, but I refused, "I'll handle them *my way*." I turned to Ivar. He was armed with a bow and eyeing the fight ahead. My focus shifted back to the scuffle unfolding before us. "You two cover me, when I land, brace yourselves." They both nodded. "Let's clear them out."

Together we charged forward, ready to fight. Wolves and men fought one another as archers perched behind trees in the distance, firing arrows. Leander clashed against a wolf, using his sword to fight it off. He kicked the wolf onto the ground and struck his blade through its throat. Ivar fired arrows, his aim precise, knocking down Vaud wolves in my path as I continued forward. A lone wolf charged me, slamming into my arm as I swung, sending the wolf aside hard into the dirt. It whined as I slammed my boot into its skull. Two arrows zipped past me, directing my attention to the wolves ahead, falling as Ivar cleared my path. I looked back to him, nodding my thanks, then began to sprint forward. My legs ran at full speed toward a table ahead, launching my body high into the sky.

"NOW!" I yelled, warning the two. Leander threw his sword deep into the ground, holding tight, as Ivar ducked behind a boulder bracing for impact.

My fist slammed into the earth creating a crater beneath me. A thunderous boom echoed at the impact of my power that sending a blast of air, followed by a wave of debris. The fae among the trees died instantly from the collision of the high pressure wave. Men and Vaud wolves were flung back as hard dirt and rocks slammed into them. The Vargrs and men of Ydalia's tribe were able to break free from the fighting as Leander and Ivar motioned for them to flee north. The remaining Vaud wolves and Emilios' men retreated in fear.

The world fell silent, my ears ringing from the blast as I climbed from the deep hole I created. Ivar and Leander stood waiting for me at the edge of the crater. They were covered in dirt and grinning.

"Next time, warn me to shut my mouth, Fenix," Leander spat.

"You didn't shut your mouth?" Ivar laughed as Leander rolled his eyes. I rubbed my wrists as they ached from my impact on the ground. "You really are powerful, Jarloth," Ivar reached his hand out to me, "I pledge my loyalty to you."

I firmly shook his hand, "Just call me Fenix." He nodded.

Leander cleared his throat, "If you two are done, we really need to get going. We can catch up to Tove if we—"

"We're not meeting Tove."

Leander tilted his head, "Why not? She's injured...so is Ydalia. They're traveling with an entire tribe of Vargrs to the Bottomlands, they're going to need our help."

"Tove can handle this, Leander. Besides, she wants us to help Ivar." Ivar looked surprised.

"We head south to Tartarus."

My mind waded through perpetual darkness. No emotions, no feelings. Complete emptiness.

The only form of presence was his voice.

"Cymar."

The voice was faint, similar to a whisper, only softer. My existence clung to the trail of his voice as it guided me through the dark, senseless void.

I slowly regained consciousness as my senses returned. Pain grew, my head pounding as I strained to open my burning eyes. My sight was blurred. Every inch of my body ached and throbbed. I attempted to sit up, failing as I struggled with the pain in my head.

"Fuck." My shaking hand reached for my head, hitting a bulging knot, which caused me to wince.

"You sure know how to take a beating, girl." My eyes darted to the sudden, unfamiliar male voice.

Next to me, seated in a simple wooden chair, was an unnaturally large man with a giant scar across his face. He was monstrous. He had a temple shave and long, wild, strawberry-blonde hair, tied atop his head. His full beard was braided with intertwined beads that fell to his bare chest. His green eyes clashed against the dark red paint smeared across his face and his entire upper torso was exposed. Tattoos, scars, and painted markings covered his bare, ripped chest and arms beneath a thick winter fur cloak. My eyes studied the markings across his skin.

Strange. His hand rested on the pommel of the sword, sheathed at his waist, ready to attack.

"Who are you?" I strained, pulling my eyes from the man, absorbing my surroundings. I had been laid across a simple bed in a cold and empty stone room with a single frosted window. *Where am I? What happened?*

The man leaned forward, his sword scraping against the hard stone floor, "The real question is, who are *you*?" His presence was intimidating. I wrestled with the urge to scream as I pushed against my pain, sitting up. Every inch of my body shouted in anguish.

"I am of no importance, sir," I winced. A strange sensation burned against my skin. My hand reached for my right bicep in a reflex, feeling something foreign on my arm. Frantically pulling the ruined sleeve of my tunic away, I saw a giant, fresh claw mark burned across my skin. It was almost identical to the man's scar across his face. The color drained from my face as I gawked at the large wound and began to panic.

"What did you do to me?!"

The man stood abruptly, stepping closer to me. His hand gripped the handle of his sword.

"I *saved* your ass. Now, tell me who the hell you are." His voice was deep. I ignored his command and stared at the deep burn on my skin, tears forming in my eyes. I couldn't risk giving him my name. "Suit yourself," he turned and made his way to the door on the opposite end of the barren room, "I'll return later." His fist hammered against the door. Footsteps grew from the other side as the lock clicked and the door swung open. The man stepped halfway through before turning back to me, "I expect a name when I return." He exited the room slamming the door sharply behind. I could hear the lock click as his heavy footsteps faded away. I was a prisoner.

I burst into tears. Every emotion washed over me.

My body fell back onto the stiff bed as I pulled my knees deep into my chest. My throat burned with sadness as I cried, my chest aching with despair. I was lost and alone. I shut my eyes tightly, forcing myself to fall asleep as I hoped to wake from this nightmare.

My thoughts drifted as my tears shuffled me off into a light slumber.

The door slammed, abruptly waking me from my dreamless sleep. The same unknown man from before had returned. I sat up, grimacing, as he stopped a few feet from the bed.

"Are you ready to give me a name?" His hand remained atop the handle of his sword. I silently shook my head. He sighed, "Will you at least tell me what you were doing in the Silas?" *The Silas?*

I sat confused, trying to remember what happened.

Aodhan and I were on a boat...headed to Seamarke...not the Silas. There was a storm...the Sephtis attacked.

My eyes widened at the recollection of my memories.

The serpent destroyed Ivar's ship...Ivar! I'd lost sight of him during the destruction of the boat. I remember... falling into the dark sea.

My head ached at the memory.

Something rammed into my skull...then...then it all went black.

I could hear his blade scrape its leather sheath as the man withdrew his sword, aiming the tip toward me. "I *need* a name, girl." My body froze with fear. I couldn't risk giving him my name...but I didn't wish to die over it.

I studied the man for a moment before reluctantly giving in to his demand.

"My name is Cyrene..." My stomach became sick, "Princess Cyrene." The title tasted sour and felt foreign in my mouth.

The emotion on the man's face shifted as he cautiously lowered his weapon. "You're Kea's daughter?" I nodded softly, confused at the familiarity of my mother's name.

"Please, no one can know I'm here—"

"Don't play games with me, girl." He stepped closer, "Is your mother the late Queen Kea?" I nodded again. The man turned and swiftly exited the room, slamming the door behind. *Fuck.*

I slowly rolled from the bed struggling to stand, my ankle swollen from the ropes of Ivar's ship. My bare feet touched the floor causing me to gasp. It was ice cold. I limped slowly across the room, shivering as I reached for the handle of the door when it suddenly swung open. Standing in the doorway was the man from before, only this time he wasn't alone. Next to him was a much larger, beastly older man. I cautiously stepped back as the older man ducked through the frame of the door and stopped directly in front of me. He was dressed similar to the first man. He wore winter furs, darker than the other man's, his branded scar burned across his chest, along with similar markings and tattoos. His hair was akin to the color of my own, a bright auburn, with the addition of numerous white streaks that clashed against his deep emerald green eyes.

The red-haired warrior towered over me as his eyes peered into mine. The first man spoke from behind.

"She claims to be the daughter of Kea, a princess."

I kept my eyes locked on the red-haired man. He grunted.

"Does she bear the mark?"

The first man nodded, "Right arm." The older man's eyes shot to my arm as he effortlessly ripped the sleeve off my tunic, exposing the fresh brand. He lifted his large hand, pushing against the claw mark with his fingers. I yelled, instinctively pulling my arm back, but his hold was too strong.

"It's real," he whispered, removing his hand. I stepped back, clutching my aching arm as my eyes glared.

"How old are you, girl?" I refused to respond. "ANSWER!" My body flinched at his demand. I remained silent, refusing to answer. I wouldn't let these fuckers bully me.

"Told you she was stubborn," the first man smirked, walking next to the red-haired man. "Does her age really matter? She has the cristna... you know what that means." *Cristna?*

The older man whipped back toward the door grunting, "Get her cleaned up, Farouk. She can join us later." He ducked through the doorway and left. Farouk whistled. Two ladies shuffled into the room carrying fresh winter clothes, soaps, and a wash pail.

"Get the girl ready for tonight. Lord Baldyr expects to see her cleaned up." *Lord Baldyr?* The two ladies bowed their heads and staggered to my side. Farouk left the room, shutting the door behind him. I gazed through the frosted window. Snow capped, rocky mountains filled the sky.

I was in Tartarus.

The ladies carefully tended to the open wounds across my face. The deep gash across my head had to be sewn by hand. I held back tears as the needle dug into my skin over and over. Once they finished closing the cut, they smeared a natural ointment across the wound.

"Helps with the pain, dear," one of the ladies whispered sweetly to me. The ointment smelled of cloves. She smothered the brand on my arm with the same ointment, careful not to apply too much pressure. My jaw clenched, fighting back screams of pain as she did so. The ladies continued silently scrubbing my scrapes and bruises as my mind wandered.

Tartarus was the southernmost region of Devas. The territory was mountainous, rigid, and cold. The climate was similar to The Glatteis, but said to be harsh, near impossible to dwell in except for Tartarians. They were the only ones known to survive in these conditions. Tartarians were said to be amongst the most skilled warriors in Devas: brutish, aggressive, monstrous, and stubborn individuals. Not much was written about Tartarus in any of the books in the library back at court, though I once heard a rumor that wild beasts roamed freely in the region.

The ladies revealed to me the clothes they brought—simple, thick winter attire. My hands gently removed my damaged tunic and trousers revealing numerous dark, swollen bruises and bloodied cuts along my skin. The women rushed to clean every inch of me while I stood exposed, shivering in the cold room. My discolored and damaged skin was unrecognizable. After inspecting me one last time, they pulled the warm, thick clothing over my head carefully so as to not anger my injuries further.

Once I was properly dressed, they tenderly brushed and styled my hair into a long intricate braid with smaller braids woven throughout. One of the ladies left, quickly returning with a thick brown fur cloak and leather boots. She knelt onto the stone floor, carefully placing my feet into the dark winter boots one at a time, lacing them tight enough without irritating my swollen ankle. The other lady fastened the thick fur across my shoulders. It was heavier than I expected, causing me to hunch as my back adjusted to its weight.

Both ladies stood and observed me for a moment before bowing and leaving the room, locking the door behind them.

I paced to the frosted window. Faint golden light peaked through the crystallized ice as my eyes scanned the wintry scenery stretching far out into the distance. A weird sense of peace and freedom emerged from inside. I may be a prisoner, but I was away from everyone. Far away.

My eyes stared out into the wintery landscape for sometime as I was lost in my wandering thoughts. The door unlocked, startling me. One of the ladies from before peeked her head around the door motioning for me to follow her. I hesitated before silently limping behind the older woman. She walked slowly, allowing me to keep pace. Trailing behind the woman, we proceeded through ancient, towering, cold stone hallways. Torches illuminated our route as we continued through what seemed to be a grand, historic palace.

Eventually, we came to two gigantic wooden doors that stretched high above. The woman pushed the doors open revealing a large dining hall, the walls made of similar stone from the rest of the palace. Large wooden pillars lined the dining hall, arching across the peak of the room with hand-carved beasts etched across the bases. Dozens of game trophies were mounted onto every wooden post as lit candles rested atop the posts on mounts, casting a warm light across the room. The dining hall was filled with empty wooden tables and benches—except for one.

Half-burned candles and a feast plastered the top of a table in the center of the room. Lord Baldyr was seated at the head of the table in a large throne-like chair, Farouk standing directly next to him. Both of the men stared as I stepped into the room, wary of my surroundings. The lady closed the doors behind me. My heart raced as I glanced at the men nervously.

"Sit." Lord Baldyr's baritone voice startled me. I inched closer to the table, eyeing the benches. There were two long pews on either side of the table and one short bench opposite Baldyr. My eyes glanced from the men to the table, deciding on the seat furthest from them both. Farouk smirked as he took a seat on the right side of Baldyr. A third lady entered the room and poured the three of us each a glass of wine. I tried to refuse when she came to me, but she ignored my gesture. She then proceeded to fix the lord and Farouk's plates in silence. My skin prickled, feeling the men's eyes leering over me as she came to mine. I fidgeted against my seat, uncomfortable with the intense situation. The lady curtsied to the lord as he waved her off. She left the hall leaving me alone with the strange men. *Shit.*

Lord Baldyr cleared his throat and spoke, "Eat. You seem to have been through a lot... You must be famished." He grabbed the meat from his plate with his bare hands, ripping it apart with his teeth. Farouk's eyes remained on me, watching as he drank his wine. I looked down at the food in front of me. It smelled heavenly. Seasoned meats, vegetables, and warm fresh bread. My stomach growled at the heavenly aromas. *When was the last time I ate?* My lessons in manners disappeared as hunger took control of my actions. My teeth frantically tore into the meal like an animal as my hands shoved more food into my mouth. I was uncontrollable. Farouk chuckled as I ignored his scoffs, slurping the wine like it was water and gorging myself.

"Can't recall ever seeing a princess eat like *that.*" Farouk took another sip as I shot him a glare, my cheeks stuffed with vegetables. He spat his drink out, coughing and holding back his laughter. Lord Baldyr glared at me. *Fuck.* I swallowed my mouthful and tried to compose myself.

"Shit, girl," Farouk wiped his face, "you got a little kick to you." Lord Baldyr pushed his plate back. His eyes fogged over as he slouched in his chair, staring off into the distance. I pushed my plate aside as well. *Remember where you are, what they did to you.* My hand lightly brushed the brand on my arm. It stung.

"It'll heal." I glanced up to see Farouk eyeing my arm. "First week or so is the worst. Soon you'll forget you have it. You're lucky, girl," he pointed to the same brand across his face and grinned.

"Why did you do it?" I spat the words as I squeezed the claw mark on my arm, grimacing at the immense pain. His eyes squinted, glaring at me perplexed.

"I didn't give you that mark." He shifted away from me and took another sip.

"Well, who did?!"

He whipped back towards me. "No one! You were born with it!"

I gawked at him as he threw his cup across the room. I stood, lifting my sleeve and pointed to the mark.

"This is not some birthmark. This is a brand like fucking animals get when claimed! *Someone* did this to me and I demand to know who!"

Farouk shook his head. "You know nothing, girl." He slowly rose from the bench and walked to my side, grabbing my arm, "This *cristna* is something all Ursii have. You *earn* it." He threw my arm down and walked back to his seat and whistled. A lady staggered into the hall with more wine. She gave him a new cup and filled it. He snapped his fingers. She turned to leave but he yanked her back and snatched the pitcher of wine, "*Now* you may go." She left as quickly as she had come.

"What the fuck is a cristna?"

Farouk groaned as he chugged his glass and poured himself another.

"A cristna is a sacred marking we must bear." He motioned to his face.

"We?"

He rolled his eyes, "Yes, *we*. Ursii," he opened his arms motioning all around, "we all wear our mark with pride. As should you."

The fuck is an Ursii? "I'm not an Ursii or whatever the fuck that is; I'm a princess."

Was I still a princess? Could I even be a princess if Serifos wasn't my real father?

"If your mother is Queen Kea, as you claim, how is it you know nothing of Ursii?" Farouk seemed annoyed.

"Why would I?" I asked sarcastically. The words seemed to hurt Farouk. Anger flashed across his face as he launched from the bench, shoving it back as he moved. He spat at the floor and glared at me.

"I'd mind your manners, girl," he pointed in my direction, "you are here by *our* choice in *our* home—"

"Sit down, Farouk," Lord Baldyr commanded.

"No!" he shouted, turning to Baldyr. "She doesn't get to sit here, in our presence, and disrespect our kind! *Fuck Kea!* She shouldn't have kept the truth from her!"

"I said ENOUGH!" Lord Baldyr erupted from his chair, slamming his fists into the table, causing everything to shake from the impact. His hands had changed from human to that of a beast. Fear washed over me. *What the fuck?!*

Farouk went silent but remained standing.

Lord Baldyr hung his head low at the sight of my fear. He dragged his changing fists back toward himself and stood; his hands had returned to normal. He didn't look at Farouk or me as he spoke, his words low and deep.

"Don't you *ever* dishonor Kea again. Brother or not, I will kill you." *Brother?* Farouk's eyes narrowed from Baldyr to me, visibly pissed. The lord's giant fists were clenched at his sides, his tattooed, ripped chest huffed as he waited for a response from his brother.

Farouk bowed, "Forgive me, Brother." He snatched his cup and the pitcher of wine from the table and stormed from the hall, glaring as he passed me.

Lord Baldyr sighed. His body relaxed as he returned to his seat. "Please forgive my brother." I too returned to my seat. "He's quick to anger. Most Tartarians are, but Farouk more than most."

"Did you two know my mother?" He froze as my question floated down the table. My eyes studied him as I took a sip from my cup.

"She was our friend...and a Tartarian herself." I choked on the bitter wine.

"I'm sorry," I frantically coughed as he observed me, "my mother was from *here*?" He nodded. I fell back into my chair baffled at the idea of my mother, High Fae Queen Kea, being a Tartarian.

"Did she not mention this place?" One could feel the hurt behind his words as he asked the question.

"Unfortunately, my mother died a few days after my birth, Lord Baldyr." My voice fell flat. He watched me a moment before speaking.

"Did King Serifos not speak of her homeland?"

My head lowered, shaking as my voice changed. "I do not wish to speak of him."

Baldyr leaned forward, his large arm resting on the table.

"Your father never once mentioned her past?"

The word stung my heart. "He is *not* my father!"

Lord Baldyr slightly tilted his head, curious as he leaned further over the table.

"What do you *mean* King Serifos isn't your father?"

Shit. I shouldn't have snapped so quickly. What was I thinking? My eyes turned from him, my cheeks flushed.

"I'm exhausted, I think it would be best if I lay down and rest." I rose from the chair, Baldyr mimicking my movements.

"Cyrene," I paused at the sound of my name, "why would you think Serifos isn't your father?"

I sighed, turning back to face him. Tears formed in my eyes as pain throbbed in my heart. "Just look at me!" I extended my arms and motioned to my body. "I look nothing like Serifos or Keres or Cecelia! I'm a *bastard!*" I couldn't hold my emotions back, tears trailed from my eyes. My throat burned as I lightly sobbed into my hands. My heart felt broken.

Lord Baldyr stood and watched me awkwardly as I continued to cry uncontrollably into my palms.

A sudden, familiar shriek interrupted my cries. I glanced up to see Aodhan soaring through the room. *Thank the Gods he was alright.* He fluttered his wings and circled me before landing on Baldyr's shoulder. My eyes stared at the two of them confused, as I wiped the tears from my face.

"You found him."

Baldyr gazed at me with a perplexed look. He glanced at Aodhan, stroking his head with tenderness and the hawk purred.

"You know this bird?"

My sniffles filled the room. "Yes, he is my companion."

Baldyr halted mid pet and withdrew his hand. He peered at me, then back to the hawk.

"Aodhan," my voice softly called the bird's name as I extended my left arm. He hopped from Baldyr's shoulder and landed atop my arm, skipping to my shoulder and nestling into my hair. "It's good to see you too, little sir." A small smile appeared on my face as the hawk nudged me, purring.

"Cyrene." I looked back at Lord Baldyr. My smile melted as he paced closer with caution. He stopped a few feet away, falling to his knees and bowing his head. The gesture was a complete surprise, throwing me off guard. *What was he doing? Lords were not supposed to kneel to anyone.*

"Please, forgive me, Cyrene," his words ached with sadness, "you are correct. Serifos isn't your father... I am."

My heart stopped beating as I held my breath. Lord Baldyr remained kneeled, head hung low at my feet. *No, there was no way he was my father. How could he be?*

"No," the whispered word escaped from my mouth. He lifted his head, slowly. His green met mine. I pulled my gaze away and looked at Aodhan, "My father is unknown. He hurt my mother...assaulted her... resulting in my birth."

Baldyr quickly rose, standing high above me. "Why would you say such a thing?!"

"Keres informed me himself. It's one of the reasons I left the High Fae Court. I have no place among them. I'm a monster's child." His muscles tensed as he leaned closer towering over me, his cristna level to my eyes.

"No one would *dare* disrespect *my mate* in such a way," he growled the words down to me.

His mate?

I gaped up at Lord Baldyr as he strained to control himself. "What do you mean *mate*?" Baldyr ignored my question. He whipped around, stomping back to his chair, huffing and mumbling to himself. "What do you mean by mate?!" I demanded. He grabbed one of the wooden benches alongside the table and threw it across the dining hall in anger. His strength was bewildering.

"Of course you didn't know! Why *would* you?!" He bellowed as he marched aimlessly around the room, kicking and tossing furniture as though they weighed nothing. "Fucking Serifos! That bastard *knew* you were my child!" He turned and pointed to me, "Look at you! You're the spitting image of Kea and myself!" He continued to angrily mumble as he destroyed the feast, slamming his fists into the table.

The doors to the dining hall creaked open as Farouk stepped inside casually sipping a cup of wine. He strode to my side and watched as his brother roared.

"Told you, did he?"

My head whipped in his direction. "You *knew*?"

He took a sip and laughed. "It's a bit obvious, girl. You resemble your mother, but you have your father in you for sure. Anyone with eyes can see it." I kept my gaze on him as he continued to drink, unbothered by what was unfolding in front of us. His eyes were the same color as mine, his hair was lighter, but auburn strands peeked throughout.

"Not to mention," he pointed to Aodhan, "you wouldn't be able to form your little bond with that bird if you weren't Baldyr's child." I glanced at Aodhan then back at Farouk.

"What do you mean?"

He smirked, "Gods, you have so much to learn, girl. *Fylguirs* can only form bonds to their family's spirit animals. That hawk there," he motioned his cup toward Aodhan, "is your father's. Found him when he was young, and now he seems to have found his way to you." He took another sip. "We wondered where the little fucker had wandered off too."

"If Lord Baldyr is my father, like you claim, then why the secrets? Why would Keres say such things? Why lie about my father?"

Farouk rolled his eyes at me, annoyed. "Are you seriously asking me that?" I anxiously nodded. He groaned, "Your mother and Baldyr weren't just mates, they shared the pairing bond. Serifos, enamored by her duende ability, stole your mother." A window shattering drew our attention back to Baldyr. His arms had transformed into those of a bear as he continued destroying everything in sight. "Typical Ursii behavior. And he says *I* have a temper."

"What is an Ursii?"

He looked at me once more.

"*Ursii* are Tartarian warriors that have the ability to transform into a bear. Not an average bear, no, Ursii are far more powerful. That mark on your arm, your *cristna*, is proof that you are one of us. And that you've had your first transition."

I could change into a bear? But I hadn't... Had I?

I twisted my arm and observed the claw-like brand. The memory flashed across my mind. *The shipwreck...I remember...auburn claws. My claws. It was real.*

"Why the brand?"

Farouk rolled his eyes. It seemed he was easily annoyed by my questions and inquisitions. "I already told you, all shifters are marked with them once they shift. As Ursii, we wear the *Scratch of Bjorn*." He pointed to his scar across his face. "Other shifters have them too, though I don't care for them." I tried to process all the information. *Other shifters?*

Baldyr slowly approached us, panting. "Forgive me." His arms had returned to normal. "As you'll see, we Tartarians are a bit quick to anger." His voice was low, his words filled with soft notes of sadness.

I stared at the man before me. He towered above Farouk and me, built like a beast. His long auburn hair mimicked the colors in mine, his sad emerald green eyes were identical to mine. I felt the truth churning in my bones as my eyes studied his cristna. It was scarred across his tattooed chest. He bore markings of streaked red paint, similar to Farouk, across his arms and chest. A single blue mark was printed into his forehand.

"What do the symbols mean?" My question took him by surprise.

"The red ones represent our station here in Tartarus," Farouk spoke from behind.

"What of the blue one?" I pointed to Baldyr's forehead. He spoke this time.

"It signifies to other Ursii that I am their Alpha."

Lord Baldyr of Tartarus. Alpha of the Ursii.

My father.

Without any thought, I threw my arms around Baldyr's waist. He hesitated before embracing me.

"Welcome home...my child."

Home.

Chapter 15

I slammed my lover's beautiful body hard against the wooden post of my bed. The wood creaked at the impact of his body. My eyes caught a glimpse of a faint smile on his blurry face. He stood tall, watching me. I could feel his appetite growing with my own, we were starving. My hands impatiently ripped his tunic from his body, drinking in his beauty. Before he could make a move, I shoved him roughly back onto the bed, taking control. A soft chuckle escaped from his throat. He bit his bottom lip. Mine. I crawled over his body, my hair lightly brushing against his skin, ready to pounce. I hadn't dreamt of my lover since the Sephtis attack. It had been too long and my body yearned for him.

My soft lips ran across the scar on his collarbone, kissing it gently. He growled, tightening his grip on my backside. I grinned, licking my way to his neck and inhaling his scent. Gods, he smelled amazing. My lips found his and all my control disappeared. He sat half way up and embraced me completely. It had been too long. He dragged me closer as my legs straddled his warm body, my knees sinking into the mattress. He continued to kiss me, running his hands under my tunic, smoothly up my back. My arms wrapped around his neck, trailing my hands through his long, wavy dark hair. I struggled to breathe as he plunged his tongue further into my mouth, his cock growing beneath me only exciting my body more. He gripped my shoulders, pulling me down towards him. *Not yet.* I bit down hard on his lower lip as a moan escaped his lungs. I grinned, feeling him dig his nails hard into my skin and dragging them along my back. My body arched, enjoying the sting of his fingers along my spine.

"Don't tease me, Princess," he warned deep into my ear as he bit my neck.

"Or what?" I mocked.

He moved so swiftly. He lifted me from the bed and slammed me vigorously against the cold stone wall. I gasped, aroused by the aggressive control he took. He wrapped my legs around his waist, yanking my tunic off to leave my chest completely exposed. A carnal growl grew from his lips as they pressed against mine. My legs tightened around his waist squeezing him tightly. He extended his arms against the wall, bracing himself as he moved his kisses from my mouth to my breasts, running his tongue along my nipples. My body arched in response. *More.*

He pierced my hardened nipple with his teeth, tugging lightly. "Behave, *Cymar*, or I'll have to punish you," his voice rasped. My hand tugged at his hair, forcing his face down, level to my own. I could feel his eyes burning into mine.

"Is that a threat," I leaned against the wall, licking my lips, "or a *promise*?" I swear his eyes glowed as a sinister grin broke across his blurry face. He dropped my legs, stepping back as I caught myself. Fire burned in my bare chest.

"It seems as though I'm going to have to *fuck* that attitude out of you, Cymar."

I snickered, "You can *try*." His grin grew, flashing his canines, as he swiftly moved toward me. He slammed his arms against the stone wall, hovering an inch from my body. His lips brushed across my face as his mouth floated over mine. My breathing increased.

"I'm going to take my time fucking you," my heart raced as he slowly unlatched my belt, "and when you *think* you can't take anymore," he whipped the belt from my trousers, "I'm going to fuck you harder," he wrapped the leather belt tightly around his palm, "longer..." he ripped my trousers, exposing my body, "but I won't quit..." he seized my neck with constraint, his long hair pouring onto my face, "until you're *begging* me to stop." He stroked my mouth with his thumb. Excitement and fear washed over me. My mouth opened to breathe, his grip tightening as his thumb slid across my lips. I opened wider, letting him slip inside. His arms flexed as I sucked harder, his grip on my face tightened. "What else can you do with that pretty little mouth of yours, Princess?"

I lunged, pushing against his strength, our mouths meeting and exploding with passion. I struggled to breathe as he released my neck and lifted me once more, carrying me across the room to a nearby table. With one arm he swiped the contents from the table onto the floor and threw me on top, my head slamming against the wood. He broke from my grasp and slid the torn trousers from my legs. My arms reached for him, scrambling to untie his trousers.

He shoved me back against the table. "I told you," he growled, roughly flipping me around bending me over the table top, "I'm going to take my time." He took the leather belt from his hand and snapped it. The crack of the leather sent a shiver up my spine. He whipped the belt against my ass cheek. I whimpered, wanting more. He pulled my arms behind my back, wrapping the belt around my wrists and pulling tight as he bound them. He knelt down, his hair lightly brushing my legs as he kissed his way up my inner thigh. I closed my eyes, forcing back my moans as he inched higher. "I'm going to make you scream," he purred, shoving my legs wide open. My center became wet at the mere sound of his intentions. *Oh Gods.*

He gripped my cheeks, biting me softly. I moaned into the wood of the table as his tongue traced the outside of me so tenderly. He teased me endlessly, quickening his pace as he slithered inside me. My thighs flexed as he licked me fiercely, my back arching as my body fought against the binds around my wrists.

"Oh no, not yet, *Cymar*. We're only getting started." I could hear him smiling, his breath hot against my skin. He slapped my ass as a racy smile appeared across his face. His hands moved from my backside, taking hold of my waist, gripping me as he brutally thrust his tongue back inside me. I moaned at the intense sensation. He continued, increasing his movements.

"Mm, you taste like heaven, Princess." He continued to devour me. My breath quickened, my hands struggling against the constricted leather as he pushed deeper. *Fuck. Oh fuck!* He could feel my body beginning to climax. My legs shook as fire burned through my veins. The erotic bliss was too much. I tried to fight the wave of euphoria, but it washed over me, drowning me in ecstasy and causing me to scream.

My body jerked and flinched as he continued, gripping me harder, until my heart felt as though it was bursting. Slowly, his tongue retreated as I dripped around him. He stood, replacing his tongue with a single finger, steadily inserting it inside me.

He leaned over me, continuing his strokes as he stared down at me. "I told you," he smiled, inserting a second finger, "we're not finished yet." Paralyzed with pleasure, I couldn't speak, incapable of forming words. Only moans. He felt amazing inside me. I began to sweat as he inserted a third finger, his free hand tugging at the belt causing my head to rise. My breasts rested on the table as my nipples rubbed the hard wood with each thrust of his hand. He could sense my excitement growing. He slowly withdrew his hand causing me to twitch, inhaling rapidly at the break he granted me, though it was short lived.

My eyes glanced back at him and watched as he undid his trousers. His lower half was blurry—same as his face. *What the fuck? Seriously?!* I groaned in disappointment. He laughed, as if knowing why I was upset.

"Soon."

Before I could question his response, he forcefully shoved himself inside me. Pain and pleasure ruptured as I raised my head and cried out. *Oh Gods!* His cock felt enormous, struggling to fit inside me. We both stood still a moment, enjoying the sensation before he pulled back and fiercely pushed himself inside me again. My body began to explode at the feel of him.

"No, not yet," he whispered in between his panting. He continued entering me, harder, faster and deeper with each thrust. I whimpered as my body began to burst. He gripped my backside and a fist full of my hair, yanking my head back as I peaked with a scream.

"Please, stop," I begged. The pleasure and fulfillment he gave me was too much to bear. He slowed to a halt, slowly pulling himself from inside me. Moans burned my throat as he took his time before stopping at the tip, ramming himself deep inside once more. I shouted at the flood of enjoyment, soaking his cock as he pulled from my body.

"You got off lucky tonight, Cymar." I jolted, gasping as he licked me one last time. "Next time," he slapped my ass causing me to cry out, "I won't be so nice."

Warm sunlight leaked through the glass window, waking me. Despite the cold air that filled my room, I was sweating profusely. My dream lover had exhausted me. My hands wiped the sweat from my forehead, my gash mostly healed and scarred over.

After learning that Lord Baldyr was my father, he asked me to stay here in Tartarus, and I accepted his offer without hesitation. He'd given me my own chamber and access to the library, where I spent days learning all there was to know about Tartarus, Ursii, and my father himself. I'd begun lessons with Farouk on how to properly shift into my Ursii skin and even started training in the Tartarian ways of combat. In between lessons, Farouk, Baldyr, and I exchanged stories of our lives and spoke of my mother.

I learned that the three of them grew up here in this palace together. My father's ancestors had been the ruling family of Tartarus for centuries. My parent's families had always been close, as had my parents. As they matured, they realized their connection wasn't ordinary but instead a pairing bond. They were mates. One night, they snuck away and performed a sacred ceremony, binding themselves for eternity. Their marital bliss didn't last long, and soon it all came to an end. During a meeting of all the rulers of Devas, Serifos, a mere prince at the time, was enamored by my mother's beauty. He publicly announced his intentions to marry her, knowing she had no choice but to accept. My father, knowing he couldn't stop Serifos, returned home alone, devastated. Eventually, Serifos and my mother were married. Not a year after their wedding, she gave birth to Keres and Cecelia. It wasn't until the death of Marius, and the crowning of Serifos and my mother, that my father saw her again as the new Lord of Tartarus. When he laid eyes on her after all those years, he said she glowed, feeling the love she had for him through the pairing bond. They snuck away and had one last passionate night together before he had to return home. They were both heartbroken when he left. He never knew of my existence, assuming she kept the truth of my father a secret to protect us both.

It broke my heart hearing the love he still had for her. I could feel the despair behind his voice as he told the tales of their youth. I tried to not pester him much on the topic, but Farouk assured me that it meant much to my father to share stories of my mother with me and that I had reminded them so much of her.

I was thankful for every moment I had with my newly found family.

I winced, sore from my days of training, as I sprang from my warm bed and hurried across the stone floor to dress myself, a simple task I welcomed after years of fussing from ladies in waiting. I enjoyed the lax customs held here in Tartarus, welcoming the simplistic lifestyle. I brushed and styled my hair in many intricate braids adorned with beads, a custom I had *finally* mastered after many failed attempts.

My hand reached for my thick, dark winter fur as faint pain shot through my right arm. I winced, moving the sleeve of my tunic, examining my cristna. It had begun to heal, forming a raised scar just as Farouk had said. I grabbed a small glass jar from the table beside my bed and unscrewed the lid. I'd been dressing the brand with the clove ointment given to me by Farouk. It helped greatly with the pain. I carefully lathered the thick herbal ointment across the raised claw mark. It stung lightly but smelled divine. I returned the jar to the small table and adjusted my furs over my tunic. My eyes caught my reflection in the small mirror propped against the wall in the far corner of my room. This was the most authentic and happy I had ever felt. I smiled and rushed out my door.

It was time for breakfast and I was ravished.

My lungs inhaled the rich aromas of hearty stew, fresh bread, and herbs as I made my way through the stone halls. My steps quickened with each growl of my stomach. I pushed open the doors to the dining hall to see almost every seat and table filled with members of Lord Baldyr's counsel and fellow Ursii. They were all large, monstrous men, women, and fae, covered in markings and tattoos and dressed in traditional Tartarian attire and furs. Seated at his usual seat in the middle of the room was my father, Farouk seated in his usual place at his side. I weaved through the crowd of giant warriors and joined them.

"It's about time you joined us," Farouk chided, chugging a mug full of ale. I ignored his comment and seated myself across from him. My father, seated on his throne at the head of the table, nodded welcoming me. I reached across the table and filled my plate with a little bit of everything: bread, fruit, porridge and meat stew. It all smelled delicious.

"What's the plan for the day, Father?" I asked, ripping a piece of fresh bread, soaking it with the juice from my stew. He cleared his throat as he wiped the crumbs from his hands.

"A few scouts have informed us of a ghoul nest that seems to have infested the southern mountains."

"Fucking little bastards," Farouk grumbled as he filled a second mug.

My fingers picked at the fruit on my place. "Are ghouls usually an issue in those mountains?"

He nodded. "Most mountains in Devas are plagued with them. Tartarus' mountains are easily infested due to the harsh weather and isolation of our region. Occasionally, the ghouls will create nests in our mountains, allowing dense hoards to wander too close to our lands—"

"That's when the Ursii step in and wipe those fuckers out!" Farouk raised his mug and yelled, "URSII!"

The whole hall shouted, raising their drinks in unison, "SKOL!"

"Who do you plan to send?" I yelled to my father as the room settled. Farouk peered at me while drinking his ale.

"Farouk. He's one of the best Ursii warriors in Tartarus."

"I *am* the best."

Baldyr chuckled. "Your uncle usually is able to handle the ghouls with a few other Ursii. Ghouls aren't too difficult to flush out." The two men continued their meal as I played with my porridge.

"What if I joined you, Farouk?"

Farouk slammed his mug down mid drink, "Look, girl, I appreciate the eagerness, but ghouls are a little much for an inexperienced shifter such as yourself."

"I've mastered my bear skin and been practicing my shift. Plus, you've been training me in Tartarian combat." I looked at my father as he watched me with intense eyes, "Please?"

"Drop it, girl," Farouk sounded annoyed.

"No!" I snapped at him as he growled. "You said so yourself, ghouls aren't difficult. Let me earn my place."

Farouk turned to Baldyr. "As much as I hate admitting it," he sighed, "the girl's right. She's skilled, brother." Baldyr contemplated my plea.

Before he could answer, Aodhan soared through the hall shrieking.

The hawk circled our table before landing on Lord Baldyr's extended arm, fluttering his beautiful cinnamon wings. "What is it, Aodhan?" The bird screeched. My father's eyes met mine as Aodhan's calls registered in our minds. *Strangers?*

"Does he not know who they are?" Aodhan screeched again, flapping his wings.

"No. Seems they wish to meet with me, claiming to mean no harm." Baldyr clicked and signaled Aodhan as he flew from his arm to mine. "Farouk, gather a few Ursii in the throne room. We'll meet these trespassers in true Tartarian ways." Farouk grunted. He stood, nodding, and left the table.

"What should I do, Father?"

Baldyr rose from the table. "I can't risk you being discovered. Who knows what Emilios or Serifos will do... You stay in your room until I call for you." He turned to leave as I shot from the wooden bench, Aodhan balanced on my arm.

"No."

My father halted, his back to me.

"I didn't leave court and run away just to be locked up somewhere. This is my *home*."

He turned his head revealing a grin.

"You sound just like your mother." He sighed. "Keep up. You will join the rest of the Ursii, but, Cyrene," he turned to face me, "stay in your bear skin," his eyes were filled with concern, "and no matter what happens, remain by my side." I nodded. He turned and paced out of the hall as I sprinted, trying to keep up with his long strides.

"The hell is she doing here, Baldyr?" Farouk huffed as we entered the large throne room. Farouk and a handful of large tattooed men and women crowded the foot of the dais. A single grand wooden throne sat atop the dais in the center of the room. The room reached higher than any other in the entire palace. Its walls were made of stone, adorned with numerous tapestries, lit torches, and towering glass windows frosted by the cold outside. Lord Baldyr climbed the stairs to his throne.

"She's joining us, as is her birthright," Baldyr commanded. Farouk and the other warriors glanced from Baldyr to me. This would be the first time I'd represented Tartarians and Ursii in a formal setting.

Clutching his sword, Farouk approached me. "Listen here, girl, if you are to be a part of this audience, you *must* remain in your bear skin. Do not, under *any* circumstance, shift back. Do you hear me? And for the sake of the Gods, remain next to your father up there," he pointed to my father seated in the ancient throne. The wooden throne resembled the arched pillars in the dining hall. Hand carved etches of bears and beasts covered the colossal seat.

My boots tapped against the stone as I made my way up the dais and positioned myself next to Baldyr. "Alright, fuckers, listen up!" Farouk roared, slamming his closed fist into his bare chest. "Earlier today we received word of three foreigners entering our lands. We don't know who they are or what they want," the warriors mumbled amongst themselves, "but we stand prepared ready to fight. As Ursii you have vowed to protect your Alpha!" The warriors cheered, "and today, your vow extends from your alpha to his blood—his *heir*!" The room vibrated as cheers filled the room. "Now, change your skins and, by the Gods, do *not* break your vows!!"

"SKOL!"

One by one the warriors groaned, snarling as they shifted. Their bones snapped and broke as they hunched over, hair sprouting from every pore. They fell to the ground as their bodies quickly morphed, shaking remnants of their old skins from their backs. Where once was a handful of Tartarian warriors, now stood a line of colossal bears. The Ursii lined up on either side of the steps, ready to die for their Alpha. Farouk glided up the steps of the dais and stopped in front of me.

"And now you, Cyrene." I began to panic. I had never transformed in front of anyone but my uncle. He nodded, reading the fear across my face. "Focus." Aodhan jumped from my shoulder to Lord Baldyr's.

My lungs inhaled a deep, large breath. *You can do this. Focus, Cyrene.*

I closed my eyes and steadied my breathing. Fire burned down in the pit of my stomach and raged through my veins. My bones began to break and snap, a soft whine escaping my lips as I fell to my knees. My teeth grew to a point as my jaw pulled and stretched further from my skull. Pain washed over my entire body as tiny auburn hairs began to poke through the pores of my ivory skin, stinging as they broke free. My hands curled as my fingers cracked and curved, my nails expanding as my claws formed. I released one final cry as my voice changed, deepening into a roar. My body snapped into its bear form. Grunting, I stumbled a moment struggling to gain my footing on all fours. Farouk smiled, pleased. My eyes peered up at my father. He was seated high, beaming with pride. *I did it.*

My paws carried me, circling the throne as I positioned myself to one side of Baldyr, Farouk on the opposite. He clutched his sword close and motioned for the staff to bring the foreigners to Baldyr. From what I read, Tartarus hasn't allowed outsiders to cross their border in over a hundred years. After Serifos stole my mother, Baldyr closed the borders and refused entry to everyone, Serifos included, though I doubt Serifos would dare set foot here. Lord Baldyr was significantly larger and, being an Alpha Ursii, more powerful. Even with his lout abilities, Serifos didn't stand a chance against my father.

The doors to the throne room slowly opened.

Two armed Tartarian men entered the throne room, followed by the three foreigners and an additional Ursii warrior in his bear skin. The strange men didn't seem phased by the sight of the monstrous bears, though if they were, they hid it well. As the three men approached, dressed in simple winter attire, my eyes instantly recognized one.

Ivar.

My body struggled to contain my excitement as Ivar and the men stopped a few feet from the base of the dais. Ivar eyed the bears showing no emotion. Standing next to Ivar was an average looking fae with brown hair and dark eyes. He was tall, appearing more human than high fae despite his pointed ears. His face seemed oddly familiar. *Where do I know you from?* The third man caught my attention as he stepped forward from behind the other two. The cluster of Ursii growled a warning as he moved. He was the tallest of the three, with medium tan skin, darker than my own, and golden yellow eyes. They appeared to be glowing? His long, pitch black hair was tied behind his pointed ears, a thick alabaster streak falling loosely in front of his face. He was the most handsome fae I'd ever seen. He peered up the dais at Lord Baldyr and me, meeting my gaze. *Shit.* I shook my bear skull, breaking eye contact with a grunt.

The mysterious man spoke. "Forgive our intrusion, Lord Baldyr—"

Farouk interrupted the man, "You must have a damn good reason to come trampling across our lands... *Jarloth.*" He spat the title as he addressed the fae. *Jarloth?* My eyes glanced back down at the fae. *So this was the elusive, self-proclaimed king. He wasn't beastly at all.* Ivar had mentioned him during our boat ride from court...it surprised me to see him in the company of the fae.

The man smirked.

"I have to admit, I did not expect to witness such a mythical sight." His voice was deep and alarming. He crossed his arms, his biceps flexing. "There's not a man or fae alive that has seen Ursii in their bear skin. Outside of Tartarians of course." It was true. Farouk had told me how the Ursii kept their ability to shift skins a secret from the world. There was little to no knowledge of Tartarian shifters outside this region. *How did he know?*

"Might want to lose that cocky attitude, little lord. There's a reason no one has lived to tell the tale of the shifters here." The Ursii warriors growled.

"Ah, forgive me. Where are my manners?" He chuckled, slapping his hands together. "May I introduce my companions?" He turned, motioning toward the plain fae man. "Lord Leander Baldassare of Southern Amos." *That's why he seemed familiar. I'd seen Leander before at court... wait... Southern Amos?* Farouk's eyes glanced at me. *Fuck.* The man then raised his other arm at Ivar. "This is Captain Ivar from Seamarke." Ivar bowed in respect. The high fae turned back to Lord Baldyr, "And I am Fenix." He bowed, still grinning. "I may be from the Bottomlands of Devas, but I assure you, sir, I am no lord."

Lord Baldyr observed the trio presented to him. "Why then, Fenix, have you trespassed into our region?" His usual voice had hardened. Ivar stepped past Fenix and cleared his throat.

"Lord Baldyr, we are here for Princess Cyrene."

I froze.

Lord Baldyr gripped the arms of his throne, straining to resist the urge to shift. Farouk trotted down the dais, the pommel of his sword deep in his grasp. Fenix advanced in front of Ivar as Farouk stopped directly in front of him.

"Now, what in the Gods makes *you* think the princess is *here,* boy?" Fenix was unbothered by the silent threat behind Farouk's words. Ivar spoke from behind.

"I saw you take her," Farouk whipped his attention to Ivar, "a few weeks back. I was tasked with getting her safely to Seamarke... I failed. We were attacked by the Sephtis. I thought she was lost at sea, but I saw her, washed ashore on the Silas. She was unconscious. You," he pointed to Farouk as he stepped around Fenix towards him, his voice was traced with anger, "you and your band of fucking brutes dragged her from the sand and brought her back here. We're here to take her back."

Farouk cackled, turning to the Ursii soldiers as they grunted in unison. He whirled back to Lord Baldyr, "This fucker thinks we have the princess!" He turned back to face Ivar and wiped his eyes. "Oh," he started, placing his free hand upon Ivar's shoulder, "you see, boy, even if she were here, we'd *never* give her over to you three bastards."

Farouk spat at Ivar's feet and strode back up the stairs of the dais to his position. My eyes remained on Ivar. I pitied him. He traveled all this way to rescue me, though I didn't need it. Ivar lunged towards the steps as Lord Leander caught him, struggling to hold him back. The Ursii snarled and bared their teeth.

Farouk slithered his sword from its sheath, "You want to fight, little boy?" he smiled, "I'll give you a fight!"

Farouk lunged as Lord Baldyr reached an arm out and stopped him.

"No, Brother." Farouk lowered his sword, groaning. Baldyr looked at the trio of men speaking to Ivar. "You must be a close friend of the princess to break the border of our land, enter my home, and *demand* her. Very brave."

"More like ignorant," Farouk grunted under his breath.

"Can't say we don't have balls," Fenix shot, raising his eyebrow at Farouk who eyed Fenix.

Ivar shoved Leander's hands from his shoulder and straightened his cloak. "The princess is a good person. I made a vow to see her to Seamarke and did not fulfill my promise. My only wish is to see her safely to her destination." My heart warmed at his sincere remark.

"Stay. Join us for dinner," Baldyr spoke as Farouk exhaled with annoyance, "and *if* the princess chooses, she may join us as well." My paws wobbled under the weight of my forelegs. Being in my bear skin was difficult.

"Farouk, escort these men to our guest quarters. I'm sure they'll wish to freshen up before tonight."

"Wonderful!" Fenix lifted his arms in praise. "Lead the way, bear-man."

Farouk gave Baldyr a look of disdain as he nodded for him and said. "Follow me…you fucking fairies."

He exited the room, the men following behind, leaving only my father and me behind.

As the doors closed I turned to my father.

He unlatched his heavy winter fur and held it in front of me. Tugging deep inside, my bones cracked and quickly formed back to their usual structure. The transition from bear to fae was always easier. I gasped with relief as the weight of my bear skin lifted, returning to my normal body. I retrieved the fur and wrapped it around my naked self as my father turned away. It was entirely too large and wrapped completely around my small frame. He cleared his throat, speaking while remaining turned away from me.

"I won't let them take you...unless you wish to accompany them."

"There's no reason for me to leave here."

"Still," he shifted his head lightly, his expression concerned, "just know you have a choice."

"Father," I touched his back lightly, "I'm not going anywhere." He smiled slightly, turning his head.

"Get dressed, child. There's far too many men eager to catch a glimpse of a woman, let alone you. Gods help the man brave enough to face me if he did."

I released a faint laugh. "I can handle them."

"If you're even half the woman your mother was," he started as he turned, his bright eyes glistening, and he grinned, "they don't stand a chance." I gave him a warm smile as he whistled to Aodhan. He leaped from Baldyr's throne landing on my shoulder. "Keep an eye on her." The hawk shrieked in obedience.

I circled around and descended from the dais, shuffling through the doors of the throne room.

Aodhan and I snuck through the halls, quietly making our way back to my room. I turned the last corner and jumped at the sight of the man leaning against the wall across from my door. He turned his head as his golden eyes met mine.

"Princess Cyrene," he smiled as my name left his lips.

Aodhan screeched, leaping from my shoulder. He soared down the hall and disappeared from view. *Fuck.*

"Magnificent bird."

"Lord Fenix." I lowered my gaze, ignoring his words, fumbling to cover myself with the oversized furs. *How did he find me?* My bare feet shuffled towards the door. He lifted himself from the wall and rested his hand against my door. His face was so close. I pulled the furs higher over my mouth and held my breath.

"We've gone through an awful lot of trouble to find you." He tucked a stray hair behind my ear. I shivered at his warm touch.

"Forgive me, but I must get dressed," I snapped, shoving him aside, opening the door. He stepped on the furs as I entered the room, causing them to slip from my grasp.

"My bad," Fenix smiled as my naked body ducked behind the door.

"Hand me my cloak, sir!" I threw my arm out reaching for the clothing as he lifted the furs and sniffed.

"Cloves, amber and honey. *Lovely.*" He glanced up at my bare arm and stared at my cristna. His smile grew. I caught his expression and retreated my arm. "So that *was* you on the dais next to Lord Baldyr." I gulped as his eyes met mine.

He tossed the furs onto the floor of my room. My eyes shot from him as I began to thrust the door shut. His foot extended, catching the door before it could close. "If you don't mind me saying," he spoke through the gap, softly leaning closer, "you have a rather nice ass, Princess, or should I call you *little beastie*?"

Little Beastie? He raised his brows and grinned, turning away gracefully. I slammed the door, locking it immediately. *Fucking prick!* My hands snatched the heavy cloak from the floor and tossed it onto my bed in a huff. *I didn't care how fucking attractive he is, Fenix is an asshole.*

I tried to shake the anger and embarrassment I felt from my mind and dressed for training with Farouk.

My boots dragged through the thick, cold snow as I stepped onto the training field. Farouk was sharpening his sword seated on a large rock, waiting for me.

"Tardiness is unacceptable, girl." He didn't look up at me as he scraped the whetstone across his already sharp blade. Faint sparks shot from the impact. I threw my winter fur aside and picked up a short blade sword for myself. "You going to tell me your reason for being late or just stroll in here all entitled?" He examined the edge of the blade slowly angling the tip in my direction, his eyes examining me.

"Forgive me, *old man*, wouldn't want to waste your precious time now, would I?" I grinned, my eyes meeting his as he furrowed his brows and shot me a frown. He rose from the rock, sword in hand.

"Let's see how cocky you are after I kick your ass, girl."

I scoffed, twirling my blade before settling into a defensive stance. Farouk approached, ready to strike.

"Remember your footing." Farouk lunged. My foot stumbled, keeping my position as I counterstruck his hit. He pulled back, "Good." I aimed my sword in his direction and ran at him. He spun, kicking me in the back sending me face first into the snow. Farouk chuckled, smacking me on the back with his blade. "Try again." I brushed the cold snow from my face, groaning as I climbed to my feet. "Fix your stance." He swung, lightly cutting my arm. I winced, looking down at the thin slice on my arm. *Prick.*

We sparred for a few hours, Farouk landing a few more cuts along my arms. He finally granted me a small break. I sat on the rock catching my breath, chugging water from a waterskin.

"Who's old now, girl?" Farouk chuckled, unexhausted from our training. My eyes shot him a glare. "Here," he threw an ax in my direction. It landed sharply at my feet.

"What the fuck do you expect me to do with that?"

"Pick it up, smartass. Today you learn to yield two weapons. Tartarian warriors' skills aren't limited to a blade—we learn how to use these as well." He twirled the ax in his hand, stepping back to the center of the training field. His sword and an ax of his own firmly in his grip. I sighed, retrieving the ax from the dirt.

"Remember, even with two weapons, you need to know how to block and keep your footing." Farouk had me mimic his movements as he showed me how to wield the ax and sword together. "When an enemy attacks, swing with the blade," he threw his arm out as if cutting someone down, "then, land the final blow with your ax." He lifted his other arm, swinging the ax down into the invisible enemy's head. *Brutal.* "Use your Ursii rage. It's what makes us stronger. Now, you," he motioned for me to repeat his actions. I ran through the motions, fumbling the ax. "Grip the handle like this," he demonstrated. I followed his instructions. Within a few tries I had begun to master the two. Farouk continued showing me counterstrikes and moves as my eyes watched, studying every detail determinedly.

"Now, the real test." Farouk positioned himself opposite me, grinning. *Fuck.* I steadied my footing and nervously waited. He made the first move. Our weapons clanked against one another as we fought. Farouk seemed to be enjoying the scuffle a little too much. He knocked the sword from my hand, shoving me back into the snow. I rolled to a crouch as his blade missed, sticking into the ground. He growled, abandoning the sword and swinging the ax high above me. My head ducked, his ax scraping against a rock behind me, shooting a spark into the air. He spun to find my ax level to his chin. I smiled, panting.

"Submit, uncle."

He smirked, chunking his weapon down into the snow. "You're definitely your father's daughter."

I raised my head, confident in my skill.

I made the mistake of lowering my ax, turning to grab my sword. Farouk fell to a crouch, spinning as he swung his leg out and knocking me down flat on my ass. He stepped over me, grinning, his hands on his hips.

"You still have much to learn, girl." My eyes narrowed as he trotted off. I crawled to my feet and raised both my arms above my head, the ax in my grip. My muscles screamed as I heaved the ax toward my uncle. As the weapon whirled in his direction, he whipped around and barely dodged the impact. The ax stuck deep into the trunk of a nearby tree behind him. He turned his gaze to me, his eyes wide as he gawked.

"Seems *you* need to learn a few things as well." I snatched my sword and walked towards the palace.

Faint grunts and clanks could be heard echoing in the distance as I strolled the dull palace grounds. I continued, following the sounds, picking up a familiar scent. I followed the smell to find Cyrene and Farouk sparring in the distance. They were in the middle of an old, snowy training field. *Interesting.* I lurked closer, keeping just out of sight.

I observed the two for sometime. Cyrene was quite skilled with a short blade, not what I expected from a princess. I could see her rage as she fell into the snow. It was amusing to see her riled up. I crossed my arms, watching as Farouk nicked her arm. The smell of her blood, a faint tang, in the wind.

"Ah, what have we here?" Leander strode to my side. "Wondered where you wandered off too." He eyed Cyrene and Farouk in the distance, sighing. "She's pretty good, isn't she?"

"Oh, don't be jealous, Leander." I grinned, glancing over to him. He huffed, ignoring my tease.

"Fenix, why is Princess Cyrene training with Lord Baldyr's brother in the middle of a Tartarian training field?" His voice was serious.

"If you're so curious," I started, angling my head motioning in their direction, "why don't you go ask her yourself?"

Leander pondered a moment. "Honestly, it's nice to see that she's capable of holding her own. She needs to be able to protect herself." He sighed. "I'm going to take a small rest. Lord Baldyr expects us at dinner later." He hesitated before leaving. "Don't mess with her, Fenix. We don't need to piss anyone off right now."

"Too late."

Leander groaned, retreating to the palace. I stayed in my place, watching.

Farouk began teaching Cyrene how to wield both an ax and short sword—a traditional technique taught only to Tartarians. *Very interesting.* She was slow at first but seemed to learn quickly. My eyes remained glued on her as she moved, learning exceptionally quickly.

She had bested Farouk, raising her ax level to his chin. She stood tall, her cheeks flustered, proud of herself. *Clever girl.* As she turned away from Farouk, I sensed his next move. *Don't turn your back on him.*

Farouk spun, knocking her hard on her ass. She was pissed. *What now, princess?* My eyes watched as she rose, grabbing her ax and raising it above her head.

I couldn't help but grin at her temper as she chunked the ax past him, barely missing. *Feisty.*

Cyrene threw her sword over her shoulder and stomped away from Farouk. She quickly approached me, unaware of my presence. I stepped in front of her, causing her to trip. She fell hard into the snow, her sword landing beside her.

"What the fuck?" She spat the snow from her mouth, glaring up at me. My boot kicked the blade from the ground, catching it mid air. I examined the short blade as she slowly tried to stand.

"I like seeing you on your knees, Princess," I teased, slapping the blade against her ass. She growled. *Feisty indeed.*

Cyrene shuffled from the snow and lunged for her sword. "Give it back, Fenix!" I dodged her grasp, swaying as she attempted to seize the blade.

"I'm curious, why *are* you out here training?" I reached my arm out, holding her back, "Not very princess-like behavior."

"What do you want?" She spat, pushing against my extended arm. She seemed a bit tired.

"Just trying to figure you out is all." I lowered my arm as she slammed into my torso. Her vivid green stared into mine as the wind fiercely blew her bright hair across her face. "Here," I extended my hand, offering the sword back. She snatched it from my grip. "As much as I'd love to see you walk away, I must be going." I lifted my brow, flashing her a sensual smile.

I turned, stepping back toward the palace. "Perhaps another time, Princess," I shot over my shoulder. Her contempt for my teases amused me.

My feet dragged reluctantly up the stairs into the palace, my sword scrapping the stone as it trailed behind me. Fucking Fenix.

Farouk had exhausted all my energy, sparring for hours, and I had gained a few cuts from my missteps, though I'm sure he enjoyed knicking me. Regardless, I was thankful for his training. I'd always been well-versed with a blade, but with my uncle's continued help, I'd become far more skillful.

I stepped into the entry of the palace, surprised to find Ivar staring back at me. His eyes were wide, filled with shock as he studied the sight of me.

"Princess?" The sword fell from my hand as I ran to Ivar, embracing him in a tight hug.

"Thank the Gods you're okay, Ivar."

He squeezed me tighter as he spoke softly, "I thought I lost you, Princess." He pulled me back and fell to his knees, my hand in his. "Forgive me, Princess," his head fell, "I failed you." My heart ached at his pureness. I lifted his chin, his beautiful deep eyes staring into mine.

"You did no such thing." I motioned for him to stand. "Ivar, you are the truest friend I have ever had. In my weakest moment, you took me in, cared for me and offered me protection—no questions asked." My hand tenderly touched his cheek. "I'm eternally grateful to you, dear friend," he gave me a warm smile, "but I will not be returning with you to Seamarke."

His smile faded, "But Princess—"

"Just Cyrene. I left the title of princess behind at court…with my old life."

He nodded as he gently grasped my hands in his, "Are you sure you don't wish to travel to Seamarke? I can't imagine you truly being happy here."

My head tilted with a soft expression. He was too kind. "Yes, I'm very happy here, Ivar. This is my home now."

"Home? Princess—forgive me—Cyrene, how could you be content staying here? You don't know these people… Tartarians aren't the best kept company."

"And your *Jarloth* is?" I snapped as he lowered our hands, giving me a stern look.

"You don't know him as I do, Cyrene." *What could possibly be worth knowing?* "Fenix may seem arrogant, but there's far more to him." I doubted that. "Do you remember the stories I told you while at sea? Those are only the surface of the truth. You should hear him out, Cyrene."

I scoffed, pulling my hands from Ivar's retrieving my sword from the floor. "I'm surprised to see you in his company, Ivar." I sheathed my blade. "Truthfully, I don't care to hear what he has to say. It matters not to me." I began to walk away toward the dining hall. Ivar stepped in my path.

"It *should* matter, Cyrene. Your father—King Serifos—he's done awful things…"

I glared up at Ivar.

"Serifos is *not* my father." I shoved Ivar aside as I continued in the direction of the hall.

Ivar scrambled to connect the information. "If Serifos isn't your father…" he turned to me, "then—"

"Yes, Ivar," I whipped around annoyed, "Baldyr is my *true* father. Which is why I choose to remain here in Tartarus. I'm sorry you wasted your time, but there's no need for you here."

He disregarded the revelation and stepped close to me. "I don't care *who* your father is. If you are happy and safe, then I am grateful." My heart glowed with relief.

"Please, Ivar, *no one* can know I'm here."

He bowed, "On my honor, your whereabouts will remain a secret."

I flashed him a soft smile, "Thank you." My hand cupped his, pulling him toward the dining hall. "Now, let's go eat. I'm famished."

Together, Ivar and I entered the dimly lit dining hall. The room was silent with only Baldyr, Farouk, Leander, and Fenix present. The men were all seated around my father's table in the center of the room, Baldyr and Farouk in their usual arrangement. All eyes shot to us as we stepped through the doorway and made our way to the table. I led Ivar, his hand still in mine, as we sat on the pew alongside Farouk. I glanced across the wide spread of food and caught Fenix's sight fixated on mine and Ivar's hands.

Lord Baldyr cleared his throat, "As you can see, Princess Cyrene is safe and well cared for." He raised a wooden cup of ale, "A toast to her health." Ivar gently released my hand as the party raised their cups.

"Princess Cyrene," they shouted in unison. The men sipped the ale as I lifted a cup of my own and gestured my thanks.

Lord Leander was the first to speak. "Forgive me for saying so, Princess, but you appear more Tartarian than a princess of the high fae court."

Ivar eyed the lord.

"Is that a *problem,* boy?" Farouk's eyes burned in the lord's direction.

I quickly lifted my cup and took a swig. "I fear that shows how little you interact with female fae, my lord." Farouk bellowed a laugh as Baldyr smirked.

Fenix grinned. "That's because she *is* Tartarian, Leander."

My father and uncle slowed their movements as they surveyed Fenix. Leander looked from his companion to me.

"What do you mean?"

Ivar and I remained still. Fenix casually popped a grape into his mouth.

"You didn't know? Queen Kea—" he picked another, repeating his motion, "she was Tartarian, was she not Lord Baldyr?" He looked at my father for an answer, undisturbed.

"Yes, Kea was Tartarian." My father's eyes glanced at me then back at his place of food. The tension eased. Fenix slowly shifted his sight, inspecting me. My eyes glared back.

"Lord Fenix," my father's voice broke my focus, "tell me, how does one become a Jarloth, per se?" His question was serious but his tone teasing. Fenix leaned back in his chair, propping an arm over the top as he angled his body towards my father.

"Ahh, come now, Lord Baldyr, don't tell me you haven't heard the rumors?" My father grunted. Fenix raised his glass and took a sip. "It's quite simple really…" his tone changed, becoming serious, "have your father murdered and his crown stolen by the same prick." He took another sip.

"You mean to tell us," Farouk started, snorting, "that late king Marius is *your* father?" He pointed to Fenix.

"Yes, he was." The room fell silent. We all studied Fenix as he spoke. "My father married my mother in secret. See, she was a high fae lady from the Bottomlands, and after the death of his queen, Eydis, Marius wanted to spare my mother from a scandal. But, being mates and sharing a pairing bond, they were impatient…deciding to get married in secret. Before they had a chance to publicly announce the relationship, Serifos brutally murdered Marius. My mother witnessed the entire thing, barely surviving herself. Serifos beat her, leaving her for dead." *Fucking hell.* "But alas, she was stronger than he expected. She returned home to her brother, Lord Harold, and was nursed back to health, only to discover she was carrying me."

"If what you claim is true," Baldyr stated, breaking the gawking silence, "that would mean Serifos is guilty of treason…making *you* the rightful ruler of Devas." I shot my focus to Fenix as he looked down at his empty cup blankly.

"Indeed."

Could everything Fenix said be true? Serifos would never murder his own brother…would he? I pondered for a moment, reflecting on Serifos' actions.

Serifos stole my mother from her home—from her mate…forcing her to marry him. Did he even love her? He turned his back on his people after the death of their queen, while remaining at court as the world suffered. He offered me away to Emilios out of fear, unbothered as to how the child he raised would be treated. If everything Fenix claimed is true, Serifos would have indeed murdered his brother, his own blood for the crown… He would be truly corrupt. Evil.

"Why now?" The men focused on me as the question flowed from my mouth. "Why, if you've known this information, did you wait until *now* to challenge Serifos?" I was honestly curious to know his answer.

Fenix raised his brows. "Because overthrowing a king takes time and patience. I have chosen my actions wisely over the years, waiting for the opportune moment to make my move," his eyes flashed over me, "I hoped to strategize a bit longer, but that prick Emilios became a bit of a problem."

Emilios?

"What of Emilios, boy?" Farouk cautiously gripped his sword.

"Relax, Farouk, I too despise the Lord of Northern Amos."

Lord Leander leaned forward, his elbows resting on the table as he clasped his hands together. "An informant of ours brought forward evidence of Emilios' plan to overthrow my region. Rumor or not, that was something we obviously couldn't allow to happen."

"If Emilios seeks to reign over both halves of the Amos territories, he would rival the power of other regions in Devas." Baldyr sounded concerned.

"Unfortunately, my plan to kill Serifos was discovered, and even though I don't want the crown, having my plans to commit murder out in the open does tend to make committing the sin a bit harder. Which is *why* I chose to publicly declare my claim to the throne, hiding my true intentions. Though, I will admit, I did *not* expect Emilios to use my claim to strengthen his plan. Witty fucker, that one."

Leander motioned his hand in my direction, "That's when we think he realized marrying Princess Cyrene would not only benefit his agenda but fast track his plans. You see, bearing the title of a prince, all while being a descendant of the old Baldassare house, would give him claim to take control of both halves of Amos. He could then strengthen that power with the largest region in Devas, potentially overthrowing Serifos and taking the throne himself."

"Alas, Princess Cyrene being *here* seems to have thrown Emilios off." Fenix flashed a large grin. "By escaping as you did, there's not a soul alive who knows your whereabouts," he looked at Lord Baldyr, "outside this room, of course."

"If Emilios locates you, Princess, he would be able to carry out his wretched plan. You're the key to his power," Leander explained.

My eyes scanned the faces of the men around the table. "It's not my intention to leave Tartarus," I spoke to all of them, "Ivar has sworn to keep my whereabouts secret. Can I trust the two of you to do the same?"

"Hold on one fucking minute," Farouk launched from his seat, "you don't *actually* expect us to let them leave, *knowing* she's here, do you, Brother?"

Fenix rose and glared at Farouk, his yellow eyes glowing in the dim light.

"If keeping Princess Cyrene here, in Tartarus, benefits my plan, why the *fuck* do you think I would risk someone else finding her?"

"You better watch your mouth, boy!" Farouk snarled, his skin rippling as he fought from shifting.

Aodhan broke the tension of the room as he screeched from atop Baldyr's chair. My father's eyes met my own as we shot our gaze to the doors. Seconds later, two injured men ruptured through the doors screaming.

"Help! Alpha, please!" A young, bloodied man with blonde hair yelled to my father. He was wearing only a torn cloth, carrying an unconscious older man, across his back, cloaked only in a bloodied winter fur. The older man was barely conscious. Aodhan flew to the wooden arches above, watching as Baldyr and Farouk rushed to assist the two men. The younger man fell to the ground, exhausted, the older man falling from his back to the stone floor. Baldyr's arms changed as he rolled the unconscious man positioning him onto his back. Blood began to pool around him.

I shadowed Farouk as he rushed to the blonde older man, examining his body. His skin was obscured with deep scratches and bite marks, chunks of his flesh missing. My eyes shot to the older man as he groaned in pain. Baldyr carefully removed the soiled cloak, sighing, shaking his head with concern.

"What in the Gods happened?!" Farouk demanded as he removed

his cloak, rolling it into a wad and placing it under the young man's head.

"We tried to clear them out, but…" he coughed his words through cracked, dry lips, "they overpowered us. There were too many." He turned to Baldyr, pleading, "Please, please save him," he sobbed, "save my father." My heart tightened. Farouk glanced at Baldyr, exchanging a fraught look. *Oh, no.*

I scampered to my father and peeked beneath the blood-soaked cloak. There was a vast, deep gash across his abdomen. I could see the layers of muscle, tissues, and organs spewing from within as blood seeped from the wound.

My father hung his head, whispering in a hushed tone, "We can't save him…"

Farouk shot from the floor, yanking a lit torch from the wall as he slid a dagger from his belt. "Listen here, boy, I can stop the bleeding," he began to warm the dagger within the flames of the torch, "but it's going to hurt. *A lot.*"

My hands scrambled to my waist, quickly unlatching my belt and handing it to my father. He folded the leather belt, placing it firmly in the son's mouth. The man's eyes widened with fear as Farouk hovered the red-hot dagger over his wounds. "Now would be the time to say a prayer to the Gods." The man screamed in pain, biting the leather belt as the glowing blade kissed his wounds. The smell of burning flesh lingered in the air, making me sick to my stomach.

Fenix suddenly appeared by my side. His honey eyes studied the old man's wounds as his fingers ran along the ridges of the abdominal laceration.

"What the hell do you think you're doing, boy?!" Farouk yelled across Baldyr and me. Ignoring his shouts, Fenix slowly inserted his hand deep into the wound. The old man groaned in pain. My eyes widened, appalled at the sight of Fenix's hand inside the man's abdomen as the color drained from my face.

"Fucking hell!" Farouk screamed in horror, his eyes wider than my own. Baldyr reached to remove Fenix's hand from within the man's abdomen when Fenix grabbed my father's wrist, his focus remaining on the old man. Baldyr flinched, jolting in pain, yelling as he crumbled onto his back and clawing at his skin. His face burned bright red as his veins constricted in his neck. He flailed around the floor in excruciating pain, struggling to breathe. Farouk rushed to my father's side as I watched, helpless and petrified with fear.

Fenix lowered his free hand as my father gasped, huffing in instant relief. His face returned to normal as his pain seemed to vanish instantly. "Let me finish," Fenix growled.

I crawled to his side, watching as the pooled blood around the old man seemed to move. Streams of blood snaked along the old man's skin, returning to his injury. Fenix delicately removed his palm from within the wound, his hand soaked, dripping with the dark crimson blood. His veins were bulged in an unnatural way. He sat back, glancing at Baldyr and Farouk. "He'll live," he rose, "but he requires a healer." He walked casually back to the table where Leander was waiting. He handed Fenix the cloth so he could wipe the old man's blood from his hand. Ivar remained seated, his face twisted in horror as the events unfolded before him.

Baldyr scrambled to his feet and ordered Farouk to send for a healer. Tartarian warriors burst through the doors, aiding the two injured men. No one spoke as the injured men were carried away to be tended to.

Once the doors to the dining hall shut, Farouk charged Fenix, aggressively drawing his sword. Fenix remained calm as the blade aimed in his direction. "I should kill you now for whatever it is you did to my brother!"

Fenix scoffed. "Forgive me, lord," he glanced at Baldyr, unbothered by Farouk's threat, "but you were in my way." Farouk pressed the tip of his sharp blade into the skin of Fenix's neck.

"You're lucky I don't end you right now, boy." A devious grin grew across Fenix's face as his eyes returned to Farouk.

"What did you do to me?" I could hear the fear in my father's voice as he stepped toward Fenix. The grin dissolved as Fenix's face darkened. He remained silent, his gaze falling to the floor.

"Answer him, boy!" Farouk pushed the blade further, a small drop of blood forming.

"I took control of your blood."

Without saying a word, Baldyr stepped in front of me as I bobbed my head, peeking around his large frame.

"What the fuck are you talking about?" Farouk's eyes narrowed, his sword firm against Fenix's neck.

"Exactly what I said." His golden irises rose, meeting Farouk's.

"Impossible! You'd have to be a witch or something…"

"Or *something* is correct," Fenix's gaze shot to Baldyr's. My father's arm rose, pushing me back behind him in an odd, silent acknowledgement of Fenix's words.

"Enough of your riddles, boy." Farouk's head tilted as he spoke, "What did you do to Baldyr…and how did you heal that man?!" Fenix remained tall and silent. I threw my father's arm down, peering back around only to meet Fenix's stare. "ANSWER ME!"

"He's an *aethos*, Farouk." My father spoke, his voice firm with a hint of terror. *Aethos?* Farouk scoffed, looking from Fenix to Baldyr, bewildered at my father's serious expression. His face shot back to Fenix, his eyes widened as he quickly retrieved his blade.

"Tha-that's not possible," Farouk whispered, stumbling back, "the last known aethos was—"

"Marius." Baldyr's arms shifted, forcing me back behind him.

"Indeed." Fenix agreed, wiping the blood from his neck.

Lord Baldyr shouted for his guards. A group of Tartarian warriors and Ursii rushed into the room. "Take them to the dungeon."

"You have no reason to fear us, Lord Baldyr." Leander protested as the two men were surrounded by warriors. Ivar was yanked from his seat and thrown beside Leander and Fenix.

"Not only do you know of Princess Cyrene's whereabouts, *you*," he pointed directly to Fenix, "are a threat to all of us. I will not risk any harm coming to her. Jarloth or not, you are no longer welcome here." He waved to the warriors as they seized the trio of men.

"But—" My protest was cut off.

"*No*, Cyrene. I will not risk it." The men didn't struggle as they were removed from the dining hall.

"What the hell?!" I yelled as the door shut.

"Enough, child."

"No, what is going on? Why did you lock them up? And what the fuck is an aethos?!" *Despite my years of studying the history of Devas, the word was foreign to me.*

"He said *enough*, girl!" Farouk shot back.

"Oh fuck off, Farouk!"

"CYRENE!" my father roared, his hands still in bear form, "I have no choice! If *anyone* were to find you—"

"Ivar swore to me—"

"And what of the other two? Can you trust them as well?" My voice fell silent as I glared at him. "I cannot risk your safety. It's dangerous enough, especially now knowing he's an aethos." He turned and fell firmly into his chair, sighing as he rubbed his forehead.

"What *is* an aethos?"

"Aethos are fae with the ungodly ability to control blood. They have *Blod Seid*, a dark blood magic. King Marius was the only other fae known to be cursed with such magic and ability."

"That would mean he is Marius' son."

"It would seem so," Farouk sighed. "Regardless, *Blod Seid* is the darkest form of fae magic. Rightful king or not, Fenix is dangerous. We cannot trust him."

My eyes dashed from my father to my uncle. "Fenix just saved one of your Ursii using his *Blod Seid*. He's done nothing to show he's a threat, and he said it himself: as long as I'm away from Emilios, there's no reason to concern himself with me."

"You want to jeopardize everything on an aethos bastard you just met?!" Farouk crossed his arms.

"Enough, you two," Baldyr groaned. "Right now, the aethos and his companions are locked up and not my main concern. We need to focus on what happened to our men."

Farouk sighed. "You saw the marks. It was ghouls. I'd bet the hoard in the southern mountains overstepped into our territories."

Baldyr grunted in agreement.

"I'll take care of it." Farouk huffed.

"Let me join."

Farouk raised an eyebrow, shooting an intrigued glance at my father.

"Not today, Cyrene."

Farouk grunted, disappointed in his brother's decision but bowing his head in obedience. He swiftly left the dining hall to prepare for his task.

"And why not?"

Baldyr lowered his head into his closed fists, huffing.

"I have no energy left to handle you. Leave me."

I scoffed, exiting the room in a fluster.

As my feet shuffled in the direction of my room, my gaze caught sight of Farouk bolting toward the main palace doors. Intrigue and defiance flooded my consciousness as I observed my surroundings, sprinting quietly to follow his lead. As he passed through the large doorway, I could see a handful of armed Ursii men and women holding lit torches and mounting Tartarian war horses. "Keep up, you fuckers, I want to be back in time for a warm supper." The warriors cheered in unison. Farouk spurred his horse as the party of Ursii galloped off into the wintry landscape, rapidly fading out of view. The freezing wind howled as snow gently fell from the sky. Without thought, I clutched my furs close, waiting a moment, before stepping through the doorway. My feet scaled the steps down into the courtyard, keeping my distance, as I began to shadow the Ursii. Traveling on foot, I struggled to keep pace as I ran after them. *Fuck, you need to hurry, Cyrene.*

Soon, I found myself wandering aimlessly through the wild, frigid lands of Tartarus. Lost.

The unnaturally large, primal looking man shoved Leander, Ivar and me into a damp, dark cold room, buried deep in the depths of the palace. He slammed the dungeon door, snickering as he secured the weathered iron lock. "Enjoy your stay in Tartarus." I could hear the man's cackles as he left, the light from his torch fading. Only a small gleam of a mounted torch in the distance illuminated the dungeon room through a barred window atop the door. I slouched against the wooden frame. *Think, Fenix.* Leander groaned as Ivar crouched, sitting on the filthy floor.

"Well, Ivar," Leander hissed, "I hope rescuing the princess was worth it, because now it seems we're going to die—rotting away in this Gods' awful hell hole."

I rolled my eyes. "Always the pessimistic drama queen, Leander."

"Oh, forgive me, shall I jump for joy that we've been tossed in here, left for dead? Gods, Fenix, honestly—"

"I'm sure we'll be released…eventually. Lord Baldyr is sure to calm down. He just needs to speak to Cyrene." Ivar seemed oddly positive.

"Calm down? Do you know *anything* of Tartarians, Ivar? They don't *calm down!*"

"Seems *you* need to calm down—"

"Not now, Fenix!"

"Leander," my body lifted from the door. I crossed my arms and approached my friend, "you need to breathe. Everything will be just fine, besides," I shrugged, "I have a plan."

He sighed, "Of course you do." Leander rubbed his eyes with his fingers, annoyed.

Returning to the prison door, my fist slammed into the old wood, pounding. "Where's Farouk?! I demand to see that stout fucker of a beast!" I continued banging on the door, calling attention to myself.

Moments later, a faint light grew as the guard from before slowly approached. "Off the door, you fuckin' fairy."

"Ah, why aren't you just a lovely specimen of sunshine? Say, where might little ol' Farouk be now?"

"Gone. He and a few others left to deal with some ghouls. Now," he whipped the torch against the door, sending mini embers through the bars of the speakeasy window, "quiet down!" *Perfect.* He whacked the torch against the door once more.

"Ah, fuck," my hand clutched my face, covering my eye. The man shifted his torch to get a better look into the cell. "You burned my eye! Look!" As the man leaned in, peering at the phantom injury, I swiftly reached my hand through the iron bars, touching the skin of his face. My hands pulsated and veins expanded as I began to take hold of his blood. He whimpered, straining against my power. *Weak.* My power coursed through his body, taking control as he struggled. "Now, now," his bloodshot eyes met mine, "let's not make this any more painful than it already is." I angled my head, forcing his hand to the door, shaking as he unlocked it. "Perfect." My fingers retreated back, releasing him from my dark grip. His veins bulged, prisoner to the resonating influence I held over him.

The large man fell back landing hard against the stone floor. I swung the unlocked door open, "After you." I motioned for Leander and Ivar to exit the cell. Leander didn't hesitate rushing to the fallen man, snatching the torch and his sword. Ivar cautiously stepped outside the door, his face horrified by everything that had occurred. I patted him on the back, "Don't worry. He'll be fine in a few hours."

I searched down the corridor, locating a flight of stairs leading up from the dungeon into the palace above.

"I'll never get used to his powers," Ivar whispered to himself, stepping over the paralyzed man.

"Yes, you will," Leander tossed a dagger to Ivar. "First time I witnessed him use his aethos ability," he sheathed the sword, "I couldn't sleep for days. I'll never forget the things he did—how petrified I was watching as he did them." The two men followed behind me as we ascended the stairs.

Together, we weaved our way through the palace undetected. As we turned a corner, I could hear Lord Baldyr approaching from the distance. We quickly ducked into a room, waiting as he marched past. He was speaking to a large Tartarian warrior, unaware of our presence.

"Then do it! She didn't just disappear—find her!" *Curious.* Leander peaked his head through the doorway, motioning for us to continue down the hall. We snaked through the palace, cautiously dodging staff and warriors, eventually finding our way to a side entrance. The three of us stepped through the door. Leander and Ivar trampled down a small stone stairway as a familiar scent caught my focus. I deeply inhaled the cold air as the two men called for me to follow.

"She followed them."

"What?" Leander yelled up to me.

"The princess," I glanced down at him and Ivar as they exchanged a concerned look, "it seems she followed Farouk and his party on foot." *Oh, Princess, not one to stay idle now are you?*

"She's their problem now. We need to leave, Fenix!"

Ivar shot Leander a perplexed look. "You don't *actually* suggest we just allow her to wander off into one of the harshest, most unforgiving regions of Devas?"

"Oh, who fucking cares, Ivar?! We came here to rescue her, only to discover she doesn't need our rescuing! We need to return home before Emilios makes a move. I say leave her be. Fenix, you know I'm right."

I ignored Leander's ill-mannered comment, inhaling the cold air once more. She wasn't far. "I'll retrieve her. Then, once the princess is safe, we'll leave."

Leander bleated with contempt. "Ah, fuck sakes, Fenix," he dragged his hands across his face, resting them on his hips as he glanced high into the sky, sighing. "What do you want us to do then?"

"Oh, Leander, why not just stand there and look pretty? You're good at that," I grinned as I sprinted down the stairs, joining my companions. "Plead our case to Lord Baldyr."

"That may be a bit more difficult than you think, especially after escaping his prison," Ivar crossed his arms, "but we'll do our best. Go. Find the princess and bring her back safely."

I nodded.

"Gods, you're lucky I like you, Fenix." Leander sighed again, roughly patting Ivar's arm. "Come on then, it seems we've got some groveling to do." The two men chuckled as they reclimbed the stairs. "Oh, Fenix," Leander yelled down to me, "Do be careful. Gods know what Tove will do to me if I return without you."

My grin grew. "When am I not?"

He shook his head, "Fuck."

Inhaling deeply once more, I focused on the smells floating in the wind around me: firewood, dirt, cedar, fir, cloves—*Ah, there you are.* Her scent lingered faintly.

Ready or not, here I come, Princess.

My eyes struggled to find the trail left behind by Farouk and his party. The wind had grown, blowing away any trace of their tracks in the snow. I shivered in response to the cold climate, unprepared and lost in a land I did not know. *What have you gotten yourself into, Cyrene?*

My foot slipped on an icy stone hidden by a thin layer of snow, knocking me off balance, landing face first into the cold white powder. *Fuck.* As I pushed myself up, kneeling to stand, I heard a noise behind me. My body froze as my ears listened intently. The sound increased as if approaching me. *Footsteps.* My fingers reached into my boot, slowly pulling the small dagger from the hidden sheath. I prepared to lunge, the crunching steps growing closer. *Now!* I whipped around, swinging my arm, the dagger aimed high. Instantly, something hindered my attack, no, someone. My head jerked up to see Fenix's golden eyes peering down at me. He held my wrist tightly within his grasp.

Fenix cackled, loosening his hold as I yanked my wrist from his hand. I rose, stumbling for a moment. "What are *you* doing here? Wait, how did you escape the dungeon?" *Just my luck, running into him.* I wiped the snow from my face and clothing. "Did you *follow me*?!" My cheeks flustered.

He didn't answer my questions, only smirked at my temper. I rolled my eyes. "Come on," he reached for my hand, "let's get you back before my friends are murdered."

I slapped his hand from mine, "Fuck off."

His eyes narrowed, "I wasn't asking." He snatched my hand and began dragging me back toward the palace.

"Let go of me!" I fought to pull my hand free, but his hold was too strong.

My gaze shot from Fenix, back to the dagger in my other hand. *Fuck it.* I jabbed his hand with the small blade. He whipped around, flinging his hand free, sending me back on my ass into the cold snow. He examined his hand, a single stream of blood dripping faintly from the small incision. His eyes shot to me, glaring.

"Did you just fucking stab me?" I frantically crawled in reverse as he trailed toward me. *Shit!* My back slammed into a tree. *Shit, Shit!*

"Leave me alone!" I screamed. He halted at the fear in my voice.

There was an odd shift in his eyes. "Cyrene, I'm not here to hurt you." He kneeled at my feet, "I just want to get you back to your father. Safe." I gasped. *How did he know? Did Ivar tell him?* He smirked, reading my face. "Oh, please, anyone with eyes and a brain who's witnessed the two of you together can tell you're Baldyr's child." He reached his bloodied hand out to me, "I won't speak of it to anyone. I *swear.*"

My eyes studied Fenix's face as his hand remained extended. His expression was soft and seemed genuine—a contrast to his behavior to this point. *Could Ivar be right? Was there more to Fenix?* My eyes fell to his hand; his skin was bronzed, clashing against the bright snow. My sight traveled up his arm, across his chest and to his neck, concealed beneath his black leather cloak. His dark faded tunic was cut low, revealing his toned torso. He was extremely handsome. He cleared his throat, snapping me back to reality.

"Enjoying the view, are we?" He grinned. I furrowed my brows, plopping my hand into his as he rose, lifting me to my feet.

"I'm not returning to the palace."

"And where exactly, *dear princess*, do you intend on going?" Fenix crossed his arms as I peered up at the sky. The sun was fading, soon it would be dark. I needed to catch up to Farouk—quickly.

"The Southern mountains of Tartarus. I'm going to help Farouk and the others exterminate the ghouls."

"Do you even know where their party is currently? Or how to track them?" I glanced around, clueless, before pointing in a random direction.

"That way." I cleared my throat. "Now, if you'll excuse me," my foot stepped in the direction I had aimed.

"Nope. That's north." He turned toward me as I remained facing the opposite direction, my back to him. "You know," he stepped closer, "I *could* accompany you." I scoffed. "It'll be dark soon, and who knows what beasts wonder about these parts. Plus, something tells me you're not exactly blessed with a sense of direction." I ignored his insults. *As much as I hated admitting it to myself, he was right. I could use his help... unfortunately.*

I twirled around to face Fenix. "Fine. You may join me...but if Farouk or a ghoul kills you, it's not my fault," I snorted, full of smugness.

He grinned as he stepped even closer. "I assure you, Cyrene, I can handle Farouk and ghouls. Now," he lightly pushed past me, continuing in the direction I had pointed to, "let's hurry before it's too late."

"But that's north you said?"

"Well, I had to say *something* to convince you to let me stay." He shouted back at me as he marched forward. *Fucking prick.*

I sprinted to catch up. "How do you know the way Farouk and the others traveled?"

Fenix stared forward, "Let's just say...I have a gift." *Unlikely.*

We tramped through the snow in silence.

Before long, we discovered a rocky trail leading down into the southern mountains. "Stay alert." Fenix led the way as I followed closely behind. The sun had completely vanished. Night had washed over our surroundings, making it difficult to see far ahead.

Minutes later, a cave appeared within view. Fenix slowed as we inched closer, sniffing the air. *Strange.* As we approached the cave, I could see the party's war horses, slaughtered across blood soaked snow. I ran to the mouth of the cave searching. There was no sign of Farouk and his party.

"Did they flee?"

Fenix's eyes shot past me into the cave, inhaling deeply. *Odd.*

"No. They went inside." *How did he know?*

"Stay close, Cyrene."

I clung to Fenix's thick cloak as we stepped through the entrance of the mountain.

The cave was eerie and silent, growing darker as we ventured further. Fenix slowly made his way through the winding tunnel as my hand tightly clung to him.

"What're we doing? Where are we going?" I asked in a normal voice.

"Shh!" He stopped. "Listen..." I focused my hearing down the pitch black cave. I could hear a small, faint clicking from within the tunnel. "*Ghouls.*" Fenix whispered, softly grabbing my hand, leading me further into the cave. My skin tingled at his warm grip.

A faint glow emerged from further in the mountain. We crept alongside the wet, cold walls, closing in on the orange light. Just ahead, behind a large rock lay a burning torch. I bent down, examining the beacon. It was one of ours. I glanced at Fenix, concerned.

"They're here." His eyes bolted past me to another dim light dancing in the distance. He gently pulled me along as we closed in on the fire when someone yelled. *Farouk.*

Without any thought, I charged toward my uncle's voice, yanking my hand from Fenix's grasp.

"Cyrene, wait!" I ignored Fenix's plea and sprinted towards the direction of Farouk's grunts. I could hear him attacking something. High pitched shrieks and clicks filled the stuffy cave. *Ghouls.* As I turned the corner, I saw him.

Farouk was struggling with a horrifyingly large creature. Bones protruded the ghoul's pale, ashy skin as it hunched over, swinging its long, thin arms at Farouk with sharp, gaunt fingers. Its eyes were pitch black. The ghoul hissed, baring its sharp teeth and long thin snake-like tongue. Farouk swung his sword, slicing the wiggling tongue from the monster's mouth. It screeched, howling in pain as it fell back against the cave floor. My hands covered my ears at the high pitch scream. Thick, black blood spewed from the ghoul's mouth. Farouk huffed, panting as he lowered his sword and met my gaze.

"Cyrene?" I lowered my hands and flashed him a faint smile. Within a blink of an eye, another ghoul appeared and tackled Farouk hard to the ground. He groaned as he struggled, wrestling with the ungodly creature. My feet raced, barreling toward the ghoul, instinctively shifting into my Ursii form.

I rammed the ghoul hard with my skull, sending it flying back into the wall of the cave. Farouk rolled, grabbing his sword as he positioned himself in front of me.

"Get out of here, Cyrene!" he shouted back, shielding me from the ghoul. I growled, stepping around him. "Girl, move!" He attempted to shove me back. "Your father would never forgive me if something happens to you!"

Farouk's eyes remained on the ghoul as it clicked and chittered, prowling on all fours circling us. "Remember your training, Cyrene." The other ghoul had crawled to its feet, black blood seeping from its missing tongue. The monster gurgled as it joined in surrounding my uncle and me. "I'll do my best to protect you, but if I fall," Farouk and I stationed our bodies back to back, ready to fight, "you *must* leave me." The ghouls' sudden screams caused my ears to ring as they charged. *I'm not leaving you, Uncle.*

Farouk was able to dodge one of the ghouls as it lunged toward him. He twirled, shoving his sword into its spine. It shrieked in pain, falling to the ground. My body clashed against the other ghoul as it clawed at me, its fingers tearing across the fur of my back. I roared, stretching my jaw open as my teeth bit into the ghoul's arm, violently piercing down. I locked my jaw and shook my muzzle from side to side, tearing at the ghoul's flesh. Thick, black blood spewed from its arm flooding my mouth. The creature frantically clawed its nails deeper into my back, screeching. I yanked the ghoul's arm, ripping it clean from its body, spitting it aside. I climbed over the fallen creature, pinning it to the hard ground with my paws as it tried to wriggle free. I widened my jaw as far as I could and crunched down on its skull. The ghoul fell limp in my mouth. I spat the macerated ghoul onto the floor, faintly gagging on the acidic blood.

"Cyrene, look out!" Farouk warned as two more ghouls emerged from within the cave, darting toward me. I braced myself, ready to strike when a sudden deep, menacing growl echoed, vibrating the cave. A monstrous black wolf barreled into the cluster of ghouls, clearing my path. The gigantic beast halted in front of me. *What in the Gods?* The wolf towered high, standing substantially larger than Farouk and me—greater than any beast I'd ever seen. I peered up at the frightening wolf, its long razor sharp teeth bared as it released a deep rumbling snarl. A stark white streak of fur lined its spine and faded down across its right eye. Large golden eyes glowed as they stared down at me, meeting my gaze. I recognized those eyes.

Fenix?

One of the ghouls leapt onto Fenix's back, snarling as it snapped at his neck. Farouk pulled his sword from a second ghoul and rushed to Fenix's aid. He threw his sword, the blade hitting its mark perfectly as the ghoul screeched in agony. Fenix forcefully removed the monster from his back, hurling its body. Farouk sauntered over, ripping his sword from the ghoul's carcass. Thick, black blood soaked the blade.

"I have to say, boy," Farouk wiped his blade across the ghoul's skin, "I did not expect you to be a Vargr." *Vargr. Fenix is a wolf shifter.* Fenix growled at Farouk before turning his attention to me. He stepped closer, his paws heavy against the ground, examining my bear skin. "She'll be fine, wolf." Farouk groaned from behind. Fenix's eyes remained on me, snorting in response to Farouk. "Gods...an aethos *and* a Vargr," my uncle sat on a rock wiping his forehead, "by the looks of you, I'd say you're either a lout or an alpha..." Fenix whirled his head at Farouk and growled, "or *both*." Fenix, a Seelie *and* Alpha? *Fuck.*

As Farouk leaned over to catch his breath, movement caught my attention directing my focus from Fenix. An injured ghoul silently scaled the rock behind him. I bellowed a warning as he stared at me confused. The ghoul hissed as it towered over Farouk, raising its arm. *Move!* Farouk turned, too slow to move, as the ghoul struck him, sending him to the ground. The ghoul jumped onto his body and bit hard into his chest. He screamed in pain, attempting to fight the ghoul, "Fucking bastard." Fenix charged the ghoul as I galloped closely behind.

Farouk lay on the ground, screaming as the ghoul ripped chunks from his flesh. Fenix sprung, his mouth wide open as he snatched the ghoul by its head. He swung the creature around, ripping its skull clean from its body. I rushed to Farouk's side in a frenzy. He remained on the floor, his mouth stained red with blood as he clung to his chest. Blood gushed from beneath his fingers.

"Fucking ghouls," he spat. He tried to sit up, falling over, too weak from his injuries. The color from his face began to fade as his eyes fluttered, rolling back into his skull.

My muzzle nudged Farouk's arm. He remained still. I frantically shoved him, hoping to gain a response. Fenix appeared, back in fae form, his wild hair falling down past his chin, his cloak buttoned around his naked body. His chest and mouth were stained black from the ghoul blood. He kneeled beside Farouk and examined his wounds, sighing.

"It's bad, Cyrene." Our eyes locked as I silently pleaded, *Please, help him!* As if hearing my thoughts, Fenix placed his hand atop Farouk's chest.

Fenix closed his eyes and focused. The veins in his hand bulged, turning black as his muscles flexed. Farouk groaned faintly. Nothing happened. Fenix opened his eyes, his veins still black as he removed his hand from Farouk's chest. I whimpered. *Why isn't he waking up?* Fenix shook his head.

"I can't fix this, Cyrene, he's already lost too much, not to mention there's ghoul blood in his wounds. He needs a healer."

I panicked, pacing in circles. *No, you have to help him! We have to save him!*

"Breathe, Cyrene," I stopped at the sound of his calm voice, "we just need to get him back to the palace." My lungs inhaled deeply. *Okay, he's going to be okay.*

Fenix grabbed Farouk's shoulders and lifted him, placing him upon his back. I stepped toward him to help.

"No, I got it, Cyrene." I snapped my jaw as he grinned at my temper. "Stay in your bear skin, Cyrene." A whine left my muzzle. "I mean unless you just want me to see you naked...again." I growled, picking the torch up with my teeth. Fenix chuckled as he carried Farouk behind me, "That's what I thought, little beastie." His strength baffled me. *He must be a lout.*

"Let's get your uncle back, quickly. I can keep a good pace, but keep up. I can't handle much more shit tonight." I snorted at him, leading the way out of the cave, the torch lighting our path.

Fenix and I traveled back to Lord Baldyr's palace safely. The night had turned bitter cold, as snow continued to fall. We strode up the stone stairs to the main entrance of the palace when the doors suddenly burst open. Baldyr and a few Tartarians came racing towards us, Leander and Ivar following closely behind them.

"What in the Gods happened?!" Baldyr personally retrieved Farouk from Fenix's back, his color fading as pale as a ghost. "Quickly, call a healer!" He rapidly carried his brother inside.

My eyes glanced back at Fenix. "Go," he ushered. I hesitated before following my father inside, rushing past Ivar and Leander. The men gawked at the sight of me before running to their companion.

I remained next to my father as he laid Farouk on a table in the dining hall. He desperately poured water over the ghoul bites across Farouk's chest. His wounds sizzled as the blood boiled.

"What happened, Cyrene?" My father demanded calmly. My eyes looked up at him, filled with sadness. "It's not your fault," he reassured me, petting my head. Additional men entered the room followed by a healer. They flocked to Farouk's side and immediately began treating him. "Go to your room, child," my father kept his eyes on his brother, "I'll send the healer once they've finished with Farouk."

"My lord...his wounds...this is going to take some time," the healer stated as she cleaned the hole in Farouk's chest "but he'll live." *Thank the Gods.* "I need your help, my lord." Baldyr walked to the healer's side.

"Go, Cyrene."

I turned towards the door.

"Your mother would be proud." His words warmed my heart.

I clambered through the halls, making my way to my chamber. As I approached the door to my chamber, I realized I couldn't grip the handle with my paws. *Fuck.* My paws struggled, failing to open the door. *Come on, Cyrene!* I snapped at the handle, biting it with my teeth in frustration.

"Allow me." My eyes remained on the door as he twisted the knob. My muzzle pushed the door open, making my way inside. Fenix remained silent in the doorway. He was no longer naked and wore a casual loose tunic and leather trousers. His hair remained loose around his face, his mouth was no longer caked in the dark ghoul blood. I huffed, angling my head at the door.

"I'll go—just listen," I plopped down annoyed, "you're going to feel all your injuries when you shift back." *No shit.* "I'm serious, Cyrene, it's going to *hurt.* Your fae form isn't as strong as your Ursii one. Just, take it slow." A faint growl emerged from my throat: a warning. "Okay, I'm going...stubborn ass." He gripped the handle, "But if you need help, I'm here. Besides, it's hard to resist another chance to catch a glimpse of that ass of yours." He flashed a devilish grin and closed the door, ignoring my roar. I could hear the door creak under the weight of his body as he leaned against the wood. *Fucking prick. I swear, he must think he's some knight in shining armor. Dumb ass. I don't need his help.* Standing on my hind legs, I prepared myself.

I inhaled slowly, focusing on the shift back to my fae form. My fur slowly retreated back into my pores, prickling my skin as it disappeared. My bones cracked and snapped as my mouth shrank, stained black from the ghoul attack. I whined as my spine curved and realigned. Something felt off. I tried to remain standing, wobbling as I straightened my posture. My lungs inhaled sharply, cutting my breath short as immense pain burned into my back. I bellowed in agony. *What the fuck?!* I hunched over, limping to the large mirror. My eyes scanned the reflective glass, examining my back. Huge, deep gashes stretched across my spine. My hand shook as my finger lightly touched one of the large cuts. The lesion burned, sizzling as my skin made contact. I screamed, falling to the floor.

Fenix bolted into the room and rushed to my side. My cheeks burned with embarrassment as I tried to cover myself from his eyes. "Relax, I'm not looking. I do possess some self control, Princess." His hand grazed my back as my body jolted, screaming out in pain. His eyes darted to my burning spine. "Fuck. Ghoul blood. Must've dripped into your wounds during the attack. Their blood is normally harmless, but once it mixes with your blood, it becomes toxic." He ripped a blanket from my bed, grabbing the water pitcher from my bedside. He delicately covered my naked body with the blanket. He sighed, "I need to draw it out of your system before it travels to your heart." He rolled me gently to my side. "This is going to hurt, Cyrene." He lifted the water pitcher, pouring the cold water over the wounds. I shrieked, my lungs aching from my agonizing screams. My back hissed as the ghouls' blood bubbled. "Almost there." Tears filled my eyes as he continued. I began to feel lightheaded. Fenix placed his hand on my back, examining the gashes closer. "The water didn't evaporate all the blood." He rolled his sleeves, "Forgive me, Princess, but I need to do this." He breathed deeply, pushing his hands against my back. My eyes widened at the impact, tears soaking my face as I sobbed and cried out in pain. My skin pulsed as the ghoul blood was suctioned from my body into his hands. The pressure and pain disappeared as Fenix removed his hands, plopping down next to me. "It's done."

My breathing slowly returned to normal. My hand clutched the blanket close against my breasts as I wheeled myself around, carefully sitting up to face him. Fenix's palms were covered in my blood, his veins black and swollen as he rested his arms across his knees.

He caught my gaze. "Don't worry," he raised his left hand, rotating it as he glanced at the veins, "the ghoul blood will fade—eventually."

"Does it hurt?"

He rustled his hair, looking back at me. "Not one bit." His power astonished me.

"How does it work? The *Blod Seid*."

He shook his head and raised his eyebrows.

"Like any other ability. How does that spirit animal of yours connect to you—"

"How do you know of Aodhan?"

He smirked softly, "I know a fylguir when I see one, plus I can smell the hawk on you." I furrowed my brows in confusion.

Reading my expression, Fenix sighed, dropping his knees. "Being a Vargr, I have an enhanced sense of smell. It's how I found you earlier in the mountains." *He smelled me?*

"Okay...," my head tilted, "let me get this straight..." my mind struggled to comprehend as I turned to face him better, "you're a Vargr... with aethos abilities...and you're a lout? Correct? Am I missing anything else? I mean you're not a God are you?" I scoffed nervously.

"Gods no," he chuckled, "but I am an *Alpha* Vargr. I don't exactly enforce my position on my pack. Truthfully, I prefer for my cousin, Tove, to lead our wolves." *Fucking hell.* He was a Seelie *and* Alpha. The sheer idea terrified me.

"Why don't you enforce your position as Alpha? Don't men typically crave power like that?"

"I'm not like most men, Princess," his voice softened. "I may be an alpha *and* the rightful king of Devas...but I do not seek power. Never have. Power is a poison, slowly killing those who yield to it. It becomes a deadly addiction, never fully satisfying the poor soul who tastes its deceiving allure. No, I don't want power. I want to right wrongs—I *want* revenge." His golden eyes glared deep into mine. "I want Serifos to watch as I rip the crown from his fucking head and take back what is *mine*. Then, I'm going to torture him, *slowly*, taking my time as he suffers. He's going to pay for everything he's done to this world and only then, when the world is right, will I kill him."

We sat in silence as the intensity of his words faded.

"You're a headache, Fenix."

He laughed. I tried to rise, gripping the blanket against my naked body. Fenix shot to his feet, gently catching me as I stumbled.

"Careful. Water may evaporate the ghoul blood, but unfortunately, the pain will linger." He led me to my bed, helping me onto the mattress. He pulled the blankets over my body as my eyes suddenly became heavy.

"Rest, Cyrene."

Those words sounded familiar.

"Rest."

"*Cymar*," the whispered voice drifted into my mind, slowly waking me.

Stirring in the bed, pain shot through my body fully waking me. I had forgotten the injuries on my back. Rotating, my eyes caught sight of Fenix sitting at the foot of my bed, leaning against the wooden bedpost. His presence startled me as I pulled the blankets over my exposed body. He hopped from the foot of the bed and paced to my side.

"Farouk? How's Farouk?!"

"You uncle's fine. He's resting. How are you feeling?" *What was he doing here? And why was he being so nice?* My shoulders flinched, rotating away from him, wincing.

He sighed. "Stubborn ass." He picked up a small jar of the clove ointment. "Here," he motioned for me to move.

My eyes glared at him. "Relax," he growled, "I just want to help." I reluctantly rolled over, laying flat on my stomach, my arms sprawled under my pillows. Fenix sat next to me, drawing the covers back. He examined the slices across my skin, his fingertips lightly tracing the open cuts. I shivered at his delicate touch. "You're healing fast. Soon, these will scar over." He unscrewed the small jar. "The healer came to see you not long after you fell asleep. Your father hovered as she treated you." He grinned as he scraped his fingertips across the salve. "I doubt he was too pleased to find me in bed with his naked daughter."

I scowled as he smirked. "How long have I been asleep?"

"You've been resting for a full day. Shifters heal fast, but the quick process can take a toll on our bodies. It usually takes us a day or two to fully recover from the injuries we sustain in our second skins." *Had he stayed by my side the entire time?* He intricately stroked the ointment across my back. I instantly arched, flinching from the cold medicine. My hands squeezed the sheets, forming fists as my teeth bit my pillow. He filled the wounds with the salve, using the entire jar to treat my injuries.

My back tingled, slowly numbing from the ointment. Then my back lowered and my fists relaxed, releasing my grip on the sheets. Fenix watched me with hungry eyes.

"You know," he leaned in, his long hair gliding across my shoulder, "if you need a distraction," he ran his lips across my skin, causing me to shudder, "I would be more than happy to assist you." He tucked my hair behind my ear, purposely stroking my skin as he moved. My eyes instinctively closed as he kissed the top of my head. *What the fuck are you doing, Cyrene?* I didn't stop Fenix as he began to graze my arm with kisses. *No, this needs to stop. Now.*

My senses returned as my mind flashed back to reality. Grunting, I lifted myself from the bed and hurled my hand at Fenix's face. He effortlessly caught my wrist, stopping me before my hand could make contact with his cheek. He lifted his head, grinning. His eyes flashed down my body, devouring the sight of me on my knees, completely exposed as he clutched my wrist. He yanked my arm, pulling my body down. My back stretched, aching, as I caught myself with my free hand, still on my knees. My cheeks warmed, flushing with embarrassment and arousal.

Fenix smiled, baring his canines, "Careful, Princess," his voice was low and carnal, "some of us like it rough."

Fenix dropped my wrist and slipped from the bed. My body dropped as I caught myself, ripping the blankets over my exposed body. He glided to the door, stopping as his hand touched the iron handle. "Your father wants us to gather in the dining hall in a few hours." He flashed me an amused glance. "I look forward to seeing you, little beastie, even if it means you'll be unfortunately clothed." He opened the door, grinning as he stepped through. His footsteps faded as he strolled down the hall.

I sat back in my bed overwhelmed with emotions.

What the fuck just happened?

Dressing myself was far more difficult than I expected. Even though my cuts had healed faster than anticipated, my body was exhausted. *Just as Fenix said... Prick.*

Once fully dressed, I proceeded from my room to the dining hall to meet my father.

The doors to the dining hall were propped open as two guards were stationed outside the doorway,more guards were positioned inside the dining hall. *Baldyr's precaution, I presume.* Lord Baldyr was seated in his throne at the head of his usual table, Farouk absent from his side. *He must be resting still.* Lord Leander and Fenix were seated across the pew, Ivar sitting opposite them. I strode past the men, ignoring Fenix's playful gaze and seated myself next to Ivar. He gave me a soft, warm smile.

"It's nice to see you about and feeling well, Cyrene." My head bowed to my father. Baldyr motioned around the room pointing out the extra warriors stationed in the distance. "Can't be too cautious now can we, wolf?" His green eyes angled at Fenix.

Fenix crossed his arms giving Baldyr a beguiled look. "Not with two alphas present," he teased. My father grunted as he peered across the table at all of us present.

"Farouk is recovering as expected. Don't be surprised if he tries to come bursting into the hall any minute now."

A chuckle escaped my lips. Knowing Farouk, my father's statement amused me. "Lord Fenix," he started, tilting his head in his direction, "I want to thank you." Fenix lowered his arms shifting in his seat. His posture suddenly appeared regal. "If you and your company had not escaped from the dungeon," he stopped, glaring at the other men, "who knows what would have happened in that cave. Princess Cyrene and Farouk both could've died." Fenix bowed his head in respect. Baldyr pondered a moment before speaking again. "In return, I want to offer you my fealty." The whole room gasped at his words. The Lord of Tartarus and alpha of the Ursii was aligning himself with Fenix.

"Serifos is a disgrace to the crown and all of Devas. He cares for no one but himself and allows Keres to torment the good people of this world. If yesterday's actions reflect the type of man you truly are," he rose from his chair shadowed with nobility as he spoke, "then I would be *honored* to serve you as my king." He kneeled at Fenix's side, bowing his head. An alpha submitting to another alpha—a rare sight to behold.

Fenix rose from the pew, standing tall and powerful. "I thank you, Lord Baldyr. Tartarus is a strong, forcible region. You have the strongest armies in all of Devas and are one of the last remaining ancient realms. It is *my* honor to accept your allegiance."

My father rose, full of pride. "My king," and returned to his chair. Fenix mimicked his movements.

"Lord Leander informed me that your party wishes to return to the Bottomlands." *He was leaving? So soon?*

"Yes, seeing as Princess Cyrene here," Fenix pointed to me, "is perfectly content in her new accommodations, there's no reason for us to stay. We must return and deal with Emilios before things escalate." *Why did his words sting?*

"Very well then." Baldyr snapped his fingers as a warrior rushed to his side. "See to it that King Fenix and his men have everything they need. I want them to have a comfortable journey back." The man nodded, retreating from the room. Lord Baldyr rose from the table, the men and I following suit. "If that's all gentlemen, I bid you farewell. Safe travels, my king." As we began to depart the dining hall, a female warrior rushed into the room. An unknown, inky black raven was perched on her arm. Leander and Fenix halted at the sight of the mysterious bird.

"Forgive me, Lord Baldyr, but *this* just arrived." The woman lifted her arm revealing a small scroll tied to the raven's leg.

Baldyr looked at Fenix. "Is this bird yours?" Fenix approached the raven, stroking its head.

"My cousin's." He untied the rolled letter, silently reading its words. "Leander," he summoned, keeping his eyes on the tiny scroll. Leander rushed to his side glancing over the ink. "Forgive me, Lord Baldyr, but we must leave *immediately*." Fenix gracefully walked to the table, appointing the paper over the flame of a candle. His eyes grew dark as the page ignited. "It seems Emilios has decided to make another move." He dropped the burning page as it burned into nothing but ash. I took a step in his direction.

"What did he do?"

Fenix tilted his head toward me, his eyes locked on mine. Anger flashed across his face.

"He's planning to attack Southern Amos."

Fenix and his company prepared to depart Tartarus, the raven leaving as quickly as it arrived. Lord Baldyr had three of his war horses readied and waiting as the men stormed down the stairs into the courtyard. He stood beside me as Tartarian men helped heave satchels full of supplies across each of the horses backs. Leander held a torch as Fenix adjusted his gloves. A heavy snow began to fall, their winter furs and thick cloaks shielding them from the windy night air. Ivar approached, clearing his throat.

"I pray the Gods continue to keep you safe and bless you with happiness, Cyrene." He lifted my hand and gently kissed it. A soft smile formed on my face, quickly disappearing as he ran to join the others. My eyes caught Fenix's as the men mounted their horses.

Fenix flashed me a disquieted look, and a strange tug pulled deep inside my chest. *This isn't right.*

"We thank you for your hospitality, Lord Baldyr." Fenix shouted through the snow.

"Tartarus is at your disposal, my king."

Fenix's eyes lingered on me a little longer. "Princess," he bowed his head. The men turned, galloping into the cold night with haste. The light of their torches faded from view as they stormed north. Baldyr turned to enter the castle, stopping as he observed the troubled look across my face.

"Why did you choose to follow him?" I inquired, my eyes focused north.

He peered out into the night. "Because it was the right choice. Fenix is the rightful heir to the throne—the true king of Devas. He proved himself worthy when he saved you and Farouk. It's what your mother would've wanted." Baldyr climbed the stairs. My gaze remained locked on the distant glow of the men's torches. Something inside me screamed, begging to follow. My gut twisted watching the men begin to fade into the distance. It felt wrong staying behind. *Fuck it.*

"I'm going with them."

Baldyr paused, glanced back at me. He was smiling. "I figured you'd say that." He whistled loudly. Suddenly, a man led a readied war horse into the courtyard, stopping at the steps below me.

I glanced at the horse, bewildered. "How did you know?" My father appeared at my side, arms behind his back, smug with satisfaction.

"As I said before," he looked at me with proud eyes, "you're just like your mother." I jumped, hugging him tightly. Tears rolled down his face as he embraced me. "It's the right thing to do, Cyrene." He pulled from my arms, wiping a tear from my face. "Serifos and Emilios must be stopped. Staying here, hiding away won't prevent them from coming. Find Fenix." He pushed me towards the war horse. The man handed me a torch as I mounted the saddle and looked at my father once more. "And *don't* leave his side."

"I will return home, father. I promise." He nodded.

"SKOL!"

My eyes shot to the stairs to see Farouk standing in the doorway of the palace, smiling.

"SKOL!" My legs squeezed, signaling the horse as we sprinted north into the darkness.

Within minutes my eyes caught a glimpse of their torches far in the distance. Squeezing my legs tighter I shouted for the horse to hasten its pace. We charged through the darkness picking up speed as their light grew closer.

"Fenix!" My voice evaporated into the icy wind as my teeth chattered. I could see the silhouettes of the men and their horses ahead of me, trudging through the snow. I signaled the horse to run faster as it snorted and whined.

We continued charging toward the group, their faces appearing in sight. "FENIX!" His eyes reflected the light of his torch as he turned back at the sound of my voice. The men turned, slowing as I galloped to them. My hands yanked the leather reigns of my horse. The creature rose, kicking its front legs squealing, slamming back down into the snow. We trotted a few feet, joining the men.

"Cyrene? What in the Gods do you think you're doing?!" Ivar demanded against the wailing wind.

"I'm joining you!" My eyes shot to Fenix. "Seems my father thinks I'd be of better use in *your* company than here in Tartarus."

Leander gawked, raising his eyebrows. "*Father*? You mean to say, Lord Baldyr is your father? *Not* Serifos?"

"Oh, do keep up, Leander." Fenix smiled at my impulsive choice. Ivar looked at Leander shaking his head.

"Always the last to know," Leander scoffed, returning to the path. Ivar followed.

"Not sure being alone with me is the safest thing for you, little beastie."

"I can handle you, Fenix. Besides," my head tilted toward Leander and Ivar ahead, "we're not exactly *alone*."

"We'll see about that." *Why was I beginning to enjoy his teasing?*

A shriek from above caught our attention. Aodhan pushed against the winds and descended toward us, landing firmly on my shoulder. He screamed, repeating a message from my father.

"Seems your father wants him to keep an eye on you." I stroked Aodhan's head lifting him to my shoulder.

He chirped as my fingers brushed his head. "Something like that."

Fenix circled me, "Keep up, Princess, it's a long journey back to the Bottomlands." He rushed ahead, joining Leander and Ivar as I followed closely behind.

Don't worry, Father...I won't leave Fenix's side.

The four of us raced toward the Bottomlands. We traveled a few days before reaching its southernmost border. To help pass the time, the men and I exchanged stories of our lives. I enjoyed learning of the men's interests and abilities along the way.

Leander, the oldest of our party, was an Unseelie. *Unfortunate.* He and Emilios were distant relatives, sharing the old Baldassare house name. He seemed to despise his kin as much as I did. *Good.* According to Fenix, he was also quite fond of Tove, Fenix's younger cousin. The dynamic of the three intrigued me. Ivar was older than me but younger than the other men. He didn't know who his father was but was raised in a plain, simple life among the fishermen of Seamarke. Over time, he worked his way through the ranks of merchant ships, eventually becoming a captain of his own vessel. Leander mentioned that Ivar was also skilled with a bow—something he learned in the Silas apparently. Fenix, the second oldest of us all, spoke little of himself. Instead, he talked of his mother, Lady Hadrian. Apparently, after giving birth, she left Fenix with her brother in the Bottomlands. He grew up with his younger cousin Tove and learned of the Vargr wolves, Marius, and his abilities all from his uncle, Lord Harold. He had been raised to be a warrior from the beginning, preparing and training for the day he took back his crown. His story broke my heart.

Fenix and I would fall behind, tailing the party, conversing quietly between ourselves. He seemed oddly interested in my life. He'd ask me about my half siblings Keres and Cecelia, how I felt about them, how they treated me. It wasn't a pleasant conversation. He changed the subject, asking about my upbringing. I expressed how I always felt out of place and wished I had known my mother. Seeing my pain, he recited stories he'd heard of my mother from his own family. Hearing him speak of her made my heart glow. He seemed to truly admire her. I felt strangely comfortable discussing my life with him, but it allowed me to see Fenix in a new light.

We reached a broad cluster of trees just north of the Tartarian border. The Bottomlands was a far warmer region than Tartarus. The sun aimed down on us, causing me to sweat beneath the thick winter fur that draped my shoulders.

Fenix pointed ahead toward the treeline. "There's a creek through the trees, just down a hill. It's perfect for refreshing yourself after a long journey. We can stop here and rest a few hours before we continue north." He rode ahead, dismounting his horse, tying the reins to a nearby tree. The rest of us followed, doing the same. Ivar unlatched his cloak, rolling it into a pillow as he plopped down on the warm, green grass.

"Really?" Leander asked, "*another* nap?"

"Nothing wrong with being fully rested and prepared for whatever shenanigans you three drag me into." Ivar smiled as he crossed his arms and closed his eyes.

Leander groaned. "I'm going to stretch my legs. I need a break from you." He strode off.

Fenix had removed his gloves, unfastening his cloak as he draped it across the back of his horse. "Care for a swim?" His question threw me off guard.

"A swim...*now*?"

He grinned, raising a brow. "Why not?" He tilted his head for me to follow as he strolled toward the woods. My hands quickly unfastened my cloak, tossing the winter layers across the saddle. Aodhan hopped to my hand as I lowered my arm toward Ivar.

"Stay here, Aodhan." The hawk settled next to a sleeping Ivar as I chased after Fenix.

Fenix took my hand and guided me through the thick, green woods. Beams of sunlight broke through the heavy canopy of the trees, engulfing the lush, green foliage in a beautiful, golden glow. The temperature rose as he led me deeper into the thicket. My surroundings reminded me of a dream.

Mellow ripples could be heard nearby. Fenix helped me over a few large rocks as we stumbled down the cliff to the trickling creek that bled into a small river. Fenix began to remove his boots, loosening the strings of his tunic.

"Don't be shy, Princess," he teased, "nothing I haven't seen before." He winked, jumping into the river. Ripples danced across the surface as he rose—drenched. My canine pierced my lip, watching him intently as he combed his wet hair back with his hands.

He caught my hungry gaze and flashed me a lewd grin. "You'd get a better look if you joined me, beastie."

My cheeks blushed. A swim did sound nice, especially with the heat. *Fuck it.*

My hands ripped the boots from my feet. I stepped a few paces back, allowing myself a head start before sprinting to the edge, lunging into the warm sky. My hair gleamed in the light. Fenix smiled as my body plunged into the river. My body hit the water hard. I held my breath, sinking slowly as I descended deep into the cool water. Bubbles surrounded me, tickling my skin as they rose. Relief washed over me as my body drifted further, blending into darkness. My mind drifted as I relaxed in the cool, murky water.

Large arms wrapped around my waist as my body hovered over the sandy riverbed.

Fenix tightened his grip around my midsection as he quickly drew me upwards. We broke through the surface of the water, intertwined, gasping for air.

"What the fuck do you think you're doing?!" I coughed, shoving myself from his chest. Fenix glared at me, his hair dripping down his face.

"Don't do that." His tone was unrecognizable.

"Do *what*?" The words shot from my mouth. Fenix waded closer. His dark tunic was soaked, sticking to his built frame like a second skin. My mind struggled to focus as he inched closer.

"Don't *scare* me." *Scare him?*

"What the fuck are you talking about?"

"You hit the water and didn't come back up, Cyrene."

My eyes rolled, annoyed.

"I've told you before, I can handle myself. Don't be such a pussy, Fenix." I whipped around and began to wade in the opposite direction. "Not sure why you care anyways." I spat the words over my shoulder.

Before the words fully left my lips, Fenix took hold of my arm, whirling me through the water back to him. He gripped both my biceps and shook me. "Your father entrusted me with your safety. What do you think would happen if the heir of Tartarus were injured or worse, died? I'd be at war! *Nothing* can happen to you." He stared down at me, his golden eyes flickering with care and desire. *He's lying.* A small flame ignited inside me.

"Is that all?" I hissed back at him. My heart fluttered as he grinned.

"Were you hoping for something else, Princess?" My body ached for him. *Stop it.* My arms struggled, attempting to wriggle free, but he only clenched me harder. "Were you *wanting* me to say something else?" He leaned close, his wet lips brushing my neck.

"Stop," the word exhaled softly from my lungs.

"Your mouth may be telling me to stop," he whispered, caressing his way to my cheek, "but your body is screaming otherwise." His hot breath sent shivers up my spine, causing my skin to prickle. His ravenous eyes became level to mine as a burning tug raged inside my core. My thirst for him had become unbearable.

"If you *really* want me to stop, say the words." His honey eyes stared into mine. My breathing increased as he flashed a devilish grin. "But if you don't, little beastie, know that I will make your body ache with pleasure in ways you never thought possible." His words melted me. I couldn't resist him any longer.

Fuck it.

Carnal lust boiled in my blood as my lips rammed into his. The impact of my kiss plunged our bodies back into the cold water. His hold on my arms softened and his hand drifted to my ass, breathing into my mouth as we exchanged hot air. After days of his endless teasing and toying, I caved. *I wanted him.* We floated to the surface of the river, panting, gasping for air in between our passionate kissing. He gripped my ass cheeks, pulling my body close to his as my legs wrapped tightly around him. My hands clutched the wet collar of his tunic, pulling him closer. A rich fire burned inside. *Gods, I need more.*

My hands traveled beneath the drenched tunic traveling up his bronzed frame. As one hand wrapped around his neck, the other stroked his chest. My fingers ran across his collarbone hitting a rough mark. I fingered the bulging skin. *Wait...*

Fenix grabbed my wrist as my lips pulled from his. A serious look washed over his face as panic set in. *No...* I ripped my hand from his grasp and yanked the dark, wet fabric aside. Branded across his skin was a large scar resembling a bite mark. A cristna. My breathing increased as my heart panicked. Fear built inside my stomach as my eyes frantically scanned the mark, recognizing the scar immediately. I *knew* that mark. *Cymar.*

I pushed Fenix back, glaring at him as he tried to pull me back.

"*You*," I pointed at him, "you motherfucker."

He reached for me. "Cyrene."

"No." My arm pushed back from him. My mind became a blur as thoughts tangled inside my head. *How was this possible? Did he trick me? Was he a pathos like Emilios?! Did he alter my dreams? Was any of this real?! What the fuck was happening...*

He swam to me. "Cyrene, let me explain, *please*—"

"Stay away from me, Fenix!" I yelled, my fist making contact with his face. He glared at me, growling, as he towered over me, his cheek bright red.

"I *can't*."

"What do you mean you *can't*?" I snarled up at him, baring my canines as a growl emerged in my throat.

"You're *mine,* Princess."

I charged him, flaring my nostrils, baring my teeth. "I belong to *no one*, Fenix." He flashed his canines as he gripped my neck, tilting my head upward. Pain and pleasure twisted inside me as he tightened his clutch.

"If you don't want me," he spat, staring at me intensely, "then I won't force you...but you are my *mate*, Cyrene. I can *never* leave you be."

"Fenix!" Leander's voice floated down the hill to us. Fenix remained still staring down at me, my neck in his grasp. "Tove sent word! We need to leave, *now!*" Our eyes remained locked on one another a few moments before he suddenly released me. My body fell back into the water, gasping. He waded through the river heading to the grassy bank.

My body bobbed in the water, watching as he lifted himself onto the littoral land and stalked to Leander. My brain felt as though it would explode.

Mate.

I swam to the edge of the water, pulling myself onto the grass. I rolled over, laying on my back and stared up at the thick canopy of swaying leaves. The sun peeked through, warming my drenched body. Birds sang, their songs dancing in the soft warm breeze as my mind registered his words.

Fenix was my mate.

"You alright, Fenix?" Leander glanced from me back down to the river. Water dripped from my soaked body as I grunted, approaching his side. My cheek stung from Cyrene's blow.

"What did Tove say?" I grumbled, ignoring his question, eyeing the small paper in his hand. My bare feet stomped past him, snatching my boots as he followed behind.

"Nox just delivered this." He lifted the paper. "Emilios is approaching the border of Southern Amos. We need to return to the palace immediately." My mind struggled to focus on his words. Cyrene looked as though she was disgusted. *Was being my mate so terrible?* I marched through the tree line, Leander still talking, as the events replayed over and over in my mind.

In our dreams, Cyrene had fully given herself to me without hesitation. I knew the risk of her discovering my identity, which is why I chose to hide it and everything I knew, hoping she'd one day want me for who I am, not because we shared a pairing bond. I *needed* my mate to want *me*.

"Fenix? Did you hear anything I just said?" Leander snapped my attention back into focus. Cyrene suddenly came angrily stomping through the trees. She ignored us as she passed, heading back to the horses. My eyes struggled to control their lingering gaze as she bounced past, her scent choking me as she stormed by. *Mine.*

He sighed, "Well, she seems pissed." He looked at me, his head tilted and arms crossed.

I shot Leander a scowl, grunting over my shoulder as I continued forward, following Cyrene's lead. "I told her she was my mate."

"You did *what*?!"

Leander tried to keep up with my long strides. "Fenix, I thought we agreed not to tell her? Fenix!" I rushed from Leander to the horses. Ivar was throwing his cloak over Cyrene as my body broke through the trees. A faint growl grew in my throat as my eyes watched him as he touched her. Her emerald eyes shot to me with anger. Her wet auburn hair stuck to her face and neck, her clothing clung to her curves. *I burned for her.*

Cyrene turned away, shunning me as she thanked Ivar.

"We're leaving."

The four of us quickly mounted our horses. "We stop for nothing until we reach the palace." I uttered, squeezing the horse beneath my legs.

We galloped in the direction of our destination, quickening as we continued. All I could think of was Cyrene. I needed to focus.

The sun had begun to set as we approached the palace of the Bottomlands. Tove's red hair glowed in the distance against the warm sunset. She was standing next to Ydalia. The two women sprinted down the steps to us as we rode closer. The horses slowed to a trot as we came to the palace stairs.

"Fucking took you long enough!"

I smiled at my cousin's words, leaping from the back of my horse. "Missed you too, cousin." She punched my shoulder, smiling. *Gods, I had missed her.*

Leander, Ivar, and Cyrene dismounted their horses behind me. Tove instantly noticed Cyrene, shooting me a concerned glance. I shook my head. "Leave her be, Tove."

She scoffed, shoving past me to Cyrene. *Shit.*

Tove reached her hand out, a warm smile across her face. "Welcome to the Bottomlands, Princess Cyrene. I'm Tove, leader of the Bottomlands and personal pain in the ass to my cousin Fenix and Lord Leander."

Cyrene hesitated before gripping my cousin's hand. "Just Cyrene, please. It's a pleasure to meet you, Lady Tove."

Leander burst into laughter, stifling his chuckles as my eyes shot him a glare. Cyrene's eyes danced between the three of us. "Did I say something wrong?"

Tove released her hand, crossing her arms. "Nah. Leander just seems to forget that I can kick his ass. But please, call me Tove. The whole title of 'lady' just doesn't fit me."

Leander cleared his throat, unpacking his horse.

Tove pointed to the hawk perched on Cyrene's shoulder. "It's nice to finally meet a fellow flygiur."

She smiled. "This is Aodhan. Fenix mentioned knowing another flygiur."

Tove smirked. "I believe you met my raven back in Tartarus, her name's Nox. She was my mother's spirit animal once. Now she's mine." They continued chatting as Leander led Ivar inside the palace. Ydalia approached my side.

"Fenix, on behalf of my people, I want to thank you." She bowed her head. "You welcomed us into your home when all was lost. My wolves and I are yours to command. We submit to you, Alpha."

"My only hope is that you and your people are able to find comfort in our lands. All I ask is that when the time comes, you fight by my side."

"It would be my honor, Alpha."

Tove approached, Cyrene at her side. "Come, Fenix, there's much to discuss. The counsel has gathered in the great hall."

Cyrene whispered softly to Aodhan. "Let my father know we've arrived safely." She sent the hawk high into the sky.

Cyrene, Tove, and Ydalia climbed the stairs to the palace. I lingered behind, watching as Cyrene observed Tove and Ydalia.

My mate was here, in my home. Cyrene glanced behind and caught my stare. I flashed her a devilish grin. She flipped me off.

Feisty little beast.

Fenix's cousin Tove was beautiful. She presented herself as a rough warrior, but she was easily one of the most beautiful fae I'd ever seen. Her vibrant, wild-red hair flowed freely past her waist concealing the two swords sheath across her back. Her eyes glowed the same golden yellow as Fenix's. A giant scar stretched across her left eye and down her cheek. It wasn't a cristna. I wondered what would've caused such a deep wound.

She led all of us through the palace and into the great hall. The room was warmed by a fire blazing in a large stone fireplace. A long wooden table stood in the center of the room, various men crowding the corner arguing amongst themselves. My feet stopped as the rest of the group walked past me, taking their seats around the table. I was unsure of where my place was.

"Sit next to me." My heart quickened at the sound of his voice. Fenix stood directly behind me, his body radiating heat.

My mind was frantic after learning that Fenix was my dream lover. *My mate.* I scrambled the memories of my dreams, combing through every detail to see if it was true. I remembered feeling his cristna, counting the bumps beneath my fingertips, memorizing every inch of his bare body. My soul knew the truth. My lungs inhaled deeply. *Cedarwood, cardamom, and ginger.* It was him. I had so many questions. I needed answers.

Fenix placed his hand on my lower back, softly pushing me towards the head of the table. His touch made my core burn. I struggled to control my feelings. The cluster of men eyed me as he led me to the seat directly next to his. Leander and Tove were seated on the opposite side. Fenix sat himself at the head of the table, shooting me a wink before shifting his focus back to his counsel. He seemed so regal. Like a king.

"Lord Cormac," Fenix spoke across the table, "please review what all has transpired in my absence." An older, heavy set man rose from his seat at the far end of the table.

He cleared his throat. "As your cousin, Lady Tove, has informed you, Lord Emilios has attacked Southern Amos."

"I'm sorry," Fenix started, leaning forward, gripping the arms of his chair, "did you say *attacked*? As in past tense?" The man was petrified. "You mean to tell me, Emilios has already struck Leander's region?" The color left Leander's face.

Tove lowered her head.

"Y-yes, my Jarloth. We received word j-just a few hours ago...before you arrived." Cormac stuttered, fearful of Fenix.

"Has Emilios made his way to Leander's palace?"

Cormac shook his head. "Fortunately, Lord Leander's forces have been able to hold Northern Amos back. But it's only a matter of time. We need to prepare. We *must* strike." Fenix leaned back in his chair, pondering his next move.

"I must return, Fenix, my people in Southern Amos need me." Fenix nodded as Leander rushed from the table.

Tove swiftly rose watching Leander. "Fenix, you can't let him go alone."

"I need you here, Tove."

She scoffed, "Fenix—"

"Lord Leander can handle himself, Tove!" His voice boomed with power, silencing the room. She slowly returned to her seat.

Ivar stood gracefully. "Forgive me, Jarloth, but would you perhaps allow me to accompany Lord Leander?" Tove looked at Ivar with sorrowful eyes. Something sparkled across her golden irises as he stared back at her with deep, soothing eyes.

Fenix nodded. "Be careful, Ivar. Keep him safe." Ivar bowed. He looked at me, flashing a smile before departing the room, rushing after Leander.

"Who do we have at our disposal, Cormac?"

The man shifted his weight around. "We have Ydalia's wolves," he angled his head at the woman next to Tove. She was absolutely beautiful, resembling a goddess.

Her turquoise eyes glowed against her dark ebony skin. "Our pack may not be many," she grinned, "but our wolves will make a difference. We've been training with your pack in your absence. We're ready, Alpha."

Cormac interrupted. "Yes, the wolves of both packs have been working together. If you add Lady Tove's soldiers and Lord Leander's forces, already present in Southern Amos, we might have a fighting chance."

Fenix leaned forward, his elbows on the table as his hands clasped together. "Lord Baldyr of Tartarus has pledged himself to our cause as well." The men gasped, murmuring amongst themselves.

"If Tartarus fights with us—"

"I will not ask Lord Baldyr to join this fight. Not yet."

Cormac looked at Fenix appalled. "My Jarloth, if you don't ask them to fight alongside you in your time of need, then what is the point of their allegiance?"

"I do not need to justify my choices to you, Cormac. The Princess Cyrene is here as Lord Baldyr's counsel. She will speak on Tartarus' behalf, not me."

Cormac squinted his eyes as his mouth formed a frown. "But, sir, *you* are the true king." He looked at me with disgust. "Not some traitorous bitch of Serifos—"

Before the man could finish his sentence, Fenix burst from his chair, slamming the table forward into Cormac. The man fell back hard against the floor as the rest of the counsel scuttled away from him frightened. The room fell silent. Fenix raised his hand in Cormac's direction.

"You will watch how you speak of my *mate!*" *Mate.* The word made my heart skip a beat. Fenix's fingers pulsed, his veins bulging as his power surged. The man gasped, clawing at his chest, his face turning red. Fenix's eyes darkened in a way I'd never witnessed before.

"Fenix!" Tove yelled as she ran to Cormac's side. Fenix glared at the man, pure rage filling his now dark eyes. The veins around Fenix's face bulged, darkening as the man flailed on the floor. Tove peered up at me with pleading eyes.

"Cyrene, he needs to stop, he's killing him." Cormac's face began to shift a dark crimson, slowly fading into a hue of purple. "Stop him, Cyrene!" Fenix remained in a trance, determined to kill the man.

"Fenix, stop," I cried softly. He was too focused to hear me. My body jumped from my seat. "Fenix, *stop!*" His dark eyes darted to me.

"I will not allow anyone to disrespect you," his eyes returned to Cormac's flailing body, "*especially* in my presence."

I rushed to Fenix, stepping in between him and Cormac. "Please, Fenix." I pleaded. His eyes watched me, his irises slowly fading back to a golden honey, as he registered my fear. He softened his glare, lowering his hand as his fingers relaxed.

Cormac gasped, the color quickly returning to his face. "F-forgive me! Forgive me, my king! Please!!"

Fenix straightened his posture, tucking his hair behind his ears. His regal demeanor returned, as he spoke deeply, eyeing Cormac. "You're lucky she was here to stop me. I swear to the Gods, if I *ever* hear you or anyone else speak of my mate in such a way, I will not hesitate to drain every drop of your blood, killing you slowly." The rage Fenix exhibited was frightening. "Now, get on your knees and *beg* the princess for her forgiveness."

The man rolled onto his front side, struggling to his knees. "Forgive me, Princess! Please, forgive me! I did not know!" His sobs filled the room, all eyes on me.

My heart ached at the pain he endured on my behalf. I knelt down, placing my hand softly on his shoulder. "You're forgiven, sir." A loud whine ruptured from him as his sobs filled the rooms. I pitied the poor man, angry with Fenix for torturing him.

"We rest tonight," Fenix addressed the entire room. "Tomorrow, we will travel to Southern Amos and meet Lord Leander at his palace, joining our armies in defending his land." A few men helped Cormac to his feet. "Ydalia, ready the packs." Ydalia nodded, rushing from the room. "I will see you all in the morning." Fenix left without uttering another word. Tove stood beside me, as we watched as Fenix rushed from the great hall.

"He told you, did he?"

My eyes blinked with confusion. "You knew?"

She smiled. "We've all known for sometime." *We?* My face reflected my confusion. Tove roughly nudged my arm. "Talk to him. He doesn't bite—much."

My arms crossed. "There's nothing to discuss. He can claim we're mates all he wants, doesn't make it true."

She snorted. "Keep telling yourself that, Cyrene."

I knew she was right. Fenix owed me answers.

Tove led me to the door of Fenix's room. "Good luck."

"Thanks, Tove."

"I wasn't talking to you," she chuckled, her eyes shooting back at the door. She cupped my hand in hers. "Go easy on him, Cyrene. He may be an ass, but he means well." She flashed me a faint smile before leaving. My eyes shot back at the door. *Why was I so nervous?* I raised my fist, preparing to knock, when the door briskly swung open. Fenix stood in the doorway, shirtless. His hair was tied above his head, his white streak falling in front of his lowered eyes. My brain struggled to remember my words as my eyes absorbed the sight of him.

"We need to talk." I shoved past him, charging into the room. He didn't look at me as he shut the door. Fenix's room surprised me. A lit fire burned deep inside an elegant fireplace, throwing shadows onto the dark stone walls. Large stained glass windows stretched high across the wall, casting an array of rainbow light that danced along his large wooden bed. Deep, emerald-green velvet canopies draped across the wooden bedposts, falling onto the floor. The room was grand but comforting. Not at all as I had expected.

Fenix kept his back to me, leaning against the door. My eyes traced along his sculpted back, dozens of scars scattered along his skin. It pained me knowing he'd experienced so much.

He startled me, speaking softly, "What is it, Cyrene?" I shook my head struggling to remain focused, inhaling. The room was drenched in his scent.

"Tell me the truth." His head lifted, turning slightly to look at me, his alabaster hair laying in front of his eyes. "I want to know everything. You *owe* me that." He rotated his body, completely facing me. My heart raced as I stared at him, biting my lip. Gods, he was beautiful.

"Telling you won't change your mind," his words faded as he stepped closer. His dark skin gleamed in the light, shadows from the fire dancing across his torso as his muscles bulged. His cristna, fully exposed, seemed larger in person.

"Still," I hesitated as he closed the gap between us, "I want to know." He smiled, a faint gasp escaping my lungs as he walked past me, brushing my arm. He approached the fireplace and leaned against the mantle, staring into the flames.

"Where would you want me to start, Princess?" He crossed his flexed arms. *Focus, Cyrene.*

"The dreams. The man in my dreams—that was you?" Fenix nodded. "How come I could never fully see you? Why were you...out of focus?"

"Because you hadn't accepted the pairing bond. Obviously, you were open to it." He lightly turned his head toward me, his eyebrow raised, grinning. "But until you fully give yourself over to it and accept the bond, your dreams remain faded."

"Could you...feel them..." I sheepishly asked, recalling the devious acts between us. My cheeks flushed.

"Yes," his grin grew, exposing his canines, "your dreams weren't *entirely* dreams. The pairing bond creates a connection between mates. You can access each other's mind, thoughts, and feelings. You actually tapped into my mind once, you know? In the forest. I was in my Vargr skin when I smelled you. A pleasant surprise." *That's why the woods from earlier seemed familiar. I'd been there in his dreams.* "Until I saw what was done to you..." His gaze returned to the flames.

"Will the dreams continue? Now that I know?"

"That's up to you, Cyrene. You can choose to accept the bond or deny it."

My eyes watched him as he spoke. I felt *drawn* to him.

My mind shifted, fighting to stay on track. "You shouldn't have done that to Cormac—" He snapped his head in my direction, appalled at my words.

"*Cormac* is lucky to be alive." He growled.

"You had no right, Fenix."

"I had *every* right!" He pushed from the mantle, slowly stepping in my direction. "You might not accept it, Cyrene, but you *are* my mate." His fists started to vibrate, shifting slowly as they morphed into a strange fae-beast hybrid form. Black fur covered his thick, muscular arms. His fae-like hands were clenched, sharp claws protruding from his fingers as he growled. "I'd kill anyone who disrespects you. I may not be yours... *but you are MINE.*"

Immense power seeped from Fenix's body. His words made my heart flutter.

My eyes narrowed and my brows furrowed as I crossed my arms. "You don't even know me, Fenix." *Why did I want him so badly?*

"I know everything about you, Cyrene. I've seen your dreams and nightmares. I know your fears and I've felt your pain," his hungry yellow eyes looked me up and down, "I can feel you now, *Cymar*. I sense those urges deep inside, burning as I stand here." I swallowed, fighting back those strange urges inside.

"Why do you call me that? What does it mean?"

His wolf skin hand lifted my chin, his claws lightly scraping my skin. "It's an ancient shifter term meaning *soul mate*." *Soul mate.* Fenix had called me Cymar in my dreams for as long as I could remember. He had been there all this time.

His claw remained, holding my chin. My mind pondered, thinking about everything he had told me. "What would happen if I accepted it? The bond?" Fenix grinned, flashing his canines again.

"Well, Princess, it would mean you accept me as your mate. You would be mine and I would be yours. Our pairing bond would become unbreakable; our minds would sync and our souls would join together, forming only one soul. We would feel each other's happiness and pain, connecting on every level possible." *One soul?*

"But know this—once connected, if one of us were to die, the bond would tear, ripping apart our souls. It would mean part of the other dies as well," he pulled me closer, my chin still in his hybrid hand. "Could you bear that weight, Cyrene? Could you continue to live, half of your soul being gone, dead, ripped apart from you in the most agonizing way possible?" His eyes stared into mine, waiting for a response.

Our eyes locked. Fenix was the most powerful and beautiful fae I'd ever met. He'd suffered and lost so much in his life, and had every reason to watch as the world burned, but instead he fought *for* this world. Others may see him as the villain, but I saw him for who he really was. He had risked his own life to protect mine and Farouk's in that cave. He would sacrifice himself to save those closest to him. He deserved someone that could do the same for him. *Could I really be that person?*

"Yes, you can, Cyrene." Fenix's soft words shocked me.

"How—"

"You've already accepted me, Cyrene."

What? How?

"You began accepting the pairing bond when you stepped through that door, you just hadn't realized it."

He remained close to me, his scent filling my lungs as his hand lightly stroked my chin. My eyes stared, gazing into his honey eyes, burning with passion. I couldn't fight the truth. Standing before me was Fenix—my mate. Cymar. We shared the pairing bond, we were one.

Fenix's hand shifted back to his fae skin, still cupping my face gently. His free hand seized my waist. "Well," he smirked, "the bond isn't *fully* complete."

A look of confusion washed over my face.

"To secure the pairing bond, we must become *one*." He fiercely tightened his grip around my waist, my body jotting as he did. His fingers glided through my hair, gripping the back of my head lightly tilting my face toward his.

"What are you waiting for, Fenix? *Make me yours*."

Fenix gave me a carnal smile, "Oh, you naughty little beast."

Cyrene bit her lip, leaning into my body. *Fuck.* My body wanted her, but my mind was made—I was going to take my time, enjoying her body as I worshiped every inch of her ivory skin. She was *mine.*

My thumb rubbed across her soft, rosy lips. She released a faint gasp as her mouth widened. *Oh, princess.* All self control disappeared as I leaned in fervidly kissing her, breathing her in. I could feel her core burning with desire, desperately wanting more. She pierced my lip with her teeth, pulling as my nails dug into her skin. A tiny drop of blood appeared. She licked it from my lips causing me to growl with excitement. She smiled, leaning closer as her hands ran down my back and under my trousers. Her soft hand traveled eagerly, gripping my cock. I instantly hardened at her delicate touch. She began to stroke me, quickening her pace as my cock grew within her grip. I moaned, my chin resting atop her head as she continued increasing her pressure and speed. I could smell her arousal in the air. My hand pulled hers from my trousers, kissing her palm. My lips traveled up her arm. Her cristna had become smooth, almost fully healed. She shuttered, pain and pleasure intertwined as my tongue traced her mark. She was ready.

An eager smile formed across my face.

I pushed her back onto the bed. Her fiery hair clashed against the dark green bedding, sprawling around her face. She breathed heavily, watching me with starving eyes. I approached the foot of the bed and roughly unlatched her belt, whipping it from her body as she gasped.

"I'm going to make you mine, Cymar," my feet paced to the side of the bed, "in every way possible." I tied the belt tightly around her wrist. She gasped as I tugged the leather in place, attaching it to the wooden bedpost. I removed my own belt, walking to the other side, repeating my actions. Her hands were completely bound, stretched across the bed with little slack. I returned to the foot of the bed, her ravenous eyes glued to me. My hands gripped her trousers, tearing them from her body. I positioned myself between her legs, propping them on the wooden bedframe. My eyes ogled over her helpless body, mine for the taking.

I thumbed her mouth, trailing my fingers down her neck. My hands traveled to her chest, gripping the collar of her tunic, forcefully ripping it down the center. Her breasts bounced, her rosy nipples hard and perky. Her chest was completely exposed. *Fuck, her body is amazing, and it is completely mine.*

I began to untie my trousers, pulling my cock from beneath them. Cyrene's eyes widened with fear and excitement. She licked her lips, staring at my cock with anticipation. *Give it to me, Fenix.* The bond vibrated with an animalistic hunger. *Patience, Princess.* My hands clenched her ankles, running my palms up her legs, as I kissed her knees. She grappled against the restraints. My mouth inched closer, making its way up her inner thighs, kissing and caressing her smooth skin. I could smell her arousal.

"I told you, Princess," I whispered, my hot breath against her delicate skin as my tongue flicked her center, teasing her. She moaned, slightly arching her back pulling the leather constraints around her wrists. My tongue shoved its way deep inside her. "I'm going to make you scream." I breathed the words into her warm, wet body, her breathing quickening as my words touched her skin. I lifted her legs, resting them over my shoulders as I pushed my tongue further. I devoured her excitement as she soaked my tongue. *Not yet, Cymar.* My tongue slowly slithered from inside her. Her body flinched when I kissed her center. My lips continued along her abdomen, tasting every inch of her delicious ivory skin, finding their way to her breasts. I flicked her hardened nipples one at a time, circling each one with my wet tongue. Cyrene wanted more.

My mouth moved higher, kissing her neck as two of my fingers shoved into her. She cried out as my thumb stroked her center gently, my fingers thrusting further inside her as her body soaked my hand. Cyrene lowered her legs, wrapping them tightly around my waist, tugging me closer. She whined, silently begging for more. *Impatient little beast,* I teased through the bond. I took my time, removed my fingers from within her, soaked in her pleasure. She bit her lip as I lifted my fingers, savoring her liquid bliss dripping down my skin. *Gods, you taste like heaven.* My cock was hardened, pulsing for the feel of her tight body wrapped around me. My eyes stared into hers, burning. *You're mine.* Before she could prepare herself, I shoved my cock forcefully inside her, losing all control, fucking her with all my strength. Our erotic dreams were dull compared to this exhilarating moment.

Exchanged fire burned down through our bond. I peered down at Cyrene, watching as her beautiful body spasmed with each thrust. My hunger for her became unbearable as my cock pushed harder inside her. She was *mine.* My hands grabbed her face as I leaned over kissing her. We inhaled each other, our breaths intertwined with passionate kisses. The bond exploded, rupturing with euphoria as she came. Her head jolted back, her mouth wide open as she orgasmed, the room echoing with her cries of bliss. I could sense her disappointment at coming too quickly.

I grinned. "Don't worry, Princess," my hand softly gripped her neck as I leaned down whispering in her ear, "I'm going to fuck you until the sun comes up." A spark flashed across her emerald green eyes as I kissed her. My grip on her neck tightening before pushing my cock harder into her drenched body. Her elated screams were constricted by my hand around her throat. Her wrists pulled against the leather belts as her back arched. I wanted to go deeper, fucking her in every way possible.

My cock slid from inside her. *No, don't stop, Fenix.* I kissed her knee as my hand dragged from her neck, grabbing her hips. *Oh, we're just getting started, beastie.* I rolled her body over, her knees digging into the bed as adjusted herself, her ass raised high. Her bound arms crossed, pulling tightly against the leather. All slack in the constraints were gone, holding her tightly in place. *Perfect.* My hand grabbed her chin, tilting her face up to me as my body leaned over her.

"I could get used to this view." I slapped her ass hard. Cyrene flinched, gasping at the pain, my palm burning from the impact. My fingers weaved through her long soft hair, tugging while my cock slid inside her. Gods, she was tight. Her body clung to mine as I slowly re-entered her, deliberately taking my time. My free hand squeezed her ass as her moans filled the room. My cock slammed further while I fucked her, grunting. *I am yours, Fenix.* Her thought unhinged me, sending me over the edge as I thrust as hard as I could, climaxing heavily deep inside her wet body. *You are mine, Cyrene.*

Collecting my breath, I sensed my body wanting more.

Cyrene felt my hunger.

She pulled herself from me, slowly, my legs shaking as I fell from her body. She rolled onto her back, pulling herself up, positioning to lean back against the headboard. She motioned for me to come to her. *My turn,* she purred down the bond. I crawled to her, kissing her skin lightly as my body rose, positioning myself in front of her. My hand gripped the wooden headboard, the other lifting her chin. Her eyes twinkled as she opened her mouth. I slid my cock slowly inside her widened, wet mouth. My cock struggled to fit inside her, her lips stretched firmly around me. I groaned, gripping the wooden headboard as she snaked her tongue, stroking me while sliding her tight lips up and down my cock. My arms stretched, gripping the bed posts as my hands partially shifted into a hybrid form as she bobbed. I pushed my cock further into her mouth, thrusting harder into her. She gagged, quickening her pace. My claws dug into the wooden posts. *Fill my mouth, Fenix,* she moaned down the bond. *Choke me.* Her pleas were too much. *Oh Gods.* My head shot high, howling as I came, shaking the bed frame as I roared with ecstasy. She ingested me, running her tongue along my cock sucking me dry.

She slowly pulled away from me, allowing me to fall from her. Her tongue glided over my cock once more, purposely flicking the tip. My body flinched in response as she licked her lips, revealing a devilish grin.

"This isn't over yet," my voice rasped, smirking. My claws effortlessly sliced the leather belts from the posts, Cyrene gasping as her arms fell. She leaned her naked body towards me, dragging her arms, as her eyes burned into mine. I instantly hardened. She pushed me back onto the bed, straddling me with her knees. She sat over my abdomen, running her fingers across my hybrid arms. Her touch bristled my hair, causing electricity to shoot through my body. She held my arms, rubbing them delicately over her breasts, moaning as she pleased herself. My cock ached for her body. My claws lightly dug into her soft skin as she ran my hands down her body, resting them around her waist. Her eyes remained locked on mine as she lowered herself leisurely onto my cock.

Gods, I couldn't get enough of her.

Cyrene squeezed her thighs around my waist, riding me slowly, taking full control. My claws dug further into her skin, reaching towards her cheeks as I lightly pierced her smooth ass. She leaned back, her breasts pointed to the sky as she thrust harder, faster. My hands traveled up her midriff toward her breasts. An uncontrollable desire burned fiercely through the bond. She struggled to catch her breath as she climaxed, wetting me from within. My control dissolved as she jolted. My hands squeezed her hips, thrusting my cock as I burst beneath her. We moaned in unison as I continued to fuck her. Euphoria circled our bond, tightening it in place. I could feel our souls fusing together as we became one.

Our bodies relaxed as she gently laid across my chest, my cock still inside her. My hands shifted back to their fae form as my fingers softly ran up her bare sweaty back. I kissed the top of her head softly.

You are mine.

After a short rest, Fenix and I spent the remainder of our night having sex, getting little to no sleep. My body ached, sore and bruised from our vigorous love making. My voice was hoarse from the screams of pleasure. Being with Fenix was an addiction I couldn't satisfy. Our bond was strong. The sensation of merging my soul with his was thrilling. We were one.

Morning sunlight began to bleed through the stained-glass windows, casting a rainbow of color across the bed. My fingers stroked Fenix's chest, tracing his muscles and scars. They made their way to his cristna, gently feeling the bumps of his mark. "Why a bite mark?" I asked, feeling the raised scars.

His fingers traced my cristna as he spoke. "Ursii bear the Scratch of Bjorn. Vargrs, wolves, bear the Bite of Fenrir. We gain our marks when we experience our first shift—same as Ursii." My gaze jumped from his mark to my own, recalling my first shift, shuddering at the memory of the pain and fear as I struggled to survive.

Fenix caught my gaze, touching my face softly.

"I'm sorry you had to experience that alone, Cymar." He tucked my wild hair behind my ears. "Know that I will never leave your side. Nothing will touch you as long as I breathe. I would *die for you, Cyrene.*" He kissed my forehead. The thought of him dying made my heart clench in sadness.

Just don't die and we're good.

I'll do my best, Princess.

"Tove is approaching." Fenix rose from under my naked body, groaning as he leaned over the bed.

"How can you tell?" I rose, kissing his back. He chuckled lightly and pointed to his nose.

"Vargr bonus."

Tove's fist pounded against the door.

"Everyone has gathered outside, Fenix. We'll be ready to depart within the hour."

Fenix pulled his trousers over his legs, standing as he tied them.

"What happens when we reach Southern Amos?" I asked as he tossed me my tunic, continuing to dress himself.

"If we keep a good pace, we should arrive before Emilios reaches Leander's palace. Then, we fight." Fear fell over me as my body flinched at the memory of my last encounter with Emilios.

"Don't be scared, Cyrene." Fenix walked to my side, his hand touching my cheek as he spoke to me, sweetly. "He will never again lay a hand on you. You are my mate, Cyrene. *Mine.* No one will hurt you as long as I live. I will make Emilios pay for what he did to you, *I swear it.*" He kissed me passionately as my arms wrapped tightly around his neck. I didn't want to leave the room. Fenix slowly pulled from my grasp. "Here," he handed me the rest of my clothes. "As much as I enjoy seeing you naked in my bed, we really must be going."

I shot him a frown, reluctantly dressing myself as we exchanged kisses in between movements. *I don't want to leave. What if I lose you?*

"I'm not leaving your side, Cyrene."

Hand in hand, Fenix and I made our way down the steps of the palace into the brisk morning air. We wore layers of clothing and our swords sheathed at our waists, clanking as we walked. Tove and Ydalia stood aside a line of war horses, dressed for battle. Red and blue war paint smudged across their faces.

Why the paint? Fenix turned me to face him as Tove handed him a small vial filled with white paint. He dipped his thumb into the chalky paint, smearing it down my face, dragging it from my eyes.

Many reasons. The paint helps identify our people on the battlefield. Helps avoid confusion. The red and blue signify our wolves, the white represents 'king'. He ran the paint down his face, identical to mine.

But I am not a king.

He smiled, tossing the vial aside.

You are my equal.

The women exchanged a look as we approached.

"Sleep well, Fenix?" Tove teased. My cheeks reddened with embarrassment. *Did she hear us?* Fenix's laugh echoed in my head. *Hard not too. I'm sure all of the Bottomlands heard you, Princess.* My eyes shot him a glare as he snickered.

"Alright now, you two keep that pairing bond shit to yourselves." Tove teased as she mounted her horse. Ydalia gave me a soft smile before mounting her own.

Cormac approached, perched atop a war horse as a few other men trailed behind. They were all dressed in light armor with their weapons at their sides. He lowered his head as he trotted to Fenix.

"Jarloth, Lady Tove and Ydalia's wolves are ready, as are your men. If we can keep a good speed, we should arrive at Lord Leander's palace by nightfall, but we will need to move fast."

Fenix nodded, leading me to his horse, and leapt onto its back.

"Where's mine?"

He smiled, extending an arm. *I told you, I'm not leaving your side.* My hand gripped his as Fenix hoisted me onto his horse, positioning me in front of him. His arms wrapped around my waist as he grabbed the reins. *Don't worry, I'll try my best to behave.*

Such a tease. I nudged him with my elbow.

Fenix pranced to the front of his army. Shifters, fae, and men listened as their king spoke. "Listen up! As we ride into Southern Amos, we don't know what awaits us...but no matter what comes our way, remember *why* you fight! You do not fight for me. I may be your king, but you fight for the people of Devas! Together, we will protect Southern Amos and stop Emilios and his men. Now, keep pace. We stop for nothing.

Once we arrive at the palace, prepare yourself for battle. Stay alert and don't let your guard down."

The mass of warriors bellowed at the command of their king. Fenix kicked the horse, shooting us northward.

Fenix's army charged north.

We didn't break once as the war horses were pushed to their limits. The sun had begun to set as we crossed the border into Southern Amos. The smell of smoke lingered heavily in the air. *What is that?*

Emilios. It seems he's already reached the palace.

Panic set in. Fenix slid a hand around my waist, silently reassuring me.

Smoke smothered the air as Leander's palace appeared in the distance. The smoke rose high, drifting from within the palace. I could feel Fenix's rage as he whipped the horse, quickening its stride.

"Fenix, wait!" Tove screamed, chasing after us.

Clusters of men, fae, and wolves fought along the land surrounding the stone palace. As we closed the distance between the palace and ourselves, my eyes watched, confused as wolves attacked Leander's men.

They are Vaud—wild, rabid wolves who refuse to bend to their alpha. Somehow, Emilios has convinced them to join in his war.

Emilios' men and Vaud wolves had broken Southern Amos' barricade, flooding Leander's palace. I could feel Fenix's rage boiling as we galloped closer.

Fenix shifted his hand from my waist and retrieved his sword. *No matter what, you stay by my side. And by the Gods, do not wear your bear skin, Cyrene.* I nodded, taking the reins as he withdrew my sword, wielding both blades. His army shadowed him as we charged through the fighting mass. Vargrs shifted into large, painted wolves, lunging forward as they began breaking the lines between the two sides. Fenix's army rammed into Emilios'.

Fenix swung the blades, cutting down Emilios' soldiers as we continued, the war horse snorting as it sprinted across bodies of fallen men toward the palace. As we neared the gates, a Vaud wolf launched at Fenix and me. He lightly tossed the sword, repositioning it in his grasp, surging the blade like a javelin. The sword struck the wolf's face, instantly killing it.

We need to get inside and find Leander and Ivar. My hand gripped the reins and we galloped toward the courtyard.

We skidded to a stop as Fenix leaped from the horse, carefully pulling me down. His sword remained in hand, ready to strike. Tove and Ydalia sprinted next to us.

"Are you fucking crazy, Fenix!"

"We need to find Ivar and Leander!"

Tove huffed, dismounting her horse followed by Ydalia.

"My pack knows to secure the perimeter of the palace. Get inside, Alpha. Find your men." Ydalia turned away, cracking her neck. "I'll clear the courtyard." Her turquoise eyes glowed as she tilted her head, lifting her hand as her fingers arched. Gravel rose from the earth, shooting at a few oncoming soldiers. *What is she?* I asked through the bond. Fenix smirked, *She's a druidess.* My eyes were glued to her, watching as she lifted her other arm, raising a cluster of boulders and debris, slamming them into Vaud wolves.

Another wave of Emilios' men and Vaud wolves flushed into the courtyard.

Tove ordered her men, turning back to Fenix and me. "I can handle this." She winked, marching past me. "Here," she tossed her blade in my direction, "I have no use for this."

Fenix lightly pushed me back, giving his cousin space. She howled, hunching over as her back snapped into a curve. Her arms and legs cracked as her bones broke. She fell on all fours, her face extending as she growled, the skin around her mouth ripping as a muzzle protruded from within. Her eyes glowed yellow as deep maroon colored fur sprouted from her pores, covering every inch of her transforming body. She shook, shedding the remaining traces of her fae skin from her fur. She was beautiful. Her wolf physique was smaller than Fenix's but strong and monstrous. A Vaud wolf appeared, its sight set on Tove. She growled, the hair standing up on her spine, her ears shooting back as she charged the wolf. Their bodies slammed together as they wrestled in the courtyard. Tove rolled, pinning the smaller wolf down as she bit into the wolf's neck, twisting and breaking it beneath her jaw. The wolf went limp as Tove rose, blood staining her teeth. Emilios' men shouted, running in our direction. Tove barreled into the soldiers, knocking them aside, shredding them apart.

"Come, Cyrene. Ydalia and Tove seem to have a handle on things out here." Fenix grabbed my hand and led me inside the palace.

Leander's men ran frantically through the halls putting out small fires, no doubt set by Emilios' men. We checked every room and corridor searching for any sign of Leander and Ivar. No luck.

We climbed the stairs and explored the palace. Men and fae fought inside. Together, we helped clear the palace, searching for Leander and Ivar as we moved. We traveled the stairs, scaling the palace. Fenix was beginning to panic. As we reached the third floor, he caught a whiff of Leander's scent. "This way." He pulled me along as he sprinted. Bodies of men from both armies plastered the halls.

We came to a locked wooden door. Fenix slammed into the door, breaking it open. Inside, Ivar was on his knees scrambling to help Leander. He was propped against the wall, bleeding. The two men were filthy, covered in soot, dirt, and blood. Fenix and I rushed to their aid, tossing our blades aside.

"What happened, Ivar?"

Ivar was pushing his hands against Leander's shoulder, blood pouring from beneath. Leander groaned, covering another wound on his thigh.

"Emilios attacked this morning. We were asleep when he sent the Vaud, followed by a surge of soldiers. They broke through all our defenses. A second wave of soldiers attacked midday, storming the palace. We weren't prepared, Fenix."

Fenix rolled his sleeves, placing a hand on Leander's shoulder. His veins bulged as he strained, manipulating the blood back into Leander's body. He placed his hands on Leander's thigh, returning his blood to the wound. *He needs a healer, Fenix.*

"Cyrene, warm your dagger. We'll need to cauterize his wounds, just as Farouk did in Tartarus. Find a torch." I nodded, pulling the concealed dagger from my boot. My body lunged, sprinting down the hallway searching for a torch.

My eyes scanned the halls for a few minutes before spotting a small torch. I quickly yanked it from the wall and spun to return to Fenix when my body slammed into his. Horror filled my core as he smiled down at me, his pale blue eyes filled with delight at the sight of my fear.

Keres.

"My, what an unfortunate little surprise it is to find *you* here, Cyrene."

Fenix.

"Emilios will be pleased to know his bride is safe." *Fenix!* My mind screamed down the bond. I attempted to run past him. "Not so fast, little sister." Keres grabbed me as I struggled against his grip. He was too powerful.

FENIX!

"To think, after all this time, you were right under our noses." Keres continued to gloat as my body wriggled against him. I angled my dagger and stabbed his arm. He released me, throwing me to the floor as he yelled in pain. "You little *bitch*." He spat, blood dripping from his arm. I stumbled to my feet and began to run as he grabbed my hair and yanked me hard to the ground. My dagger fell from my grasp as my hands clawed him, trying to free myself.

"FENIX!" I screamed at the top of my lungs. Keres' smile faded as the floor shook. Fenix turned the corner in his wolf skin. His eyes darted to Keres, glaring with hatred as he snarled, revealing his teeth. He was monstrous, towering high over Keres.

Keres dropped his grip on my hair and pulled out his sword as I crawled to Fenix. *Forgive me, Cyrene.* He nudged me, helping me to my feet.

My hand stroked his large ear. *You're here now.*

Keres released a laugh. "Oh, Cyrene, don't tell me you're fucking this beast?"

Fenix growled, his spine spiked and ears back as Keres grinned, angling his sword.

Fenix, don't. He ignored me, full of rage as he lunged at Keres.

He body-slammed into Keres, sending my brother barreling into the stone wall. Fenix huffed, turning back to me. Keres crawled to his feet, his sword in hand as he ran at Fenix.

Look out! Fenix turned, catching Keres' blade with his teeth. Keres strained to pull his sword from Fenix's grasp.

Fenix whipped his head, breaking his hold as he sent Keres through the air. He spat the sword aside as my brother fell to the ground. Fenix stepped to my brother, crawling over him, growling as he lay helpless. Fenix clawed Kere's face, obscuring it with deep, monstrous gashes. Keres screamed in agony. Blood covered his pale skin, staining his stark white hair. *Fenix, please, stop.*

Fenix halted, slowly stepping away from Keres. *He deserves to die, Cyrene.*

He's my brother, Fenix. His eyes stared into mine. *Please.* He lowered his head respecting my wishes, circling me.

We began to walk away when Keres yelled.

"Coward!" His mouth filled with blood. "You let that bitch order you around? Some king you are, bastard!"

Anger fueled me as my hand snatched my dagger from the floor. I rushed at my brother, standing over his helpless body as he laid on the floor.

"You don't have the balls, sister." He spat, blood falling as he choked on his words.

I kneeled, looking down at him, my dagger in hand. Fenix stepped directly behind me, watching.

"We may share blood," the dagger twirled in my fingers, "but you are not my brother." Keres' eyes followed my hand as I inserted the dagger, slowly into his thigh. "You deserve to burn for *your* sins, brother." He bared his teeth, groaning as my hand pushed the blade further. He screamed, cursing me.

I smiled as I stepped over Keres.

Fenix proudly nudged me.

Together, we walked away, ignoring Keres' screams.

We quickly made our way back to Leander and Ivar.

Leander's wounds had been burned and bandaged in my absence. He leaned on Ivar for support, limping as they stepped together.

"Is everything okay, Cyrene?" Ivar asked, looking at my hand. It was covered in Keres' blood. My eyes peered down at my palm, Keres' ruby blood dripping from my hand. I nodded.

"It is now."

Leander groaned as he spoke. "We need to find Tove and Ydalia. Emilios is sure to send more men. We need to leave, Southern Amos is lost." Fenix snorted. Ivar helped Leander as he limped from the room. My hand wrapped around Leander's waist, helping as Fenix led the way. We slowly descended the stairs, eventually making our way to the front doors of the palace.

The palace had grown silent. The fighting men from earlier had vanished. *Odd.*

Stay alert, Cyrene.

The four of us approached the large doors that led to the courtyard. Fenix trotted ahead, pushing the doors open with his muzzle. As the doors swung open, arrows sprayed through the air. A whine echoed as a sharp pain shot through my chest. My body screamed as my hands fell from Leander, clutching my chest.

Stay back, Cyrene!

My eyes darted to Fenix, arrows pierced into his chest. I was feeling *his* pain. He wobbled a little but remained strong.

Leander and Ivar pulled me from the doorway, ducking to the side of the room, hiding from the arrows. *Fenix!* Another round fired, once again hitting their target. My body fell to the floor in pain. My eyes teared up, watching him struggle to remain standing. *No.*

I crawled to my feet and ran to his aid.

Outside, at the base of the stairs was a line of archers. Emilios stood directly behind them. An evil grin formed across his face when he saw me.

"Wait!" He raised his arm, commanding his men to stop. Fenix fell, whimpering. I dropped to his side and placed my hand across his chest. It was wet. My hand lifted from his fur. It was soaked in blood. Tears formed in my eyes as his yellow eyes glanced up at me. *Fenix.* My hand gripped the arrows, yanking them from his skin.

I'll be okay, Cymar...just-just give me a moment.

My eyes looked down to see his blood slowly returning to his body. Relief instantly washed over me.

"Princess Cyrene." Emilios voice drew my attention back to the line of men ready to fire their arrows. "What a pleasure it is to see you again, my bride." I snarled, flashing him my teeth. His brows furrowed in surprise. "Now that's not very lady-like. What would your father think if he could see you now, Princess?"

Before my mouth could form a response, Fenix rose, shaking the blood from his fur, growling as he stepped in front of me. Protecting me. Emilios raised an eyebrow. "Poor Fenix. Don't worry, I came prepared." He snapped his fingers.

Seconds later, a man approached dragging a woman behind him. *Fenix.*

We recognized her red hair immediately. *Tove.*

She was wearing an oversized tunic and nothing else. Her hands were chained in front of her, her face badly beaten. Rage ruptured from Fenix as the guard yanked the chain, sending Tove into the stairs at our feet. Her chains clanked as they hit the ground.

"Fucking prick!" She yelled at the man. He grabbed her tunic, dragging her to her feet.

"Watch your mouth, you filthy bitch!"

She spat in his face, laughing. "Men have done far worse to me. You are *nothing*."

He wiped his face.

"We'll see about that!" He slammed his skull into hers, knocking her back to the ground. Her nose was spewing bleeding. Fenix growled.

"Alright, alright. Let's calm down everyone." Emilios spoke to the guard and Fenix.

A second guard approached Emilios. He handed him a large menacing, thick iron collar lined with spikes. He fumbled the collar in his hand. "You know, when I learned of your ability, Fenix, I must admit, I was completely gobsmacked. I had no idea how to defeat you. But," he pointed to the collar, "I figured it out.

"See, I had this made just for you, Jarloth. An iron collar fit for a beast." He paced to Tove's side looking down at her. "Even had another made for your dear cousin, Lady Tove. Doesn't seem like she needs it though does she? Weak little thing. The enchanted chains seem more than enough to keep her in check." He flashed her a look of disgust, pacing back towards Fenix and me. "Ah, well, it doesn't matter. You see, not only do the spikes physically prevent you from shifting, but the enchantment, well, let's call that an extra precaution. Once you put this around your neck, you lose *all* your shifter abilities." Fenix snorted.

"Yes, yes, I know—why would you put the collar on?" Emilios paced back and forth as he spoke.

"I'll make it simple." Emilios walked back to Tove. "Wear the collar and I won't kill your darling cousin here." Emilios lifted a strand of Tove's hair. She whipped her head back. "Or you can refuse and I'll kill you both. Either way, Princess Cyrene will be coming with *me*."

"The *hell* I will."

Emilios smiled. "Dear Princess, you still haven't learned. You don't have a choice. Fenix's army fled as my men stormed Southern Amos. They ran like the dogs they are, retreating with their tails between their legs. Lady Tove here is all that remains."

"He's lying, Fenix!" Tove's words shot from the foot of the stairs. "We *ordered* them to retreat—" The guard kicked Tove's side, silencing her. Fenix watched Tove with concern.

Fenix.

My mind could hear his thoughts. He was considering Emilios' deal.

He lowered his head. *I have to Cyrene, I can't lose her.*

I choked on my tears. *Promise you'll rescue me?*

I'll never leave you, Cymar. The minute he leaves, I'm coming for you. I won't let him have you.

Fenix looked at me defeatedly before slowly stepping down the stairs. My heart ached as he stood towering over Emilios.

"Careful, Jarloth, my men have been ordered to fire if *anything* happens to me." Fenix snarled at him. Emilios unlatched the iron collar, "Come on now, we haven't got all day." Fenix shifted back into his fae skin.

Emilios beamed with pride as he latched the heavy iron collar around Fenix's neck. "Now, show some respect, Fenix." He removed his cloak and draped it over Fenix's bare body.

"Release her, Emilios," Fenix demanded. Emilios ignored his words and looked back at me. My eyes remained on Fenix.

"Interesting." He narrowed his eyes, "Princess," he turned, waving another man forward. In the man's hand sat another iron collar. "I know it's not customary for the groom to gift things to the bride before a wedding," he took the collar from the man, "but I think we can make this an exception."

"Why would you want me to wear a collar?" Fear rose from within as he slowly scaled the steps.

Fenix stared up at me. *Don't do it, Cyrene.*

"Oh, just a precaution. Since your ability is unknown to me, I figured it couldn't hurt to be safe. You see, I forgot to mention one thing," he stepped past Fenix, eyeing him as he made his way towards me. My feet shuffled back as Fenix shadowed Emilios. "The enchantment on the collar doesn't just prevent you from shifting...it blocks *all* your fae abilities."

What? Emilios glanced over his shoulder at Fenix. "Your Seelie abilities are of no use now, Jarloth." *Wait, he knows of all Fenix's abilities?*

Emilios reached my side, collar in hand. "I'm not putting that on." I stepped back another foot.

"Oh, but you *will*, Princess. That is, if you wish to save your mate."

My eyes shot to Fenix. "Ah, yes. I can smell the beast on you now, Princess. But don't worry, I'll make sure you forget all about him in due time."

My hand slapped the collar from Emilios' hand. The archers knocked their arrows in response. Emilios grabbed my arms, gripping me tightly. "You *will* obey me, Cyrene!" Fenix shoved Emilios off me as my body fell back onto the stone floor. He turned, gripping Emilios' neck, lifting him from the ground. His feet kicked and dangled as Fenix held him, straining without the use of his abilities.

"I'm going to take my time killing you, repaying you for all the pain you have caused my mate." Fenix growled the words through clenched teeth.

Emilios gasped his fingers frantically trying to release Fenix's grasp. "I...doubt...that."

Suddenly, a stabbing pain pierced my heart. Emilios fell from Fenix's grasp, smiling as he fell to the ground.

"See," he coughed, rubbing his throat, "I told you."

I gasped as immense pain shot down our bond, vibrating with agony.

Fenix turned to me, his eyes widened with fear. My dagger was plunged into his heart. Standing directly in front of Fenix, was Keres, grinning. Fenix fell to the ground. Tove screamed as I clawed my way to his side, the dagger shoved deep in his chest.

No, no, no, no, NO!

My hand wrapped around the dagger, ready to pull it from his heart when Tove yelled.

"NO! Cyrene, *don't*! The collar!" My eyes glanced down at Fenix.

The iron collar was fastened around his neck. My fingers desperately tried to pry the collar open. I tried to yank the collar from his neck. My hands tugged the iron, screaming as I strained with all my power to break it free from my mate. I was too weak. Fenix couldn't heal himself.

Tears poured from my eyes. I could feel Fenix's soul fading his body, separating from my own. Our pairing bond was tearing.

"Fenix, Fenix, please," my hands cradled his body, "don't leave me," my head laid across his bloody chest. "You can't leave me, Fenix...you can't! You promised!" My throat burned with anguish.

"*Cymar,*" he struggled, reaching his hand to my face, touching my cheek gently. My hands clutched his, kissing his knuckles. Tears poured from my face onto him. A hole began to grow in my chest, filled with the most excruciating pain I had ever experienced.

"Fenix, please, just hold on. Hold on for me. *Please.*" The light began to fade from his eyes. Our pairing bond hung by a thin thread. "FENIX!" I screamed in agony as his body went limp in my arms.

The torment I felt was unbearable.

A part of me was dying.

My head lifted to the sky as the most blood curdling scream emerged from my lungs.

My mate's limp body lay in my arms.

"Take her." Emilios ordered Keres.

My lips kissed Fenix's blood-stained lips one last time before placing him gently on the ground.

Keres reached for my arm when I whipped around, glaring up at him. My throat roared as my mouth released a low threatening growl. His smug smile faded as my bones cracked and bent. "What the fuck?"

All control of my emotions faded away with Fenix. I didn't care anymore.

My body broke and bent, shifting into my Ursii skin.

Keres and Emilios ran back, petrified.

My body positioned itself over Fenix's, releasing a roar filled with all my pain and anguish.

Emilios ripped his sword from its sheath as Keres held his own. They both steadied themselves, preparing to fight.

No one will touch you, Fenix. If I have to, I will die with you.

Keres lunged first. My claws swung, whacking the blade from his hand. He rolled, dodging my paw as he threw his arms around my neck. My head wriggled, stumbling away from Fenix, struggling to free myself from his grasp. He was too strong.

"Hold her!" Emilios yelled, dropping his sword. He had the iron collar in his hands. *No!* My body flung Keres from my neck, throwing him to the ground. My body turned toward him, growling as I opened my jaw. I roared, ready to kill when a sudden sharp pain pierced my neck, followed by a click.

Emilios smiled.

The heavy iron collar was piercing my skin. My body felt forced as it shifted back to my fae form, slamming into the ground. The sharp spikes had burrowed in my neck.

Keres stood, walking to my side. My eyes locked on Fenix, his lifeless body next to mine.

"Cymar." I cried, tears filling my eyes.

My arm sretched out, desperately trying to grab him.

"You're a fucking beast yourself, Cyrene." Keres spat, kicking my face.

Everything went black.

this is only the beginning

Cyrene looked peaceful as she slept. Too exhausted to dream but resting while her wounds slowly healed. I tried to warn her, but her stubborn ass wouldn't listen.

I lightly pulled her covers back, examining her fresh wounds. Her back was shredded from the ghouls.

"I'm sorry I didn't reach you sooner." Anger filled my veins as I stared into the deep gashes. *Fucking ghouls.* My nose caught a whiff of Lord Baldyr's scent as I pulled the sheets back over her bare back. I sat next to her in the large bed, stroking her hair, waiting for him to open the door. No words could describe the anger and confusion his face made as he ducked through the door frame and saw me in her bed. The healer shadowed him, equally puzzled, as Lord Baldyr halted, eyeing me with his emerald irises. He ordered the healer away, shutting the door as he turned back to me.

"What the Gods are you doing here?!" He roared. I could sense the anger boiling in his veins as he stepped closer, cautiously aware of my abilities. I grinned, crossing my arms as he slowly inched closer.

"Isn't it obvious?" I angled my eyes down at Cyrene.

Before I could whip out another witty remark, Lord Baldyr rushed at me. He growled as he gripped my tunic in his giant fist, lifting me from the bed, glaring deep into my eyes. His protectiveness impressed me.

"If you lay one finger on Cyrene—"

"Shh. Wouldn't want to wake your daughter now, would you, Lord Baldyr?"

He tugged me closer, a menacing rumble vibrating deep within his chest as he leaned in, glaring into my soul.

"What did you say?" His words were threatening but didn't phase me.

"I can smell your blood within hers. The minute I entered the throne room, her scent gave away your secret."

"How can you *smell* such a thing?!" He shook my body as I smiled.

"As an Alpha yourself, you already know." My grin remained as his face tightened at the realization of what I was. "Now if you could," I tapped his wrists. Lord Baldyr was hesitant, slowly releasing his grip as my feet touched the floor. He huffed, his strength straining through his muscles as he eyed me with emotion.

"You should leave," he growled, glancing at Cyrene, "now."

"I'm afraid I can't do that Lord—"

Before the words could fully leave my lips, he swung his large arm, sending me across the room. My body slammed into the large mirror, shattering it as I fell. I scoffed, chuckling lightly as he quickly approached me.

"You better listen here, *boy*. I don't care if you are an aethos, I don't care if you're an Alpha Vargr," he drew a monstrous Tartarian axe from beneath his winter furs. He angled the blade, lifting my head, "you will not dishonor my heir." His arms began to prickle and shift into his hybrid form. Monstrous half bear-half human arms gripped the axe. "Do you wish to die today, Fenix?"

My brows furrowed as my eyes glared up at Lord Baldyr, my smile fading.

"I would die a thousand deaths for Cyrene. No one, not even *you*, can keep me from her." My voice deepened as a growl emerged in my throat. Lord Baldyr's face twisted as my arms shifted into their hybrid form. I gripped the axe, pulling it closer to my neck as Lord Baldyr fought against my grip. The blade dug into my flesh as blood slowly ran down my neck.

"But could you live with yourself knowing you killed your daughter's mate?"

Lord Baldyr's eyes widened, blinking as he spoke.

"What did you just say?" He demanded.

I glanced back at Cyrene as she slept. My mate. My eyes returned to Lord Baldyr.

"Why else would I be here risking my own life and my kingdom for her safety? Don't tell me somewhere, deep inside, you didn't think such a thought."

Lord Baldyr's expressions shifted as he grunted. "How can I know that what you speak is the truth?"

"Do you really think I'd be sitting here with your axe on my throat, ready to die, just to fuck her?"

"Watch your mouth!" He pushed the blade deeper. My grin returned as my face lifted up.

"Deny it all you want, but you know I speak the truth."

"If what you say is true, then why hasn't she mentioned such a thing? Why does she reject you? Explain that."

"She doesn't know—yet. I won't force our pairing bond, and if she rejects me, I'll live with that pain. But part of her wants to be loved, wants to find her mate. How else would I know her dreams?" Lord Baldyr's face softened, a wave of sadness washing over his green eyes at the mention of her dreams. "You paired with her mother, Queen Kea. You know what I speak of is only possible for those who are mates." He pulled his axe back, lowering his weapon as his head dropped.

"Being mates and sharing a pairing bond is not as pleasant as you may think."

My hand rose to my neck, feeling the blood. I glanced up at Lord Baldyr. His arms had shifted back to their normal skin, as did my own. Where once stood a powerful Ursii Alpha now stood a heartbroken man.

"I know the risks—"

"But she does not!" His emerald eyes were filled with tears as he glanced down at me. "The day her mother died, I felt that bond ripping away. I didn't know the child she carried was mine." He glanced at Cyrene as a tear fell down his rugged face. "But I felt Kea's life fading. I felt her soul tear from my own as she passed. It was the most agonizing pain any being can experience." He looked back at me. "I don't want

Cyrene to ever experience such excruciating heartbreak. I barely survived the torment. She isn't strong enough—"

"Cyrene is stronger than you think." I growled back at him. I knew how strong she really was. She was stronger than anyone I'd ever met.

He sniffled, chuckling lightly. "I guess she is. She really is like her mother—a true Tartarian warrior. Though she has a mind of her own."

"That she does." *A real stubborn ass.*

Lord Baldyr extended his free hand to me. I hesitated before placing my hand in his as he lifted me back to my feet.

"I won't tell her of this conversation, as this choice must be hers, but if she chooses to accept you as her mate and you share the bond," his eyes grew serious as he stared into mine, "you better not leave her. In *any way*. Do not let her experience that pain, Fenix. She can *never* know that pain."

I don't plan on leaving her, ever...but I would die if it means protecting her. I would do anything for Cyrene.

I nodded. "You have my word."

Lord Baldyr pulled a dagger from his belt, slicing his palm as his eyes remained on me. He extended his palm.

"Your word isn't enough." He flipped the knife and forced it into my hand. "Show me what kind of king you are."

I gazed down at the bloodied dagger, my fingers wrapping around the hilt. A Blood Oath was sacred. If broken, Gods know what would happen. I opened my palm as I slowly drew the dagger deep across my skin. *I'd risk anything for you, Cymar.*

I gripped Lord Baldyr's bloody palm, squeezing tight. He pulled me closer, our eyes almost level. His opposite hand gripped my head as he forced our foreheads together. A sign of honor.

"You have my blessing, Fenix."

ACKNOWLEDGEMENTS

The Pairing of Beasts would not exist without the help of countless creators, readers, friends, family, and my amazing husband.

To my own Cymar, thank you. You never doubted my potential and cheered me on from the beginning. When I questioned my worth, you reassured me and reminded me of what I could do.
There truly are no words to express the gratitude
and love I have for you.

After the trial and error of the release of **The Pairing of Beasts** first edition, I'm extremely thankful to everyone who took the time and care to help make the second edition even better.

Book Notes

IMPORTANT PAGES & FAVORITE QUOTES

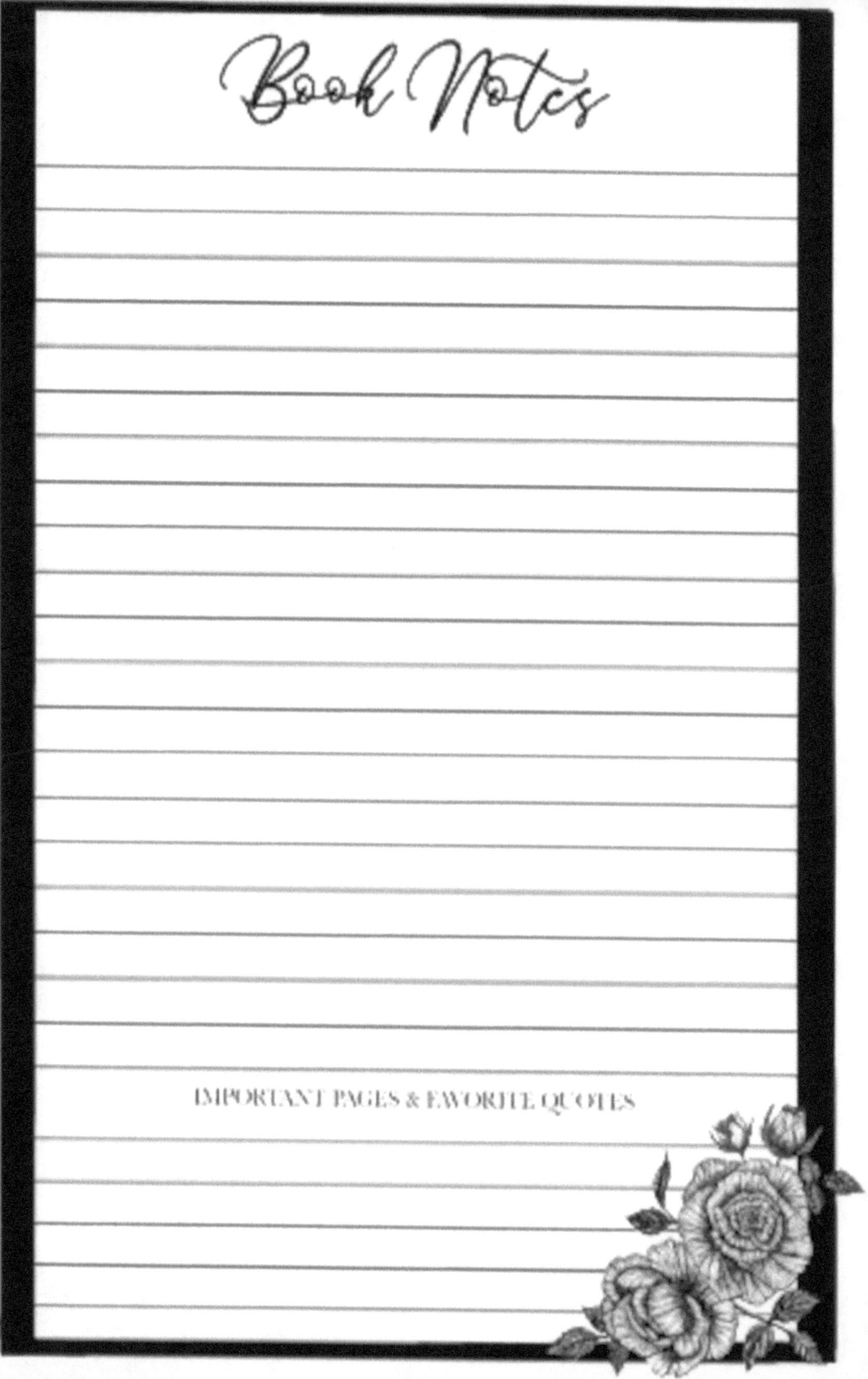

Book Notes

IMPORTANT PAGES & FAVORITE QUOTES

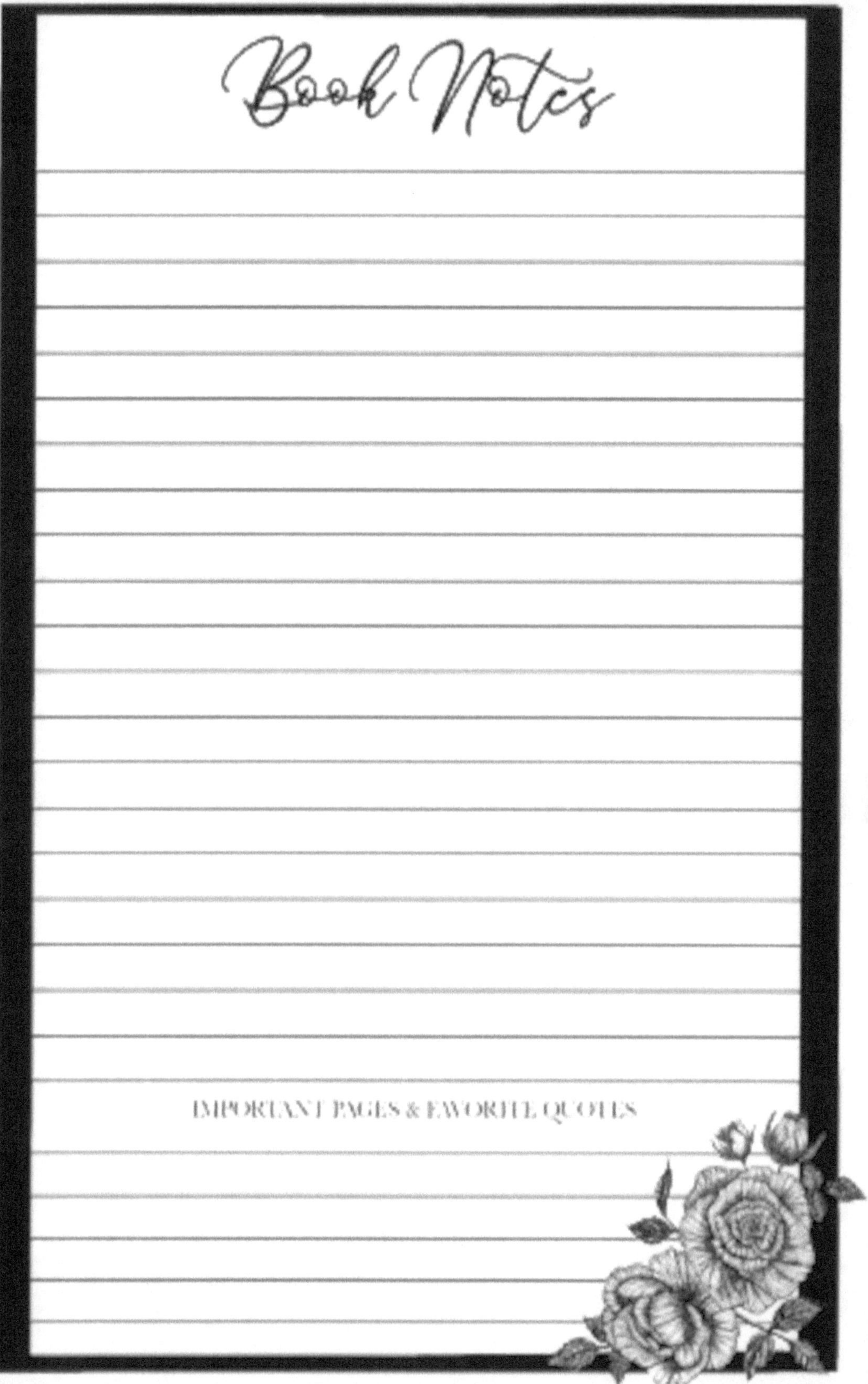

Book Notes

IMPORTANT PAGES & FAVORITE QUOTES

Book Notes

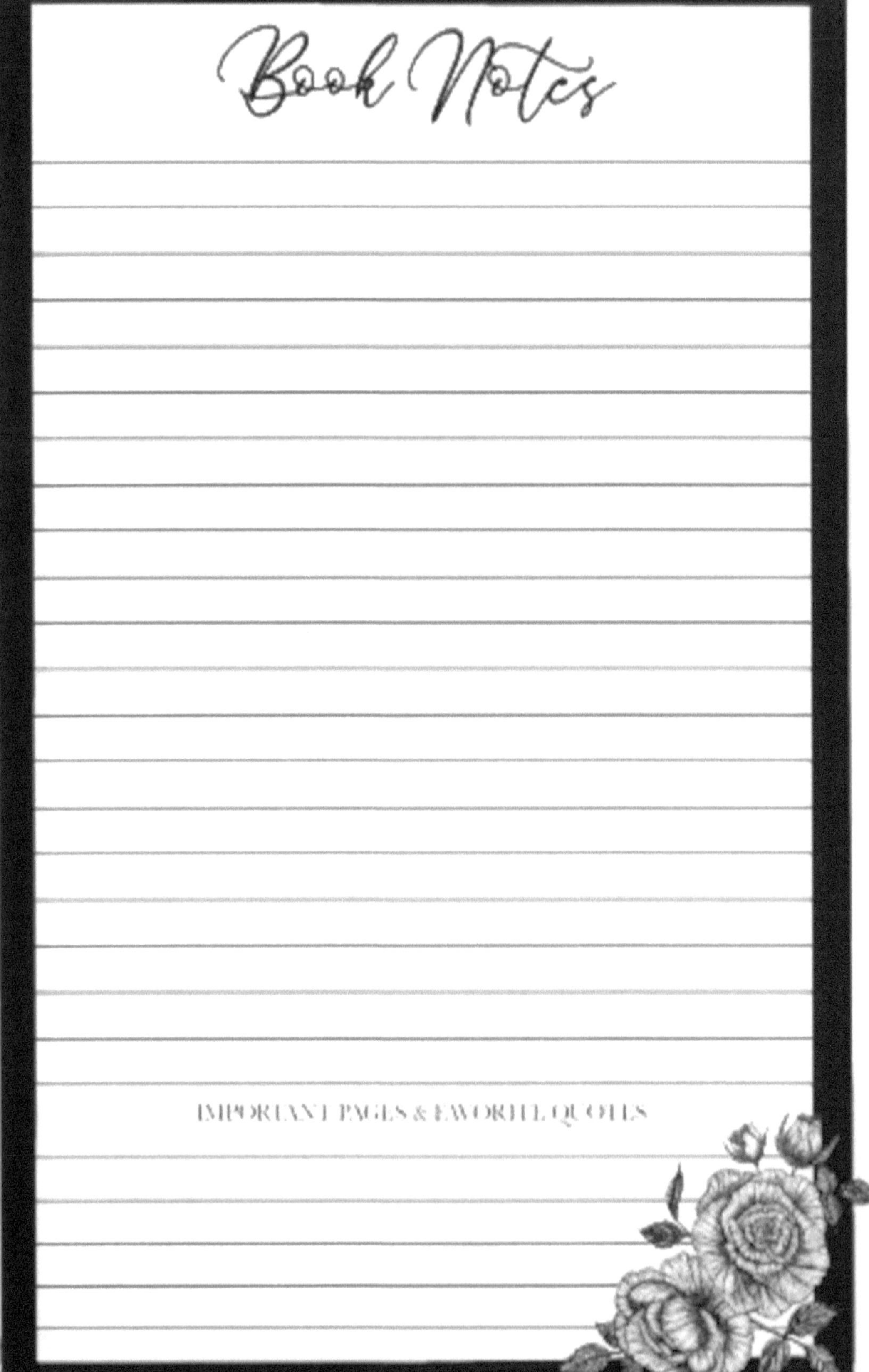

IMPORTANT PAGES & FAVORITE QUOTES

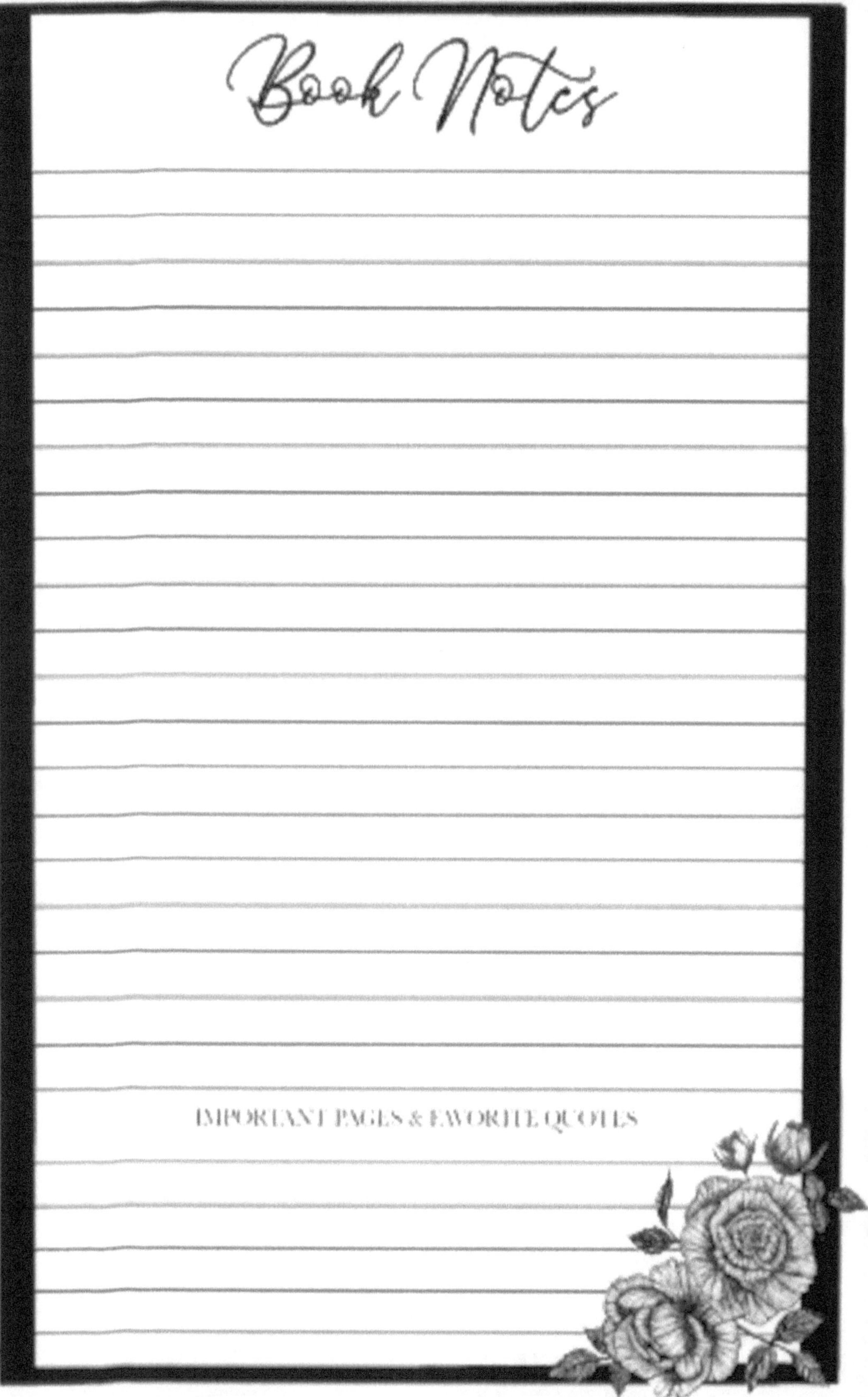

Book Notes

IMPORTANT PAGES & FAVORITE QUOTES